THE HAMBURG DOSSIER

First published in 2006 by

WOODFIELD PUBLISHING
Bognor Regis, West Sussex, England
www.woodfieldpublishing.com

© John Law, 2006

All rights reserved.
No part of this publication may be reproduced
or transmitted in any form or by any means,
electronic or mechanical, nor may it be stored
in any information storage and retrieval system,
without prior permission from the publisher.

The right of John Law
to be identified as Author of this work
has been asserted in accordance with
the Copyright, Designs and Patents Act 1988

ISBN 1-84683-035-4

The Hamburg Dossier

JOHN LAW

Woodfield

To my Grandchildren

Sam, Tom, Jon & Dani

*who gave me so much love whilst they were growing up
and who, now, as adults, are mature enough to read it*

*I would like also to express my thanks to
Kath Lewis
who gave up her time to read and correct the drafts
and for the advice she offered*

and

*The members of Phrase Writers
for their encouragement*

About the Author

Following a successful Service career, John Law set up as a Professional Investigator/Security Consultant, establishing a blue-chip client base both at home and overseas. Now retired, he lives with his wife, Marina, at Uxbridge, writing the occasional article for security publications. The Hamburg Dossier is his first novel.

Prologue

At the end of the Second World War the German economy was in chaos. Factories and infrastructure had been destroyed. Food and fuel was in short supply; raw materials non-existent. There was no work and little opportunity for the majority of the population to make a living.

By comparison, the occupation forces had an abundance. Parks filled with vehicles of all types and the spare-parts for them. Overflowing fuel dumps. Military hospitals and sick quarters containing medicines and drugs. Food in messes and warehouses, which was constantly re-supplied by a fleet of cargo, ships arriving in Hamburg harbour. All were commodities which the German population looked upon with envy. Necessities to sustain life. Necessities which some servicemen were ready to supply. So a black market was born.

The British Government, with its military policy, had to shoulder some of the responsibility. With the ending of hostilities thousands of men called up for wartime service were released back to civilian life. National Service was introduced to fill the void and all 18-year-old males were conscripted for a period of 18 months. The majority of them did not want to be in the forces and the Services didn't really want them. Most were employed in mundane military jobs as clerks, drivers, storemen, medical orderlies or cooks.

Those conscripts posted to the British Occupation Forces of Germany came as conquerors to a lifestyle they had never experienced before.

These conquerors, many whom had only just exchanged a school uniform for another, found a diffident population. Elderly people who they would have treated with respect back at home, now stood aside for them in the street. People who watched without protest as they pushed their way to the head of queues to travel free on buses, trams and trains.

They found bars, which were open all hours, full of young and not so young women, offering all types of entertainment. With the abolition of the non-fraternisation rule, they also discovered sex that until then had been no more than boastful fantasies made to their barrack-room colleagues during the shining hour. The lurid films of venereal decay shown to them during training, and the hesitant lectures by naive chaplains, were soon forgotten. Now available to them were women who were prepared to do that which had only been sniggered about during a surreptitious cigarette behind the school bicycle shed.

But they found that there was no such thing as a free roll in the hay. The women were selling the only commodity they had. Selling it to survive. Selling it to support their families; husbands, children, parents and siblings. In exchange for their favours they wanted either hard currency or merchandise that could be sold on.

To save on foreign exchange, the occupation forces were paid in script currency commonly known as BAFFs. These were coupon-like notes with a face value of every note and coin of the Realm, except the penny and halfpenny which were large and small, Bakelite discs. This currency could only be used in Service outlets; NAAFI clubs, church canteens and cinemas. It could not be used in German shops or establishments and it was an offence for a German national to be in possession of it.

Those troops who wanted German currency, to spend in civilian bars and shops, were able to exchange a limited amount of their pay through the Pay Offices. But as most conscripts were only paid 4/- (20p) a day, the number of German marks they could obtain through legal means was very small.

An artificial currency was established. Every serviceman, whether they smoked or not, received a cigarette ration which could be sold on the black market for four or five times the buying price. If they knew the right orderly room clerk, additional ration cards could be obtained. Other attractive items, vehicles, machinery, fuel, medical supplies and food, were found to have a like value.

So the people closest to these attractive items, the bored clerks, drivers, storemen, medical orderlies and cooks came into their own.

1

1947

The moonlight reflected off the hoarfrost covering the brick rubble bordering the once elegant road. It silhouetted the walls of the buildings that remained standing. A stark monument to that night three years before when the bombers raised a firestorm across Hamburg.

The canvas of silver and black was flawed by cracks of light escaping from the curtained windows of a distant bar, where a muted accordion could be heard playing a haunting gypsy tune.

Although now deserted, the street was home to dozens of people living in cellars under the piles of masonry, but not beneath the ruin in which the two watchers were standing. This building, like others with white crosses painted on their walls, still contained the remains of bomb victims, whose only interment had been the quicklime pumped into the debris.

A flash of gold showed that the door to the bar had opened and closed. Approaching footsteps echoed along the street. An indistinct shape became a man and woman with arms entwined. In another place they might have been taken for mother and son. The man was a boy; a young soldier in an ill-fitting, battle dress uniform. The woman was a head taller, twice his width and twice his age. The moonlight made her lank hair appear white as it hung from beneath the soldier's beret perched on her head. Her mouth was a black slash in a ghostlike face.

They paused in front of the watchers' hiding place. The soldier appeared to be reluctant to go on. The woman bent down and kissed him. Her hand slid down his body and fondled his crotch. 'Don't worry *liebling*. The military police don't come around here.' She dragged him by the arm. 'My house is not far away. Then you'll be safe and I'll give you a good time.'

Mike 'Davy' Jones glanced at Harry Penrose across the gaping doorway. The door and frame, if they had escaped the air-raid, had long gone the way of other combustible material. He chuckled, 'I don't need a crystal ball to see what his good time will be. His first leg-over tonight. Broke and AWOL tomorrow. CO's Orderly Room and jankers on Monday. Military Hospital on Tuesday to see the pox doctor. Or it might be rabies with that dog.'

Penrose took an unlit cigarette from his mouth. 'I hope for his sake its rabies. If this caper goes off tonight there won't be any penicillin left to cure him of the other.'

Jones blew onto his frozen fingers. 'Do you think they're going to show Harry? How good is your information?'

'This snout has never let me down yet.' Penrose's tone could not disguise the self-doubt shown by all policemen when talking about their informers. 'If he's giving me a load of bollocks I'll personally throw the little bastard into the Elbe.'

'Let me run through it again Harry. Your information is that a load of penicillin is going to be knocked off tonight. The job is going to be done by squaddies who will hand it over to civvy contacts. You don't know where. You don't know who. You don't know who the Germans are. The only thing you think you know is that the hand over will be in this street. We've been stood here like a couple of pricks for five hours and bugger all has happened. I must be bloody barmy wasting my time.'

'Nobody asked you to come Davy,' Penrose snapped. 'It was you who volunteered. If you don't like it you can piss off now.'

The next hour passed in angry silence. Groups of customers periodically left the bar and went their separate ways. Eventually the lights of the bar were turned off showing that it was 4 am.

Headlights heralded a slow moving vehicle turning into the street from a side road near the bar. It nosed forward to within fifty yards of their position and stopped. The headlights flashed on and off.

Penrose unbuttoned his duffel coat and opened the waist holster holding a .38 Smith and Wesson revolver. 'Looks like we're in business,' he whispered.

Nothing happened. The vehicle remained stationary for three or four minutes and then slowly moved forward again. As it passed their hiding place they saw that it was a Royal Air Force Police jeep containing two policemen.

Penrose looked across at Jones. 'What the fuck are they up to?'

The vehicle stopped again, the headlights flashing.

'It's well past patrol time,' Jones said, walking to the front of the ruin. 'I bet they're looking for us.'

Penrose followed him into the road where Jones put his fingers to his mouth and let out a piercing whistle. The occupants of the jeep both turned, looked through the open rear canopy and the jeep reversed towards them.

The young corporal in the passenger seat nodded to Penrose, 'The Warrant sent us to look for you, to see if you were okay Sarge. At midnight the drugs store at the Military Hospital was found to have been done and he thought you would have sorted it out by now.'

Penrose looked at him for several seconds. 'For fuck's sake,' he hissed.

He turned to Jones, who shrugged his shoulders and said, 'You win some, you lose some Harry. It looks like you've lost this one.'

Penrose slowly shook his head. 'No bloody way. I'll have those bastards.' He turned to the driver of the jeep. 'Give us a lift back to our gharry and we'll get back to Headquarters.'

Penrose and Jones were Metropolitan Police Detective Sergeants seconded to the RAF Special Investigation Branch to combat the growing black market in military stores and equipment. They had met when they both joined the force in 1938. After their probationary service both had been selected as aides to CID. Subsequent promotions brought them back together in 1944 when Jones joined Penrose in the Flying Squad.

As serving police officers they had been exempt from wartime military service, but in 1946, when those policemen who had volunteered for active service were returning to the force on demobilisation, they seized the opportunity of a 3-year secondment to the RAF. After a short familiarisation course at the RAF Police

School at RAF Weeton they were posted to Hamburg, the hub of black market activities in the British Air Force of Occupation.

The SIB offices were part of a large residential house in Sierich Strasse, near the Aussenalster lake, which had somehow escaped the wartime bombing and had been requisitioned to house the RAF Police presence in Hamburg. As Penrose drove his unmarked Volkswagen Beetle into the car park he saw that lights were on in the upper floor of the building. In the squad room, Warrant Officer Lancaster was sitting at Penrose's desk, reading a file. He looked up as the two sergeants entered.

'What you might call a bit of a balls up Harry,' Lancaster said in his soft Welsh voice. 'What went wrong?'

'I don't know sir.'

'I don't know sir!' Lancaster's voice rose. 'Millions of units of penicillin are half inched and all you can say is, "I don't know sir."' Lancaster lifted the file he had been reading, then threw it back onto the desk. 'I thought you were on top of this job Sergeant but there isn't a mention of it in your progress reports here.' He slammed his hand onto the file. 'I know you told me about it, which I am beginning to think was a cock and bull story. You told me what you were going to do tonight. Why didn't you write the bugger down? Why didn't you arrange for extra guards at the hospital? Why weren't you there instead of scratching your arse in some bloody street in Altona?'

Penrose fought his rising temper, swallowing the smart answer that was forming in his mind. The formal use of his rank by Lancaster warned him to act contrite. He might have got away with it in the past with some Detective Inspectors, but you didn't tempt fate with an irate RAF Warrant Officer with all the powers and retributions of Air Force law at his finger tips. 'Sir, my informant only told me that the job was going down tonight. He didn't know where or who was involved. I could hardly have requested extra guards for every Sick Quarters in the area. The only other snippet he picked up was that the hand-over would be in Donnerstrasse. He promised to contact me as soon as he found out any more but I have not heard from him for the last two days so it was my decision to stake out Donnerstrasse. I would have made a written progress if and when there was something more positive.'

Lancaster tossed the file into the in-tray sitting on the desk. He thought for a moment. 'Harry, is there any possibility that your snout was having you on?' The heat in his voice had cooled.

'I don't think so Sir. I have been running him for over two years now. Although he is not at the top of the tree he is on the periphery of most things that happen around St Pauli. He's in with most of the girls that work the cafés along the Reep, from whom he picks up all kinds of gossip. I haven't yet established where he got this from, but I am certain that he is too far down the pecking order to be directly involved.'

Penrose glanced across at Jones and saw that he had a smirk on his face as if he was enjoying seeing him being carpeted. He looked back at Lancaster. 'Can I ask who went out on the job at the hospital?'

'The Brown Jobs got the call. Staff Sergeant Terry Reader. He's a mate of yours, ain't he?'

'We do have the occasional beer together.'

'Did you tell him about your information?'

'No.'

'Thank Christ for that. At least we won't be the laughing stock down at the Military Police mess.' Lancaster was referring to the professional animosity that had always existed between the Military and Royal Air Force Police units. With some the hatred was so intense that there was a complete breakdown of both communication and co-operation.

'Do you want me to have a word with Terry, Sir?'

'You can, but don't you breath a bloody word that you knew something was going off. But more importantly, get to that bloody snout of yours and find out what his game is. I will want a full report on Monday morning so I can brief the Boss.'

Lancaster rose from behind the desk and looked over at Jones 'Davy, give me a lift back to my quarters. With luck I might get a couple of hours in my pit before breakfast.'

They left the room without a backward glance at Penrose who sat down at his desk and lifted up the telephone. He asked the military exchange operator for the Military Police Special Investigation Branch. The phone was answered on its second ring.

'Military Police Special Investigation Branch detachment. Staff Sarg'nt Reader, Sir.'

'Hello Terry. It's Harry. I hear you're had a busy night.'

'What's it to bloody well do with you Harry? Especially at this time of the bloody morning?'

Despite the professional rivalry, Penrose and Reader had formed a friendship and would often meet over a beer in the WO's and Joe's bar in Hamburg House, the NAAFI Club situated in the town centre. There they would exchange snippets of information and kick around ideas to help forward each other's current investigations.

'Just curious Terry. Wondering if you've come up with anything. What did the duty storeman have to say?'

'Not a lot. He was away at the mess having his supper at the time. I've only just let him go, but I'm not finished with him yet.'

'How did they pull it off?'

'Through a back window. The place is only one of those temporary wooden huts. There must have been three of four of them to carry the stuff to wherever they'd left a vehicle. Emptied all the fridges. Millions of units of the stuff. Anyway, why do you want to know?'

'I'm just wondering if it is connected to something I'm sniffing around at. Would I be treading on your toes is I had a word with the storeman?'

'Be my guest as long as you don't start sticking your nose into my business. Anyway, the duty storeman is one of your mob. An AC1 McNeil. I should let him have a couple of hours kip first before you talk to him. I've scared the shit out of him.'

After promising to get together in the near future, Penrose replaced the receiver and looked at his watch. Ten minutes to six. Hardly worthwhile going to bed. There was a busy day in front of him and there was no telling when he would get up again once he got into bed. He swung his feet onto the desk, leant back in his chair and lit a cigarette. He drew the smoke deep into his lungs. Where was Willi Winkler, he wondered.

Penrose had met Gerhard 'Willi' Winkler soon after he was posted to Hamburg, over two years before. In a bid to establish contacts, he had introduced himself to the Chaplain at the Flying Angel Mission to Seamen and soon made a habit of calling in at the club where he occasionally picked up titbits of information. The mission was situated on one side of Zeughausmarkt, a quiet, sleepy triangle at the east end of the Reeperbahn. Although having both a comfortable restaurant and a bar, in the hope of keeping the seamen on shore leave on the straight and narrow, there were a number of nearby café/bars staffed with available and willing "hostesses" whose aim was to capture a wandering sailor and relieve him of his money before he found his way to the bright lights and hard action of the Reeperbahn. Next door to the mission was the basement bar of the Café Koch, the twinkling lights of Anita's Bar directly opposite and on the base of the triangle stood the Café Arnold.

Penrose had been aware from the start of the small, slim, foxy-faced man slinking around in the shadows, accosting passing sailors and directing them to one or the other of the bars. Eventually the small man, Willi Winkler, approached Penrose and asked if he was looking for a woman. When Penrose declined his invitation, Willi asked if he had any cigarettes to sell. Penrose always carried a carton of cigarettes, as a means of payment for information, which he sold to Willi and then invited him to join him for a drink.

Through the red, velvet curtains hanging on the inside of the door of the Café Arnold, either to keep the cold night air out or the cigar scented air of the bar in, Penrose entered a world of low lighting. Just inside the door, on the right, was a small raised stage on which a three-piece band was playing and to the left was a zinc-topped bar which ran down that side of the room. Tables surrounded a tiny dance floor; each occupied, either by a man and woman or with women alone. Penrose's entrance brought an array of smiles from the unattached women, which quickly faded when Willi entered behind him and guided him to a solitary table at the end of the bar. Slowly, over a number of glasses of beer, Penrose spelt out who he was and suggested to Willi that it might be beneficial to Willi's future prospects, and indeed his liberty, if they could come to some working arrangement.

Willi, a former driver in the *Wehrmart*, was not in the top league of black-marketers. He was a small-time wheeler and dealer, touting for various bars, picking up the occasional carton of cigarettes or tin of coffee. But he was streetwise enough to realise that if he was to progress in his chosen profession a little protection would not come amiss. Seeing Penrose as a provider of that protection, he agreed to act as an informer and would meet with Penrose two or three times a week at the top of St Michael's tower, away from prying eyes and ears.

Their last meeting had been at midday on Friday, two days before, when Willi had told Penrose of the street talk of the impending theft of the penicillin. Although his information had been sketchy, Willi had been adamant that the raid was going to take place although he didn't know where or who was involved. He had promised that he would try and find out more and get back to Penrose later that day. He hadn't made contact and Penrose had been unable to find him in his usual haunts.

2

Penrose drove slowly over the bridge dividing the Inner and Outer Alster lakes as he headed towards Damntor and the British Military Hospital. On a track, parallel to the bridge, an S-Bahn train, the overground rail system, clattered by in the opposite direction towards Hauptbahnhof, the main station. Although it was a brilliant, sunny morning, it was bitterly cold. Pedestrians were wrapped up against the weather by an assortment of clothing. Without exception, all the men wore a type of blue ski-hat and carried a scuffed briefcase. The women, scarves wrapped around their heads, were pulling low, four wheeled wooden handcarts. From time to time they would form small groups where they would attempt to barter disposable possessions carried in the briefcases and handcarts, in exchange for something to satisfy the inner man. Penrose could not help thinking that on a day like this, in more happier times, the people would have been attending the churches and, with some scepticism, listening to the parable of the loaves and fishes.

He turned into the British Military Hospital, a former civilian hospital that had been extended by rows of wooden huts, and parked opposite the guardroom, next to the ET centre.

Early Treatments Centres were established at all military units. Here, soldiers going out on the town could collect a supply of prophylactics and paper envelopes containing a sliver of soap, lint, cotton wool and a tube of obnoxious smelling ointment. They were also required to enter their details and date and time of collection in a register. The idea being that those who were unfortunate enough to contract a social disease, which was an offence under Service law, would escape prosecution if they had signed the register and had forgone after-play to hygienically wash and clinically apply the ointment, both inside and out, according to the printed instructions. An examination of the registers would show that it was difficult to estimate who was the most sexually active; Mickey Mouse, Donald Duck or the various unit padres, more often those of the Roman Catholic faith. Even then, few of the French letters were used for what they were intended. The vulcanised rubber sheaves were found to be more efficient rolled down over a rifle barrel to keep out rust and dust. They were also used as a means to smuggle contraband when troops were going on leave to Britain. Ill-gotten gains, such as watches or jewellery, could be knotted inside a sheath and immersed in a partly used jar of Brylcreem. However, HM Customs at Harwich docks were soon aware of the scam and found that it was quicker, less messy and more profitable to confiscate all jars of Brylcreem and substitute them with new ones.

Penrose entered the guardroom where an army Orderly Corporal was leaning back on a chair, balanced on the two back legs, reading a copy of Reveille. He did not look up as Penrose entered, just said, 'Yeah?'

'I want to see AC1 McNeil.'

'Who are you?' asked the Corporal, still scanning through the paper.

'Sergeant Penrose, SIB.'

The chair crashed to the floor on all legs, the paper vanished onto a shelf beneath the counter and the Corporal sprang rigidly to attention. 'I'll send a runner for him right away Sir. You can use the back office. Would you like a cup of tea?'

Some ten minutes later a knock came on the door of the back office and a small, slim, acned-faced airman entered. He was wearing a two-piece, khaki denim, fatigue uniform and it was very obvious that this had been thrown on after hastily rising from his bed without washing or combing his hair. As he stood to attention before Penrose he was visibly trembling. Penrose indicated to a wooden chair and told him to sit down.

After introducing himself, Penrose said, 'Tell me about last night.'

McNeil swallowed. 'I was duty storeman Sergeant. I went for my supper Sergeant and when I got back I found that all the fridges had been emptied and a window at the back was open, so I phoned the Orderly Sergeant, Sergeant.'

Penrose sighed, took out a packet of cigarettes, lit one and inhaled deeply. 'Good. Now let's fill in a few gaps and forget the Sergeant bit in every sentence. How long had you been duty storeman?'

'All week. Last night was my last night.'

'What were your hours of duty?'

'Start at five Sarg... er and finish at eight the next morning.'

'What time did you go for supper and what time did you get back?'

'I went between half past nine and ten and got back just after midnight.'

Penrose mashed his cigarette end into the lid of a cigarette tin acting as an ashtray. 'That's a bloody long time for supper. Were you having a five-course meal?'

'No. Just egg and chips. But my mate Ginger was duty cook so we sat chatting.'

'What about if someone needed to draw medical supplies? How were they supposed to find you?'

'No. That doesn't happen. We don't issue stores from there at night. We're only there to see that the fridges keep to the right temperature. Like I told the other policeman, if someone wants me, I leave a note on the door saying where I am.'

'How far is the mess from your stores? Could you have heard anything?'

'About five minutes away. The stores are over the back by the fence and the mess is in the main camp.'

'Is there any other occupied building near your store?'

'Not at night, no.'

'What were you and Ginger talking about for two hours?'

'Trains.'

'Trains?', an incredulous Penrose asked.

'Yes, trains. We both like trains and are always talking about them.'

Penrose studied the boy sitting on the other side of the desk, comparing him to the usual run of villains he had dealt with back in London. He had listened to every conceivable story offered as an alibi but never once had anyone told him that they had spent two hours talking about trains. 'Have you got a girlfriend McNeil?' he asked.

McNeil blushed, 'No Sarge.'
'Do you go out drinking?'
'No Sarge.'
'So what do you do when you're off duty?'
'Me and my mate Ginger go looking at trains up at the railway yard.'
Penrose shook his head in amazement. 'What gives with you and your mate Ginger? Are you shirt-lifters?'
Tears welled up in McNeil's eyes and ran down his cheeks. 'No Sarge. Nothing like that. You're being horrid. Not like the other policeman. He was kind to me.'
Penrose looked at him in astonishment as he began to cry, his tears mingling with the snot running from his nose. McNeil rubbed the sleeve of his jacket across his face and sniffed.
'Okay son,' Penrose said, 'that will do for now. I'll need to talk to you again. Off you go.'

Penrose was still chuckling to himself as he drove along Jungfernstieg, once the home to Hamburg's most elegant shops. He couldn't imagine Terry Reader being kind to anyone, least of all the snivelling, train-spotting specimen he had just been interviewing. Just wait, he thought, until I meet up with him. I'll pull his leg something rotten.
He turned right into Rathausmarkt and circled the City Hall, a 19th century, neo-Renaissance monstrosity that had somehow avoided serious bomb damage. He was heading for St Michaelis church, known affectionately as the Michel, in the hope that Willi Winkler might keep their usual Sunday rendezvous. As he neared the dock area the bomb damage became more intense. The 300-year-old Michel stood alone in a sea of devastation. Although the building had suffered extensively in the bombing raids, the 434 foot, redbrick tower, with its patina dome, which for centuries had welcomed generations of seamen as they sailed up the Elbe, was still sound.
Penrose climbed the 449 steps in the tower and emerged into the bell room where five large bells were suspended. Attached to the walls, circling the bells, was a heavy, wooded staircase that took

Penrose out onto a viewing platform, 271 feet above the ground. He circled the platform. It was deserted. Below him the whole of Hamburg, or what was left of it, lay before him. He pulled his duffel coat tighter to his body against the cold wind that was blowing off of the river and leant on the railings at the south side, the direction from which Willi would come. Drawing on a cigarette, he gazed down at the distant, 100 foot statue of the Iron Chancellor Bismarck, perched on a knoll above the St Pauli Landing Stage, and wondered, not for the first time, how both that and Michel tower were still standing when all between had been flattened.

Two cigarettes later, Penrose decided that Willi, who was normally punctual, was not coming. He descended the tower and drove to his office where he intended to spend the afternoon compiling a written report for presentation to Warrant Officer Lancaster the following morning. As he passed through the control room the duty policeman stopped him. 'Sarge. An Inspector Rossmann from Davidwache has been trying to contact you. Could you give him a ring?'

Penrose had met Inspector Rossmann of the Hamburg Kriminalpolizei on a number of occasions. Although the re-formed German civil police operated under the direction of the Occupation Control Commission and had no jurisdiction over the occupying forces, there was liaison between it and the Service police.

From his office, Penrose telephoned the Inspector.

'Rossmann'.

'Good afternoon Inspector. Harry Penrose here.'

'Ah Herr Penrose.' Rossmann replied in his precise English. 'It is very good of you to call me back. Do you know a Gerhard Winkler?'

So, thought Penrose, the prodigal has surfaced. 'Yes Inspector. We do a bit of business together. What trouble is he in now?'

'I think Herr Penrose it is better if we spoke face to face. Would it be presumptive of me to ask you to come to my office? It is most important.'

'No trouble at all Inspector. I'll be with you in about thirty minutes.'

As Penrose headed for St Pauli, that had been the red light district of Hamburg since ships first sailed up the Elbe, he wondered what Willi had done to end up in the hands of the police. Davidwache, the police station responsible for St Pauli, was situated halfway along the Reeperbahn, where in times past rope makers used to wind ship ropes along its 600-metre length. Now, even this early on a Sunday afternoon, the bars and clip joints were in full swing.

Inspector Klaus Rossmann was waiting in the entrance hall of Davidwache. A tall, serious looking man in his late 40s who was rarely known to smile, he had been a professional policeman for over twenty years. He had never been a party member or involved in the Nazi machine. With a slight bow, he solemnly shook Penrose's hand and steered him towards the basement steps which, Penrose knew, was not the direction of the cellblock.

'So what's the little bastard been up to Inspector? What trouble is he causing you?'

They were walking along a brightly lit, white tiled corridor and stopped at a dark painted wooden door on which was a plate bearing the word *'Leichenschashaus'*.

'He is not in any trouble Herr Penrose.' Rossmann indicated the sign. 'Do you understand that?'

Penrose shook his head.

'It means, in your language, morgue.' Rossmann said. 'I am afraid Winkler is dead.'

Although death was no stranger to Penrose, he was swallowing hard as he followed Rossmann into the room. On an examination table in the centre of the room lay a body. It was fully clothed and showing signs and damage of having been immersed in water. Drawn tightly around the neck was a ligature, a length of hemp rope. There was no doubt that it was Willi Winkler although he looked smaller than Penrose remembered.

'He was pulled out of the river this morning,' Rossmann said. 'We are waiting for the medical examiner to come and give us the cause and time of death, but I do not think the cause is in question.'

~ *The Hamburg Dossier* ~

Leaving the basement they went upstairs to Rossmann's office where they faced each other across the desk. 'So Herr Penrose, what was your connection with Winkler?'

Penrose's mind was racing, not knowing how much he should divulge to the German police. 'What makes you think I had any connection with him, other than knowing him as part of the street scene?'

From one of his desk drawers Rossmann took a waterproof pouch. He tipped the contents onto the desktop. 'This was on the body. It is Winkler's identity card, inside of which was this piece of paper.'

He pushed the piece of paper towards Penrose who saw that his name and telephone number was written on it and the words '*Der Taucher.*' Penrose looked at Rossmann. 'Would you translate that for me?'

'*Der Taucher.* The Diver. What does that mean?'

'The Diver?' Penrose replied. 'It doesn't mean a thing to me.'

'But, Herr Penrose, it must have meant something to Winkler for him to connect it with your name. So why don't we, how do you say, quit stalling and put our cards on the table?'

Penrose thought for a moment and decided to give Rossmann a sanitised version of his dealings with Willi. He told him that he had been using Winkler as an informant and of the information Willi had given him about the theft of the penicillin. Rossmann listened without interruption, occasionally making a note of a particular point. When Penrose stopped speaking, he ran his pencil down the list he had made, looked up and shook his head slightly. 'Is it not a pity that we do not cooperage more? Maybe that will come one day. Have you no leads to who organised this raid on your hospital?'

Penrose shook his head. 'The only lead I had is lying on a slab downstairs.'

'Do you agree Herr Penrose that it could be connected to what happened to the unfortunate Winkler?'

'It is possible. Yes.'

'So it is possible that the findings from our individual investigations might be of mutual benefit?'

Penrose smiled. 'I follow your drift Inspector.' He rose from his chair and held his hand out to Rossmann. 'We must keep in contact.'

3

Monday morning. All the field investigators were at their desks, drinking tea and smoking, while they awaited the arrival of Warrant Officer Lancaster to conduct "morning prayers". That daily briefing when each investigator would talk about the progress of his current cases, giving his colleagues the opportunity to comment or suggest an angle he had not thought about.

The hum of conversation died as the Warrant Officer entered the room. 'Good morning gentlemen.' Lancaster glanced around the room, his gaze falling on Penrose. 'Right Harry. Let's start with you. I believe you've had a bereavement.'

'That's right Boss. My snout was pulled out of the river yesterday morning.' Penrose went on to tell about his visit to Davidswache the previous day and his conversation with Inspector Rossmann.

Any leads?' Lancaster asked.

'Nothing yet as far as I know. Of course it's a Kraut investigation, but I think that Rossmann may well include me in the loop.'

'Have you put yourself in the frame Harry?' Jones asked from across the room. 'As I recall, on Saturday night you did say that you might chuck the little bastard in the Elbe yourself.'

Penrose laughed. 'At that time he was already a floater. Went in sometime on Friday after someone tied a length of rope around his neck.'

'Do you think it could be connected to the hospital job?' Lancaster asked.

'More than possible Boss, but Willie had his fingers in many pies. Although I didn't get a good look at it because the medical examiner had not yet done his business, I couldn't help but think that the rope around his neck was from a kitbag. Then there was the word *"Taucher"*, Diver, written with my name and telephone number.

Jones snorted. 'Don't forget the diver,' he said in a sloppy voice. All in the room looked at him in silence. Red-faced, he continued, 'You know. Tommy Hanley. ITMA. The guy that pops up and says "Don't forget the diver."'

Lancaster bristled. 'If you haven't got anything useful to say Davy keep your bloody mouth shut.' He turned back to Penrose. 'Doesn't it mean anything to you Harry?'

Penrose shook his head. A voice from the back of the room said, 'We ain't got any Navy here, but could it mean "frogman"?'

Again Penrose shook his head. 'I thought of that, but they tell me that frogman in German is *Froschmann*. This is definitely "diver".'

'Let's move on,' Lancaster said. 'What about the break-in? Do you think the storeman was involved?'

'Not in the commission of the crime Boss. While it was happening he was having his supper and talking trains with his mate, Ginger. Whether he knew anything about it beforehand, I don't know. I didn't want to lean on him too hard as it is Terry Reader's job. I'm having a pint with Terry tonight, so I'll be able to dig a bit more. And I'm going to take the piss out of him. The storeman reckoned that he was kind to him. Tell me about the so-called hard men of the Military Police.'

'Has any of the stuff surfaced yet?'

'No Boss, not as far as I know. I wouldn't expect it to yet. They'll be diluting it before moving it on. But I'll start enquiries with the civvy hospitals and doctors.'

The meeting broke up an hour later and Penrose wandered down to the translator's office. Inge Lang looked up from her desk as he entered. Her deep blue eyes lit up, She rose, checked that the door was closed, then wrapped her arms around Penrose's neck and kissed him deeply.

Penrose put his hands on her hips, feeling the firm body under her dress. She was a 24 years old, 5' 5" tall, slim, high-breasted blonde. Her father had been a merchant navy captain who had been lost at sea in 1943. Because of her perfect English she had found employment as a translator with the Control Commission. She was already working at the police headquarters when Penrose first arrive there. There had been an instant attraction between them and they were now accepted as an item. Or, as Inge would say, 'I am Harry's *schatz*.' She lived with her mother in a two-roomed apartment in the north of the city.

She leant back, her hands cupped behind Penrose's neck, the lower half of her body tight against his. 'I waited all weekend but you never came.'

'Sorry sweetheart. I was all tied up. Business that all went wrong.'

'And tonight?'

'I'll be there. I might be a little late, but I'll be there.'

'You look tired Harry. Will you be tired tonight?'

Penrose smiled as he clasped her buttocks and pulled her closer. Pressing his lips to her ear, he murmured, 'I'm sure you'll have a cure.' As she moved her body against his, he pushed her away. 'Don't tempt me *liebling,* I've got work to do.'

She giggled. 'Yes, it is better that you should go. I felt a *klein mann,* that was not so tired, stirring. Till tonight then.'

It had not been the most productive of days, thought Penrose as he entered the Sergeants' Mess as night was falling. Although the penicillin investigation was not his, he still felt that it was connected to the demise of Willie, in which he had a vested interest, so he had been making inquiries at the civilian hospitals and the medical administration at the Control Commission. There had not been any reports of a quantity of suspect drugs coming onto the market. Now was the time for a quick shower and shave before meeting Terry Reader. As he was checking for mail in the mail rack, the Cook Sergeant crept up behind him.

"Allo 'Arry. Are you seeing the luscious Inge tonight or are you eating in the mess?'

'I'm off out Cookie. I hope to get a better bit of supper than you can provide.'

The Cook Sergeant leered, looked around before leaning neared to Penrose. 'Is yer car unlocked?' he asked in a soft voice.

Penrose nodded.

'I'll put a bit of sommink on the back seat. A nice bit of fillet and some odds and ends. Put a bit of lead in yer pencil.'

Some months before Penrose had caught the drunken cook in an out of bounds bar in one of the seedier parts of the city. Instead of reporting him, Penrose had driven him back to his billet and had never referred to the matter again. Aware that the gesture had saved his stripes, the cook had taken it upon himself to provide a few luxuries to supplement Inge's mundane diet. Although it was against regulations, Penrose never refused the offerings, as he knew of the difficulty that the civilian population had in obtaining their meagre amounts of food.

'Very good of you Cookie, but don't get yourself into any trouble.'

The cook tapped the side of his nose with his forefinger. 'Don't worry about me 'Arry. You take care of that little gel. I like 'er. You should make an 'onest woman of 'er.'

AC1 McNeil was shivering as he waited at the tram stop for Ginger to appear. He wished that he would hurry up. They had both had the day off, which had been spent at the main railway station watching the trains departing for all over Europe. Now they were going to the NAAFI Club for a fry-up and then to the forces' cinema.

A Volkswagen stopped beside him and passenger side window was rolled down. McNeil peered in and smiled when he recognised the driver.

'Hello Mac. I wonder if you could spare me a couple of minutes?'

'I'm waiting for Ginger. We're going to the pictures.'

'It's all right. Ginger knows I'm here. He told me where to find you. He'll be another ten minutes yet, I'll have you back before he gets here.'

McNeil hesitated for a moment then got into the car. They drove into a nearby side street and stopped in front of a bomb-out building.

'We think we've found some of the stuff that was nicked last night Mac. We don't want to disturb it as we are hoping that whoever dumped it there will come back for it. Can you come and see if you can identify it?'

Trustingly, McNeil walked into the pitch-black entrance. Behind him The Diver looped a kit bag rope around McNeil's neck and used it as a garrotte. As a deeper black enveloped McNeil, he wondered where Ginger was.

Penrose turned off of Damntorstrasse into Drehbahn, a small side street. On the corner of these streets stood Hamburg House, the town's NAAFI Club. The main entrance was in Damntorstrasse but a side entrance in Drehbahn gave access to the Warrant Officers and Senior NCO's bar. Shadowy figures lurked in the dark entrances of the small shops in the side street; small-time, black marketers hoping to buy a carton of cigarettes or a tin of Nescafe from the soldiers and airmen using the club. Immediately next to the entrance of the Wo's and Joe's club was Welckerstrasse, known to the troops as Winklestrasse, one of Hamburg's two brothel streets. Painted on the wooden screens at either ends of the street, in both English and German, were the words, 'Out of bounds to HM Forces and people under 16 years'. Penrose thought it ironic that the site for the NAAFI Club should be bounded on two sides by an out of bounds area. It was like waving a red rag to a bull as the drunken squaddies rolled out of the club. Sheer bravado made them chance a run through the street with the inevitable result of being arrested by one of the Service police patrols as they emerged.

Penrose was already halfway down his second pint when Terry Reader arrived. He went to the bar and collected two beers before joining Penrose at the table.

'Sorry I'm late Harry. I got held up.'

'Don't worry about it mate. How's your day been?'

'*Schlecht* Harry. Bloody awful.'

'So I can take it that you are no further forward on the hospital job?'

Reader took a swallow of his beer. 'It looks like that they had the stuff away over the fence, into the parkland behind the store. But the ground is that rock hard with the frost, there are no tyre tracks. Nobody saw or heard anything. None of the stuff has surfaced. Anyway, why are you so interested? And what were you doing ringing me up in the early hours yesterday?'

Penrose took out his packet of cigarettes and offered one to Reader. 'Look Terry, don't blow your top, but I wasn't being straight with you yesterday.' Reader looked hard at him as he continued. 'I have got an interest in the job. It might have some connection to something I'm involved in.'

Reader listened as Penrose told him about the information Winkler had give him and the finding of Winkler's body. Then he said, 'Do you think servicemen are involved?'

'Could well be Terry.'

'Like the storeman, McNeil?'

Penrose smiled, 'You suspect your mate?'

'What you getting at Harry?'

'He told me that you were kind to him.'

'Kind to him!' said Reader, his voice raising an octave. 'Kind to him! Could I be kind to anyone? I had the little bastard bouncing off of the walls. So much so, he was in no fit state to tell me anything. I was going to re-interview him today but he had slipped away somewhere.'

'So you had the hysterics too?' Penrose said, with a smile. 'I don't think he was involved. He hasn't got the bottle for anything more dangerous than watching the trains go by.'

'Well,' Reader said, leaning across the table. 'How did they know that he would have left the store.'

'Like he told you. He left a note on the door.'

'He never told me anything like that.'

'Then it must have been your oppo, whoever was with you. The kind policeman.'

Reader looked blankly at Penrose. 'I didn't have anyone with me. Do you think anyone would volunteer to turn out at midnight on a Saturday?'

For a moment Penrose sat very still, mouth agape. 'So who was the kind policeman? I think that young man has got a lot of explaining to do. Do you mind if I hook up with you tomorrow and put my two pennyworth in?'

Penrose left the club as the 11 o'clock curfew was approaching. The lower ranks were spilling out of their bar and swarming towards the tram stop, watched, from across the road, by patrols from both the

~ The Hamburg Dossier ~

Military and RAF Police. Occasionally, a reeling individual, who didn't have a mate on either side to help him along, was apprehended and placed in the back of one of the police jeeps.

The streets were deserted as Penrose drove north to Lattenkamp. Here the bomb damage was less severe with blocks of buildings still standing and habitable. In front of the stark, four storey building, where Inge and her mother had the use of two rooms and a bathroom, he removed the rotor arm from the car's engine before picking up the brown paper parcel from the passenger seat and entering. Inge and her mother lived in one of the ground floor flats, sharing it with another family. Before the war they had lived in the affluent, riverside suburb of Blankenese, home to most of the city's ship owners and sea captains. After Captain Lang's ship had been lost with all hands in 1943, Frau Lang and Inge had been forced to seek cheaper accommodation in the city, which was subsequently destroyed in a bombing raid. The city authorities had allocated them their present home.

Inge, wearing a full-length, woollen dressing gown answered his knock. She pulled him into the icy hall where she throw her arms around his neck pulling him into a deep kiss. Behind her he was aware of one of the doors opening a crack and one of the other occupants peering at them. The door closed as they broke apart. The Lang's kitchen was a little warmer. One end was curtained off where Inge's mother had her bed. She was sitting at the kitchen table and gave Penrose a slight smile.

She was only in her late 50s but looked twenty years older. From photographs, that Penrose had seen of her, arm in arm with a handsome, young seafarer, it was easy to see where Inge got her beauty. But the loss of her husband, and subsequent events, had borne heavily on Frau Lang, resulting in the pathetic lady now seated at the table.

'*Guten Abend Frau Lang.*' She spoke very little English and Penrose's conversations with her were limited to greetings and good-byes without Inge's help. He sat down at the table, placed the paper parcel in front of her and untied the string. 'There you are. A bit of *essen* for you.'

Her thin fingers slowly peeled back the paper to reveal the contents. In addition to the huge slab of steak wrapped in greaseproof paper, the cook Sergeant had included bacon, butter, cooking fat, cheese, tea, a bag of carefully wrapped eggs, tinned milk and a small tin of Nescafe.

Her eyes lit up. She clasped Penrose's hand. '*Danke Harry. Danke*'

Penrose, not knowing what to say, winked at her. Inge came up behind him and draped her arms over his shoulders. 'Do you want something to eat Harry? There is still some soup on the stove.'

'No thanks sweetheart, I had a meal at the club with Terry Reader. I wouldn't mind a drink though.'

He watched Inge as she bustled about, putting away the food, whilst the kettle boiled, and then she made a pot of tea. Penrose knew it would be tea. The tin of Nescafe, worth its weight in gold on the black market, would be traded on. He sometimes wondered if Nescafe was ever drunk or just sold from hand to hand.

They made small talk whilst drinking the tea. Finally Inge collected the cups, swilled them under the tap and said. '*Komm. Schlafen*. We both have to work tomorrow.'

After kissing her mother goodnight, she led him back into the hall at the far end of which was her room. It was sparsely furnished. Just a double bed, which Penrose had acquired, and an upright chair. There was no floor covering. Inge's few dresses were draped over a string fixed across a corner, her underclothes and smaller items folded in two cardboard boxes.

The room was freezing. Inge took off her dressing gown. She was naked underneath. As she dashed towards the bed, her nipples became erect and goosepimples appeared on her body. She slipped beneath the goose-feather filled *decker* which she drew up to her neck. She looked at Penrose, who was slowly undressing, and said, 'Hurry up. I'm freezing. Come and warm me up.'

As he climbed in beside her, she wrapped her arms and legs around his body. He turned his head towards her and they kissed, her tongue probing deep into his mouth. Her left hand moved around his chest, toying with his nipples, before slowly moving down to his groin. He felt the first stirring of an erection. She grasped him, pulled her mouth away from his and whispered in his ear, 'I feel that you are no longer tired. Show me that you're not. Love me.'

After they had made love, Penrose lay on his back, staring at the ceiling. Inge leant over him and rubbed her forefinger across his lips. 'What do you say in your language? Penny for you thoughts.'

He looked at her. 'Have you given any thought to what we were talking about last week?'

She buried her head into his shoulder. 'Oh Harry *liebling*. You know I can't. There is nothing more I would like to do than to marry you. But I can't leave my mother. What would she do if I went to England with you? You also know it is not possible.'

He felt the wetness of her tears as they ran onto his skin. 'I'm not going to take no for an answer. I've got few weeks left here. I'm going work on you ever day until you see sense.'

'Harry, you know it is not possible. Let us just enjoy the time we have left together.' She moved onto him, covering his body with hers. 'Love me again *liebling* and then *schlafen*. We must work tomorrow.'

4

Inge and Penrose ran the gauntlet of good-natured, ribald comments as they walked into the Headquarters the following morning. Leaving her at her office door, after promising to try and see her that evening, Penrose went to see Warrant Officer Lancaster to whom he made his excuses for missing the morning prayers. Then he drove to the British Military Hospital.

There, in the guardroom, he found Terry Reader, leaning on the counter, drinking a mug of tea. Reader put down his mug. 'Hello Harry. You look a bit rough. Been getting your leg over all night?'

Penrose grinned. 'None of your bleeding business. Anyway, why are you hanging around here? You could have started without me.'

'Can't find McNeil. He didn't turn in for duty this morning. I've got a couple of runners out scouting for him.'

'Wonder what his game is Terry? Maybe he was out last night having his leg over as well.'

The Orderly Corporal, who had been listening to their conversation, snorted. 'That would be a first. He'd run a mile if he saw one. A train going in and out of tunnels is the only thing that gets him excited.'

The ringing of the telephone interrupted their laughter. The Orderly Corporal answered it, listened, then said, 'He's here sir.' He handed the receiver to Reader. 'It's your office Staff.'

Reader placed the receiver to his ear. 'Staff Sergeant Reader.' After listening, he said, 'Do we know who it is?' He glanced across at Penrose. 'OK. I've got Harry Penrose with me. We'll nip over there, have a looksee, then I'll get back to you.'

Reader slammed the receiver back into the cradle, then turned to Penrose. 'Civpol have just reported the discovery of a soldier's body in a house in Celleralle. That's just up the road from here. They want me to go over there, so you might as well come.' He turned to the Orderly Corporal. 'Can you arrange for a Medical Officer and an ambulance to meet us there?'

~ 26 ~

As they drove into the street that was once Celleralle they saw a black, German police car parked outside of one of the few buildings that were still standing. Two German policemen, dressed in black tunics, grey trousers and leather, coal-scuttle helmets, which always reminded Penrose of the hat worn by British postmen prior to the First World War, stood in front of the vehicle. Peering from the back of the car was a bedraggled, old man wearing a yellow armband which indicated that he was partially sighted.

One of the policemen saluted the two Service investigators as they approached and indicated the doorway behind him. Penrose followed Reader into the building. At the base of a pile of rubble, which had once been an internal wall, lay a body dressed in Air Force uniform. It was face down the head was turned away from them. Reader turned to Penrose. 'Looks like it's your shout Harry. It's one of yours.'

Penrose approached the body, carefully watching where he was treading to avoid disturbing anything that might be of evidence. As he drew near he could plainly see the thin, rope looped around the neck and tied tightly at the back of it. Moving sideways to get a better view of the face, he saw the protruding tongue and eyes, classic indications of strangulation. For some reason, he was not at all surprised to see that the victim was AC1 McNeil.

As he returned to the doorway he said, 'Look's like we've found the missing train spotter Terry.'

Outside, whilst waiting for the arrival of the ambulance, they found that the German policemen's English was very limited. To pass the time, Penrose took out his cigarette packet and offered it around. Both the policemen took a cigarette, which they put inside their helmets, indicating that they would smoke it later. Penrose knew that more than likely the cigarettes would be sold.

The ambulance arrived with an excited looking Royal Army Medical Corp. Captain. 'Not a lot for you to do here Doc', Penrose said. 'You can't do anything other than confirm that the person is dead.'

'Who are you?' the doctor asked.

'Sergeant Penrose, RAF SIB'

'So you are not medically trained or competent to declare if a person is dead or not? And, I would be obliged if you would address me as Sir.'

Terry Reader, standing behind the doctor, grinned at Penrose and raised his eyes to the heavens. Penrose, keeping a straight face, replied, 'No, I'm not competent. But if I see a person sprawled out with a ligature around his neck, cold as ice and in complete rigor, I don't figure he is sleeping off a heavy night. So, Sir, if you will follow me, step exactly where I step, because that is my area of expertise, examine the man and then tell me if, in your medical opinion, I am correct or not.'

As the doctor followed Penrose out of the building after confirming that McNeil was dead, he called across to the medical orderly, who was standing with the driver, 'OK Smith. You can go in and bring him out now.'

Penrose shook his head. 'Sorry Sir. He has to stay there for a while yet. Not very dignified, but there is a lot more I have to do before I can allow the body to be moved. The ambulance will have to remain here so I will give you a lift back to the hospital. I will take a statement from you later.' He turned to Reader. ' Can you hold the fort here while I nip back to the hospital Terry? I'll have to phone it in and get a photographer down here. Also keep the Kraut police here and the guy in their car. I'll have Inge brought along so I can talk to them.'

It was nearly an hour later before a staff car containing Warrant Office Lancaster, a police photographer and Inge arrived. She looked very pale as she got out of the car. Although she had attended various scenes in the past, Penrose knew she had never been to a scene of violent death before. He smiled at her. 'Don't worry sweetheart, you don't have to see anything nasty.'

'So what's going on now Harry?' Warrant Officer Lancaster asked.

'I'm waiting for a pathologist to come from the hospital.' As he was speaking, a staff car drew up. 'This might be him now. Whilst I take him and the photographer to the body could you and Inge talk to the policemen and get their story.'

A short, jovial looking man, carrying a medical bag, got out of the staff car and introduced himself as Lieutenant Colonel Balfour. 'Sorry I've taken so long. I was over at Luneberg Heath where a young man met his end when his mate started up the tank he was sleeping under. So, what have you got for me?'

Penrose led him and the photographer into the building. The pathologist observed the scene from a distance whilst the photographer took a number of photographs of the body from various angles.

'I don't think we are going to get too much evidence from this scene,' the pathologist said, taking two thermometers from his bag. He placed one on the pile of rubble and then approached the body. 'Let's see how cold he is. Help me get his trousers down Sergeant.' After inserting the second thermometer into McNeil's rectum, he waiting a while before recording the temperature, then he turned the body over and examined the hands. 'Just in case there is any thing on them, or under the nails, I'll bag them.' He took two white, paper bag from his case and taped them around the hands. 'There is no point in removing the ligature here. I'll leave it and cut it off when I do the autopsy.' He recorded the reading of the thermometer he had placed on the rubble, then packed his bag. 'OK Sergeant. Get him away to the mortuary. I should be able to deal with him this afternoon.'

The body was wrapped in a rubber sheet before being loaded into the ambulance and conveyed to the hospital.

Penrose joined Inge, WO Lancaster and the two German policemen. 'What's the story here Inge?'

'They were flagged down by Herr Busch ......'

'Whose Herr Busch?'

Inge indicated the old man in the police car who was peering myopically through the rear window. 'He flagged then down and told them that he had stumbled over the body in the building.'

'What was he doing in the building?'

'He's an old man. He had to answer the call of nature. He didn't see anything until he tripped over the legs.'

'Penrose looked again at the old man. 'I don't think he is our perpetrator.' He took out a full packet of cigarette which he handed to Inge. 'Get a short statement from him, then give him these and send him on his way.' From the way that the policemen looked at the packet of cigarette Penrose knew that they would not be in Herr Busch's possession for too long.

Penrose, Reader and Lancaster rejoined the photographer inside the building where they carried out a detailed search of the scene. They found nothing that should not have been there or anything that might be connected to the crime.

'What's your next step Harry?' Lancaster asked Penrose as they left the scene.

'First I'm going to pop over to Davidswatche and have a chat with Inspector Rossmann. There can't be any doubt now that this is connected to Willie Winkler's death and also the theft of the penicillin. Then I'm going back to the hospital to find out what McNeil was doing yesterday and to take a statement from the pathologist.' He looked at Reader. 'Do you want to double up on this job Terry?'

Reader shook his head. 'No. I've got too many jobs in the bag already. I'll suspend enquiries into the penicillin. Just keep me informed of your progress. If you crack this you'll have done my job for me.'

Inspector Rossmann formally greeted Penrose with a handshake and, '*Guten Tag*', before invited him to take a seat on a chair facing his desk. Penrose wondered if he ever relaxed or even smiled.

'So Herr Penrose, I hear that there has been a development which you are now involved in.'

'How the hell do you know Inspector? The development, as you call it, is less than three hours old.'

Rossmann's lips parted slightly. He can smile thought Penrose. 'Herr Penrose, we may be under occupation but this is still my city. Very little happens which I don't hear about. Especially what the military police are up to.'

~ The Hamburg Dossier ~

'So Inspector. Have you discovered who sent Winkler to his Maker?'

'Unfortunately not as yet. We are making life very uncomfortable for our criminals but none of them yet seem to know anything. My feeling is that the answer will be on your side of the fence.'

'Why do you think that Inspector?'

'Firstly the rope around his neck. We have some of the finest rope makers in the world around these docks and all tell me that the piece of rope is of British manufacture. Secondly, we are compiling a dossier on Winkler's business dealing which seemed to be mainly with British troops.'

'Well he was a small-time wheeler and dealer in the black market Inspector.'

'Thirdly, you now have a crime with a similar *modus operandi*. I think that is too much of a coincidence Herr Penrose.'

'Tell me Inspector, what were the findings of your Medical Examiner?'

'Winkler was killed by strangulation and put in the river sometime on Friday night or early Saturday morning.'

'If he was in the river from then until he was found on Sunday morning, why was he not swept downstream ending up in the North Sea?'

'Maybe that was the intention Herr Penrose. But we believe that the wake of a passing ship pushed the body to the riverside where it became jammed in some pilings by the Customs House and remained there until it was discovered. Tell me Herr Penrose, when did you last see Winkler and where?'

'Midday on Friday. At the top of Michel. It was then that he told me about the penicillin job. He was going to do a bit more digging and then get back to me. He never did.'

'Digging Herr Penrose?'

'English slang Inspector. It means that he was going to ask around and see what more he could discover.'

'And at that time he did not make any mention of *Der Taucher,* the Diver?'

'No.'

'So we must assume that it was something he discovered while he was doing, what do you say, digging?'

'It looks that way Inspector. Has nothing come to light in your inquiries?'

'Just a little. One of the criminals we spoke to remembers that he overheard a group of men discussing a deal involving spare parts for vehicles and that the Diver was mentioned as the supplier. He cannot remember where or when this discussion took place but he believes that the Diver is a British soldier. Others we have spoken to deny any knowledge of the Diver.'

Penrose grinned and shook his head. 'It looks like you are putting the ball into my court more and more Inspector.'

'More English slang Herr Penrose?'

'Yes. To put it crudely, all the shit is being thrown my way.'

Rossmann not only smiled, he burst out laughing. 'That's the joys of being a policeman Herr Penrose. We are expected to shovel it against the tide. It has always been so.' He took out a handkerchief and wiped the tears from his eyes.

So much for German humour, thought Penrose. He stood up and offered his hand to Rossmann. 'I better go and find my big shovel Inspector. I'll be in contact with you.'

Much to Penrose's surprise, Rossmann rose from his seat and said, 'I'll walk down with you Herr Penrose.'

Outside of the building Rossmann said, 'This is not over Herr Penrose. I think this is just the beginning.' He grasped Penrose's hand and shook it again. 'Keep in touch Herr Penrose. Maybe we can come to a private arrangement and exchange our progress reports. We will sort this out together.'

5

Penrose entered the British Military Hospital and followed the signs to the pathology department. He found Lt. Col. Balfour in a small office adjoining the post-mortem room smoking a foul-smelling, blackened pipe

'Ah Sergeant! Come in. Come in. Push those files off of that chair and settle your arse down.' Penrose could never understand why forensic pathologists always seemed to have a sense of humour. 'I haven't got much to give your at the moment. I haven't had a chance to start on your man yet. He is still deep in rigor, must have been a bloody sight colder than he looked. What I can tell you is that, according to my calculations, he met his end between six and eight last night.' He pushed a paper bag towards Penrose. 'That the ligature. A length of thin rope. It was drawn around the neck and then knotted behind. Not self-inflected. It happened where he was found. The post-mortem lividity is fixed to the front of the body which shows that he was not moved before he was found.' He picked up his pipe, studied it before reaming around in the bowel, then put a match to it, puffing out a cloud of smoke. 'I don't think I am going to find anything else to help you when I open him up. Anyway, I'll get my report to you. Is there anything you want to ask at this point?'

Penrose shook his head.

'Right then Sergeant. I'll let you get about your business. The best of luck with your investigation.'

The rear of the cookhouse was like all Service cookhouses wherever they are found in the world. Two troughs of boiling, bubbling water in which the sated soldiers washed their cutlery and mugs, and a sweet odour from a line of bins containing the waste food which would become pig swill.

Inside, the odour was of rancid fat and boiled cabbage. Penrose entered a small office where a Senior NCO was working at a paper-strewn desk. He stared at Penrose for a few seconds before saying, 'Yes Squire? What can I do for you?'

Penrose produced his warrant card. 'I want to have a few words with one of your cooks. He goes by the name of Ginger, is a friend of an AC1 McNeal and is interested in trains.'

'Oh, that'll be Fatty Herbert, Private Herbert. He's working in the kitchen at the moment. Tell you what Squire, go and make yourself at home in the rest room next door and I'll send him to you.'

The rest room would not have won a Michelin award for cleanliness. A long, narrow table along the centre of the room was strewn with old newspapers, copies of Tit Bits and Men Only and unwashed, tea-stained mugs. Dirty cooks' whites spilt out from a line of lockers along one wall. As Penrose surveyed this picture of hygienic excellence a short, portly figure dressed in cooks' whites, which were marginally cleaner than those spilling from the wall lockers, enter the room. His moon face, adorned with steel-rimmed, Service spectacles, was surmounted with shock of bright, ginger hair. He gazed at Penrose then, with a nervous, half-grin, said, in a soft voice, 'Private Herbert Sir.'

'Come in Ginger. Sit yourself down. I want to ask you a few questions about AC1 McNeal.'

Ginger bristled. 'That blooming sod. I haven't seen him today. He didn't come into breakfast. But when I get off duty I'm going to have a few words with him.'

'What about Ginger?'

'Well. We were supposed to be going to the pictures last night. I was going to meet him at the tram stop. But as I was coming out of camp I saw him talking to someone in a car. He got in it and they drove away before I got there.'

'Do you know whose car it was Ginger?'

'No. We always go to the NAAFI Club on the tram. I went down there last night thinking I would meet him there. But he never turned up, or at the pictures. You just wait till I see him.'

Penrose looked at Ginger with pity. 'Ginger,' he said quietly, 'I'm afraid you're not going to see your friend again. He's dead.'

Ginger sat with his mouth agape. Behind his thick spectacles his eyes misted up. 'No. Not Percy. He can't be. He's my mate.' He leant forward across the table and buried his face in his hands.

For some minutes Penrose left him to his grief, then gently touched him on the shoulder. 'Ginger. You've got to help me. We have got to find out what happened.'

Ginger slowly sat up. He took off his spectacled and wiped his eyes with his sleeve before replacing them.'

'Right Ginger. How long have you known er, what's his name, Percy?'

'Since he came here. About six months ago.'

'Why were you mates? It's a bit unusual for a pongo and a Brylcreem boy to be mates, isn't it?'

'We found that we both liked trains, so we became mates. We liked to go to the station and look at the trains.'

'Is that all you used to do?'

'No. We sometimes used to go to Hamburg House for a nosh up. We would go to the pictures and sometimes just walk around the town.'

'Did you ever go drinking together.'

'No. We don't drink.'

'What about women? Did you ever go out to pick up a bit of pussy?'

Ginger blushed a bright red, very near the colour of his hair. 'No. We don't have anything to do with women. You never know what you might catch.'

'Okay. So what about men?'

Ginger looked perplexed. 'What do you mean Sir?'

'What I mean Ginger is did you live up to your nickname? Ginger, ginger beer, queer?'

Ginger jumped to his feet. His soft voice rose to a squeak. 'No. That's filthy. We are not like that.'

'Okay Ginger. Settle down. I believe you but I have to ask these questions.'

~ The Hamburg Dossier ~

'You must be that policeman who Percy said was horrible to him. When you asked him about the penicillin being pinched.'

'What do you know about that Ginger?'

'Only what Percy told me. The store got broken into when he was having his supper.'

'That's right.' Penrose agreed. 'Either when he was having his supper or talking to you about steam trains. Did he always come for his supper about 9.30 and spend the next couple of hours talking to you/'

'Yes. Except last Tuesday. He was late. Didn't get to the cookhouse until about eleven o'clock. I had to cook him something as the supper was all gone'

'Why was he late?'

'He said that the policeman kept him talking.'

Penrose's head jerked up. 'What policeman Ginger?'

'I don't know. Percy said that he was checking the safety of all the stores in the hospital. He told Percy that it was a secret and he was not to tell anyone but he told me because I was his mate. Percy said he was nice. When he found out that we liked trains he said he would get us a pass to go into the marshalling yards so we could get up close to the engines.'

'Was he a RAF or a Military policeman?'

'I don't know. Percy only called him the policeman. He didn't say if he was a red cap or a snowdrop.' Ginger was referring to the colour of the cap covers of the respective police arms.

'What did you do yesterday Ginger?'

'After breakfast we went to Hauptbahnhof and spent the day there watching the trains coming through. I had made us some sandwiches. We came back to camp about five and arranged to meet at the tram stop at six. He was there before me but he got into the car.'

'What about this car? What make was it?'

'A Beetle.'

'Colour?'

'I don't know. It was dark. It could have been black, blue or brown.'

'Had you ever seen Percy get into a car before?'

'No.'
'Had he ever spoken about anyone who owned a car?'
'No.'
'Right Ginger, I want the truth to what I'm going to ask you now. I'm not going to nick you, I just want to find who killed your mate.'
Ginger went ashen. 'Oh no. Did somebody kill Percy?'
'I'm afraid they did. Did you or Percy ever do any business?'
'What do you mean Sir?'
'Did you ever sell anything on the black-market? Have you sold any rations, did Percy sell any stores? Did either of you sell cigarettes? I want the truth.'
Ginger went red. 'We did sometimes sell cigarettes.'
'Where and who to?'
'To a bloke who stand around the corner from Hamburg House.'
'What did you use the money for?'
'Nothing. We were saving up. We're going....' He hesitated. 'We was going to try and go to Switzerland on leave. They have some lovely trains there.'
'One last question Ginger. Did either of you know a bloke called The Diver?'
Ginger looked blank and shook his head.

After recording a written statement from Ginger Penrose visited the Hospital Adjutant from whom he established that no security survey had been carried out on the hospital stores. Next, accompanied by the Orderly Officer, he carried out a search of McNeil's bed space. There was little to find. The bed was neatly made with a pair of pyjamas folded under the pillow. Hanging in an upright locker were a working uniform, a sleeveless leather jerkin and the denim overall that McNeil had been wearing when Penrose interviewed him. On the floor of the locker was a bundle of webbing equipment and an empty service kitbag complete with the rope fastener. Stuck on the inside of the door were two prints of the Flying Scotsman and the Master Cutler steaming through a country scene. On the middle shelf of a bedside locker was a folded service shirt, a change of underclothes, woollen socks and a set of PT kit. In the drawer were a well-thumbed copy of a Bible and a bundle of letters. All the letters were from McNeil's father. The contents showed that McNeil came from a religious family, his father advising him to stay out of trouble and to attend church regularly. Penrose wondered if the family had yet been visited by a Service padre stationed near their home, who would have broken the news of their son's death, bringing anguish to them. At the back of the drawer Penrose found an envelope containing 600 Reichmarks. Written on the envelope was 'Me and Gingers Holiday Money'.

Leaving the Orderly Officer to arrange for McNeil's effects to be taken into storage, Penrose wandered out of the hut where he stopped and lit a cigarette. Blowing out a stream of smoke, he muttered under his breath, 'Poor little bastard. Not much to show for eighteen years of life. He and Ginger are never going to see those Swiss trains.'

6

As Penrose passed the open door of Inge's office, she called to him, 'Inspector Rossmann has sent over a copy of his report. I am translating it now.'

'Can you give me a run-down on it now honey?', Penrose replied, entering the office and sitting down in a chair facing her desk.

Inge picked up a sheaf of paper and sorted them out into separate piles. 'Okay, first we have the medical report by a Doctor Tempel who says........'

'You can skip that sweetheart,' Penrose interrupted. 'I know how he died and I don't think going through it again is going to help me at the moment.'

Inge carefully put the medical report to one side. With a knowing smile, she indicated the remaining papers and said, 'So, what do you want to hear?'

'Is there anything on Willi's background?'

From the pile of papers Inge drew out a single sheet. 'Not too much. His name, date of birth and the address he was living at, all taken from his identity card. They are trying to obtain details of his military service. They say he was unmarried and had no known next of kin.'

Penrose's head shot up. 'Not married? He was always talking about his wife. I can't remember if he ever mentioned her name but he was always going on about his wife. How she used to give him a hard time if he was not making any money. Did they visit his address?'

Inge shuffled through the papers again. 'Here we are. 164 Fishers Allee in Altona. Only the basement is inhabitable. The people living there have been there for eight months. They have never heard of Gerhart Winkler. A shopkeeper opposite remembered Winkler being there two years ago, soon after the end of the war, but has not seen him for over eighteen months. He did not know where he went to.'

'So who is this wife?' mused Penrose. 'Where the hell can I find her?'

~ *The Hamburg Dossier* ~

Inge tidied the pile of papers. 'Why not ask the people he worked or mixed with? When I first came to work here I knew nobody. Now, by listening and asking a few questions, I know all about everyone's family even though I have never met them.'

Penrose leant over the desk and pecked Inge on the cheek. 'A wise and beautiful head on such young shoulders. Why didn't I think of that?' Penrose stood up. 'I may well be late tonight *schatz*, so don't wait up for me.'

'So I am not so wise.' said Inge, with a pout. 'I should have kept my suggestions until early mornings.'

Penrose reached the door before turning around. 'The only suggestion I want to hear from you in the mornings is that we should get married.'

Inge smiled and shook her head before saying, 'Go on. Get out of here.'

Penrose had only just time to settle at his desk and say to Jones, 'Is there any tea in the pot?' before Warrant Officer Lancaster bustled into the Investigators' office.

'So Harry. What's happening? Have you solved it yet?'

'Wishful thinking Boss,' replied Penrose. 'I've got the where, when and how, but the why is a bit dodgy and the who, well I haven't a clue.'

'What's the dodgy why Harry?' Lancaster asked.

'The possible motive. It's so iffy that it would sound crazy. The poor little sod seemed to lead a blameless life. Going off to look at his trains with his mate Ginger, having a nosh-up in the NAAFI, going to the pictures and reading his bible. His only transgression was to occasionally sell a few fags so he could go on holiday to Switzerland to look at more trains. Never upset anyone. Certainly not enough to make someone want to do him in.'

All the investigators at their desks had ceased what they were doing and were listening intently.

'Go on Harry,' Lancaster said.

'So that leaves only one thing,' continued Penrose. 'The break-in at the store.'

'Do you think he was involved with that?' Lancaster asked.

'No. But I think he knew someone who was. Someone who he could identify, so he had to be got rid of.'

'So who's this somebody?' Lancaster asked.

'The who? I don't know Guv. Well I do but I only know him as The Policeman.'

'This is getting like some kid's game.' said Jones. 'What with divers and now policemen.'

'What policeman Harry?' Lancaster asked.

Penrose related what Ginger Herbert had told him. He went on, 'I've checked with the Crime Prevention Section and they were not carrying out a security survey. They contacted their counterparts in the Military Police who also denied they were doing anything. So what we are left with is someone posing as a policeman who was casing the store last Tuesday night. Someone who spent some time with young McNeil, who promised to get him a pass to visit the marshalling yard. Someone who young Percy McNeil could finger.'

The listeners sat in silence. Lancaster took one of Penrose's cigarettes from the packet on the desk, lit it, and then asked, 'You think there is a connection Harry?'

'I do Boss. And I think it is connected to Willie Winkler's murder, so I am going to try that route. The German police have made no mention of Willi's wife but I know he either had one or was shacking up with someone who he called his wife. I'm going to find her and see what she can tell me.' He looked across at Jones. 'Fancy trawling the ladies of the night with me Davy?'

'Sorry mate', replied Jones. 'I've just collared a job over at Celle. Some WAAF has made a complaint of rape.'

'So what are you hanging around here for? Don't you remember what they taught us at Peel House? In the case of rape speed is of the essence to acquire the evidence.'

'Yes. That all very well in theory,' said Jones with a laugh. 'But the dirty deed took place on Saturday night and it has taken her until today to decide if it really happened or if it was her imagination. So I guess, now, at least I hope, she has had a few washes since then. I'll have my tea first and then get over there.'

'Okay Boss,' Penrose said to Lancaster. 'I'll do it solo.'

As Lancaster walked out of the room he said, 'Watch yourself then Harry with them women. Don't get carried away. Put your number on the soles of your boots so we know who you are without having to pull you out.' Chuckling, he slammed the door behind him before throwing it open again. Sticking his head in the room, he said to Penrose, 'And don't forget to give me a written report.'

During the afternoon and evening the dry, bitter cold of the last week had given way to a steady drizzle. Sitting in his parked car in a deserted Zeughausmark, Penrose had been watching the entrance of the Café Arnold for nearly two hours. He was waiting for a particular woman, but he was beginning to think that because of the weather she might forgo business that night. He had decided to wait until the bar of the Seamen' Mission closed, when some still thirsty sailors in search of female company might make their way across the road to the Café Arnold instead of going further afield. He also hoped that the lady in question might have the same idea.

He saw a shadowy figure come from the direction of the U-Bahn station. A flick of his finger activated the car's wipers, clearing the windshield, showed him that it was the woman he was waiting for, Lisa Lotte Klose. Wearing a long, leather coat tightly belted around her 5' 5", slim body and a dark beret angled on her long, jet-black hair, she walked with a poise that could have graced any fashion catwalk. Originally from the east of the country, fleeing before the Russian liberators, her classic features betrayed the gypsy genes inherited from distant Slavic ancestors. Although still in her early twenties, she was accepted as the leading figure amongst the women who plied their trade in the Café Arnold.

Penrose waited three or four minutes before following her into the bar. The clientele were thin on the ground. Six women were sitting at tables around the dance floor, two of them with young men who, by their bearing and haircuts, were obviously servicemen in mufti.

Penrose's entrance had drawn expectant looks from all the women before they looked away. The two with the men showed some concern. They whispered to their companions who both glanced at Penrose then hunched over their glasses of beer. The three-piece orchestra was resting, chatting amongst themselves.

Lisa was at the back of the room, sitting alone in a corner banquette. She looked at Penrose then turned her head and stared into the distance. Penrose crossed to her table and slid into the seat beside her. 'Hello Lisa.'

Slowly, she turned her head towards him. 'What you want?' she said in attractive broken English.

'Just a little chat,' Penrose replied.

'Fuck off.'

'That's not very friendly,' Penrose said as he sensed a movement at his shoulder.

It was Herman the waiter. With his gold-rimmed spectacles, he always reminded Penrose of Himmler. *'Bitte mein Herr?'*

'Can I buy you a drink?' Penrose asked Lisa.

She did not reply. Penrose turned to Herman, *'Bringen Sie mir ein Glas Bier Herr Ober und ein trinken fur Lisa.'*

Lisa broke into peals of laughter. Her outburst caused the other women to turn and stare at her. Her laughter seemed to ease the tension that had settled on the bar.

'What's so funny?' Penrose asked.

'Your German. You speak it very funny.'

'Well, at least it has made you to talk to me. Why don't you want to?'

Lisa took a cigarette out of a packet that Penrose had laid on the table, placed it in her mouth and then leant towards Penrose, waiting for him to light it. She inhaled deeply before answering. 'Because you are a big liar.'

'About what?' Penrose asked.

'You say you are a driver but we know you are MP.'

'Where did you get that idea Lisa?'

'You come here a long time with Willie, but you never go with any of the girls. We make fun with Willie saying you are queer boys. Willie get mad and say you are policeman and he work for you. Now Willie *tot* - dead. You get Willie killed.'

Penrose shook his head. Before he could reply Herman came to the table and placed a glass of beer in front of him and a glass that could have contained anything from cold tea to coloured water, known as the hostess' drink, in front of Lisa.

Penrose waited until Herman was out of earshot before saying, 'Okay, I am a policeman but I am not interested in what you or any of the girls in here do. I'm not anti-vice, I'm criminal. Have I ever caused you or the rest of the girls any trouble? Have I ever caused any problems for your boyfriends when they have been in here after curfew like those two over there?' He indicated the two men sitting with the women by the dance floor.

Lisa shrugged her shoulders and said, 'Yes. That is true. What do you want to talk to me about?'

'Willie. I liked Willie. Now I want to find who killed him.'

The band suddenly came to life as four seamen entered the bar. They looked around, inspecting the available women, before seating themselves at two tables on the edge of the dance-floor.

Lisa helped herself to another one of Penrose's cigarettes. 'Go on,' she said.

'Do you know anything about Willi's wife?'

'Pussy? She not really his wife. They not married but live together.'

'Where do they live?'

Lisa shrugged her shoulders. 'I don't know. Somewhere off the Reeperbahn.'

'Is there anyone who can tell me where they live?'

'Maybe Pussy tell you.'

Penrose looked at Lisa in astonishment. 'How the hell can she tell me if I don't know where she is?'

'I know where she is,' Lisa said. 'She will be at work.'

'At work! She'll be at work and poor old Willie not yet in his grave?'

'Yes. She very sad for Willie but Pussy always say "Business is business and love is bullshit".'
'Where does she work Lisa?'
'Herbertstrasse. Number 6. Now you buy me another drink?'
Penrose signalled to Herman to bring to bring another round of drinks. He turned back to Lisa. 'How long has she worked there?'
'Very long time. She start there before the war.'
'Lisa, do you know anyone known as *Der Taucher*?'
'*Nein*. Who he?'
'He might be a British soldier. He might use that name in the bars.'
'Okay. I ask around. Then you come and see me again?'
'Just be careful when you are asking. I don't want you to end up like Willie.'
After Herman put the drinks on the table, Lisa helped herself to a third cigarette. 'Have you got girlfriend?'
'Yes.' Penrose replied.
'Which bar she work?'
'She doesn't work in a bar.'
'Ah! So she good girl. You need a bad girl like me.'
'I'm sure you're not a bad girl Lisa.'
She rubbed her hand up and down the top of Penrose's thigh. 'I can be a very bad girl and make you very happy.'
Penrose grasped her wrist and removed her hand from his crotch. 'I'm sure you could Lisa, but what about business being business and love is bullshit?' Another group of seamen entered the bar. 'I think your business is just arriving and mine is down the road.' He signalled Herman for the bill. After paying, he pushed his nearly empty packet of cigarettes towards her and said, 'I'll come and see you again.'
Leaving the warmth of the bar, Penrose headed into the drizzle towards his car.

7

Herbertstrasse was Hamburg's second brothel street. Penrose slowly walked up the slight slope of Davidstrasse towards its entrance. Passing around the offset, wooden screens, bearing the out of bounds warning, he entered a short, narrow, cobbled street with a continuous terrace of small dwellings on either side. Behind the windows of the houses were women in various stages of undress. Some of the windows had closed curtains which showed that the occupant was at work, but where the curtains were open the lighting was so low that it was nearly impossible to judge the dubious ages of those plying for hire. Despite the late hour, the street was crowded with men, of various nationality and colour, wandering up and down, peering at the goods on offer and some at open windows trying to reduce the asking price.

As he walked down the street Penrose was solicited by the occupants of each window he passed whom either tapped on the glass to attract his attention or called through small transom windows set into the larger panes of glass. The curtains of No. 6 were closed so he continued to the halfway point of the street where a small, arched cul-de-sac gave access to four more brothels off of the main thoroughfare. Here Penrose sheltered from the rain waiting for No. 6 to open again for business.

The RAF Police patrol jeep parked in front of Davidwache, directly behind, although the patrol didn't know it, Penrose's car. The two members of the patrol continued an argument that had been going on for the past fifteen minutes.

'For Christ sake Lofty lets call it a bloody night,' the observer, Corporal Bill Sharp, said. 'It's one o'clock on a wet Wednesday morning, it's passed curfew hour and the day before pay-day. You ain't going to find anyone about now.'

Sharp was a wartime policeman, now anxiously awaiting his demobilisation to come round. His enthusiasm for the job had long evaporated. On the other hand, the driver, Corporal Lofty Wilson, was a National Serviceman of six months standing. He was a giant of a man who enjoyed intimidating not only the unfortunate serviceman who fell into his clutches but also his colleagues. He was known as a 'brown nose' and suspected of passing on tales to the superiors. No one in the anti-vice patrol section was keen to work with him.

'The patrol is not due to finish until two o'clock Jack,' Wilson said. 'We've got time to do a pass along Herbertstrasse. You can please yourself, but I'm going.'

'Reluctantly, Sharp got out of the jeep. He know that if he didn't go with Wilson the section Flight Sergeant would know about it later that day. He turned the collar of his greatcoat up around his neck and fell into step beside Wilson.

Penrose watched the curtains to No. 6 being drawn back before wandering over to the window. A tall, thin, angular woman was sitting on a stool behind the window, wearing a lacy, black brassiere, which exposed more of her minute breasts than it concealed, and a pair of black, French knickers. She opened the small transom window.

'*Deutsch?*' she asked.

Penrose shook his head, 'English'.

'Okay. I speak English,' she replied. 'Short time. One hundred Reichmarks.'

Penrose nodded and moved to the adjacent door that she unlocked and allowed him access. The room was sparsely furnished. A narrow bed against one of the wall, along which was a full-length mirror with a second mirror fixed to the ceiling above the bed. Two, upright, wooden chair. On one of the chairs was an enamel bowl containing water, a tablet of soap and a wash flannel. In spite of the low lighting provided by a red bulb in a standard lamp at the back of the room, Penrose could see that the woman was in her late thirties. Her short, blonde hair was a product of peroxide.

She held out her hand. 'First *Geld*. One hundred Reich marks.'

Penrose handed her a bundle of notes which she counted before putting them into a tin box that was under the bed. She turned back to him and hooked her thumbs into the waistband of her knickers.

Penrose raised his hand. 'Don't bother with that. Are you Pussy?'

She froze. Her knickers had been pulled down to the top of her thighs, exposing a line of jet-black, pubic hair. A look of concern appeared on her face. 'Who are you?'

'I'm Harry Penrose. I want to ask you about Willie.'

She hauled her knickers back up. 'You are the policeman who Willie worked with?'

'You might say that,' replied Penrose. 'Have the German police spoken to you yet?'

'No. They don't know about me and I don't want to get involved with them.'

'But surely you want them to find the person who killed Willie?'

'Look Mister Harry. Very bad people did this thing to Willie. If I speak to police then very bad things will happen to me. Willie is dead, finish. I still have to live.'

Penrose offer her a cigarette. 'Look Pussy, I want to find out who killed Willie. Please trust me. Talk to me. Do you know who might have killed him?'

Pussy went over and sat on the bed, her arms crossed over her breasts and her head bowed. After short silence she looked up at Penrose. 'Last week Willie was meeting the big gangsters in the bars in Grosse Freiheit. On Friday he say that he had something important to tell you. He went out that night to see you. That was the last time I see him.'

'Friday night?' Penrose asked, mystified. 'I saw him at midday on Friday, but not at night.'

'Sure,' replied Pussy. 'When he left he say he would go into the bar near our house and telephone you.'

'I didn't get a phone call from him. Did he ever mention anyone called *Der Taucher*?'

Despite the red tinted lighting, Penrose saw Pussy face go white. Her clasped hands, dangling between her legs, tightened. 'Willie say that is a very bad man. He is big gangster. Willie say he is Englishman. I don't know who he is.'

'Does Willie have any papers at your house Pussy?'

Pussy jumped. 'You no come to my house,' she said, in a raised voice.

'I don't want to Pussy. But if you find anything, you could bring it here and I'll call and see you again. Now I'll let you get back to business.'

As Penrose moved towards the door, Pussy stood up and suggestively slipped her hands into the top of her knickers, pushing them down slightly. 'Sure you don't want a short time? Only one hundred marks.'

Penrose laughed. 'Business is business and love is bullshit. Is that right Pussy?'

'Sure,' she replied.

He was still laughing as he left the house.

The Anti-Vice Patrol came around the barrier just as Penrose was approaching it. Jack Smart recognised Penrose and was set to ignore him and pass him by. However, Loft Wilson side-stepped in front of Penrose and stopped his progress.

'Are you a member of His Majesty's Forces?'

'Forget it Lofty,' Smart said, as Penrose attempted to step around Wilson, who put out his massive arm to outmanoeuvre him.

'Leave this to me Jack,' he said before again saying to Penrose, 'Are you a member of His Majesty's Forces?' His raised voice attracted the nearby punters who turned their attention from the windows to watch the street theatre.

'Let's move out of here into Davidstrasse and sort it out there,' Penrose said, aware of the stares of the crowd.

An evil grin appeared on Wilson's face. Knowing that he was now the centre of attention, he said, 'We will sort it out here. Let me see your identity card.'

Penrose cast an appealing glance at Sharp who again tried to intervene. 'Lofty, let's get away from this crowd.'

'No Jack. I will do it my way.' He prodded Penrose in the chest. 'Your identity card, now.'

Penrose reached into an inside pocket. Wilson, who had been expecting a blue identity card of the Royal Air Force or a brown of the Army, blanched when he was confronted by a white SIB warrant card bearing the Provost Marshal's signature in red ink.

Whilst he floundered, hoping for support from Wilson who had suddenly seen something of interest in one of the nearby windows, Penrose hissed at him, 'Out into Davidstrasse, now arsehole.'

Beyond the barrier, in a deserted Davidstrasse, Wilson began apologising. Penrose was in no mood for his apologies. Probing Wilson in the chest, he said, 'Look. Just piss off Corporal. If you've blown me out in there I'll have your guts for garters. You've got a lot to learn. I think that your white cap bears heavy on your head.'

He turned on his heels and walked down the hill leaving the patrol to stare after him.

From the shadows of the cul-de-sac, The Diver watched Penrose's confrontation with the patrol. He breathed a sigh of relief as they left Herbertstrasse, thanking his lucky stars that they had stopped Penrose and not carried on along the street where they could not have failed to have seen him.

He walked across to the window of No. 6. Pussy watched his approach and opened the small window as he stopped and peered at her.

'*Deutsch?*' she asked.

The Diver shook his head. '*Nein. Schwedisch.*'

Swedish was not in Pussy's range of languages. 'Speak English?'

The Diver nodded.

'Okay,' said Pussy. 'Short time, one hundred Reichmarks.'

The Diver nodded again. She indicated the adjacent door.

When The Diver entered the room he checked that the curtains had been tightly drawn. Pussy held out her hand. 'First *geld*.'

After she had deposited the money in the tin box under the bed, she stepped out of her knickers and unhooked her brassiere. Crossing to The Diver she pulled off his topcoat and jacket, which she threw across the empty chair, and then attacked his trouser belt and fly buttons. 'Come on. *Schnell, schnell.* Time is money.' She turned and walked to the other chair at the foot of the bed, straddled the bowl of water on it and began to wash herself.

The Diver, kitbag rope in hand, darted behind her. The reflection of his sudden movement in the mirror attracted her attention. A look of sheer terror appeared on her face. Her intake of breath was cut off before she could release the scream that was building up inside her.

Dragging her by the rope around her neck, he threw her face down onto the bed, toppling the chair and bowl of water as he did so. Lying along her back, he pulled hard on the rope ends. Her struggles excited him and he found that he had an erection. Forcing her legs apart with his knee, he entered her and thrust again and again as he pulled harder on the rope. Pussy did not feel him climax. She would never feel anything again. Only her lifeless eyes stared at him from the wall mirror.

8

It was 6.30 in the morning when Inspector Rossmann made his way through the collection of parked police cars in Davidstrasse to the barriers of Herbertstrasse where two uniformed policemen saluted him.

'Is the other end of the street also sealed off?' he asked. When he had received the confirmation he added, 'Good! Only let the women who normally work here enter. I will want to speak to all of them.'

In the narrow street, uniformed and plain-clothed policemen were talking to a handful of men who had ventured there in the early hours. A number of the working girls, mainly the older ones who had worked throughout the night with little success but were still hoping to make a few marks with the pre-dawn trade, stood at their doorways, protected against the cold morning chill by heavy coats thrown over their scanty working attire.

Outside No. 6 Rossmann met his assistant. 'So Manfred, what have we got?'

Manfred consulted his notebook. 'The victim is a Karin Averbeck, working name Pussy. She is 39 years of age and lives just around the corner at 169 Hopsenstrasse. She was found by her cleaner who arrived at her usual time of 6 am. Pussy, I'll call her Pussy, normally finished work at about three o'clock. This morning the cleaner noticed that the curtains were still closed and suspected that Pussy might have an all-night client. She quietly opened the door to Pussy's room. The light was still burning and she saw Pussy lying on the bed. She ran down to Davidwache to report it. I got here about ten minutes ago.'

'Whose inside now?' Rossmann asked.

'Doctor Tempel, the Medical Examiner.'

Rossmann moved to just inside the entrance of the house. Floodlights had been erected. Their harsh light showed how tatty the room really was. Near the foot of the bed were an upturned chair, a washing bowl and an empty tin box. Doctor Tempel was bending over the body sprawled on the bed, taking a swab of the skin between her legs. He turned as Rossmann greeted him.

'Ah! Good morning Klaus. Looks like our man has been at work again. Same method, same type of rope, but this time he left a little something else. Immediately before or during her death someone had sexual intercourse with her.'

'So our man is also a pervert,' Rossmann remarked. 'I'll leave you to finish up Doctor before I do my examination.'

Rossmann went outside where he found his assistant talking to a plain-clothes officer. 'Sir,' the assistant said, 'this officer has been talking to a woman who works opposite. She saw a man leaving No. 6 last night who was stopped and arrested by a British patrol. It was an Air Force patrol. She did not see Pussy's curtains open again after the man left.'

'Fine. Leave it with me,' Rossmann said. 'I'll contact the British authorities.'

It was past nine o'clock when Penrose arrived at the police headquarters. Standing outside was Jack Sharp, one of the patrol corporals from the previous night.

'Hello Sarge,' Sharp said. 'I want to apologise for last night.'

'That's okay Jack,' Penrose replied. 'I realise it was your bloody partner. You didn't have to get out of bed on your day off to come and apologise to me.'

Sharp looked embarrassed. 'Well, actually Sarge, I was called in to give a statement about last night.'

Penrose laughed. 'Looks like your mate got his two pennyworth in first. Still, don't worry about it. I was on duty and my activities are recorded in my diary. Anyway, I'm glad I've seen you. Maybe you can help me. I'm looking for a bloke I can use.'

Sharp smiled. 'Well you wouldn't have found one where you was last night.'

'Leave it out Jack. What I want is a jack-the-lad, someone who knows his way around the town. Someone who can get into places where I might have a bit of trouble. Do you know anyone?'

'Yeah. There is a guy stationed with the Regiment at Celle. He comes into town every weekend to get his end away. He's a bit of a joke with our section but he's harmless. He does a bit of business, mainly to get his weekend beer money. Look, meet up with me on Saturday and I'll point him out.'

As Penrose walked towards Inge's office, framing in his mind his excuse for not going to her home the previous night, he passed the open door of Warrant Officer Lancaster's office, who called out, 'Just a minute Harry.'

When Penrose went into the room he was surprised to see the section commander, Squadron Leader Mark Johnson, sitting, out of sight, in the corner.

'Morning Sir, morning Boss,' Penrose greeted them. 'Sorry I'm a bit late. I was working late last night.'

'We know,' Lancaster replied. 'Do you know a Karin Averbeck?'

Penrose shook his head. 'Don't mean a thing to me Boss. Should it?'

'What about her other name? Pussy of Herbertstrasse?'

'That's Willi's girlfriend. I found her last night. So, what about her?'

'She's dead Harry.'

Penrose looked at him and then at the Squadron Leader. 'Ah, Jesus Boss. What the hell's going on?'

'I don't know Harry. I was hoping you did. You see, your friend Inspector Rossmann has put you in the frame for it.'

Penrose's mouth was agape for some seconds. 'That's a load of bollocks. You've got to be bloody crazy Boss to believe something like that.'

'I'm afraid not Sergeant,' Squadron Leader Johnson said. 'It is being taken very seriously. The Provost Marshal's department at Bückeburg is sending up two investigators. Till then, I have to suspend you and ask you to remain in this office awaiting their arrival. Will you hand over your warrant card to Mr. Lancaster?'

The next forty-five minutes passed in an uneasy silence. Squadron Leader Johnson had returned to his own office whilst Warrant Officer Lancaster shuffled files from in-tray to out-tray in an attempt to appear busy. Penrose's mind was in a whirl. What was going on? Was it all connected to the theft of the penicillin? Why were his possible witnesses being killed? Was the killer anticipating his every move? Was there an attempt being made to frame him?

Footsteps along the corridor heralded the arrival of the Bückeburg investigators. Penrose knew both of them. Flight Lieutenant Jack Adams and Flight Sergeant Dick Baker were pre-war Metropolitan CID officers. Now, as two of the most experienced RAF Police investigators, they were mainly engaged in bringing war criminals to justice.

After greeting Lancaster, they turned to Penrose. Dick Baker gave him a wink. 'So Harry,' Jack Adams said, 'lets see if we can sort this mess out. First, I'm going to take you to Davidwache so Inspector Rossmann can have a chat with you. Then we will see how it goes from there.' He turned back to Lancaster. 'Have you got an interpreter we can use Mr. Lancaster?'

'We have Inge Lang,' Lancaster replied.

'Do we have to bring her into this Boss?' Penrose interjected.

'What's the problem?' Adams asked.

Lancaster looked across at Penrose. 'Inge is Harry's bit of stuff.'

'I don't give a shit about your personal life Harry,' Adams said. 'I just want to make sure I know what is being said and that we lose nothing in the translation.'

Inge sat beside Penrose in the rear of the car, clutching his hand. Her face had turned ashen when she had been summoned to Warrant Officer Lancaster's office and told what she was to do. She kept glancing at Penrose between staring out of the window, in fascination, at the sights of St Pauli. Despite having lived in Hamburg all of her life, she had never been in that area of the city before. Nice people didn't go there.

Chairs had been placed in a semicircle before Rossmann's desk to accommodate the RAF contingent and two additional German policemen from Rossmann's staff.

After formal introductions they settled down and Rossmann opened the proceedings. 'May I start by saying that I am very sorry to see you in this position Herr Penrose.'

'And what position is that Inspector?' Penrose replied.

'A murder suspect Herr Penrose.'

Penrose shook her head. 'You've got the wrong man Inspector.'

'I hope so Herr Penrose. Tell me. Did you visit Karen Averbeck in Herbertstrasse last night?'

'I know, or rather knew, her as Pussy. But yes, I did visit her.'

'Why did you keep her identity a secret.'

'No secret Inspector. I didn't know she existed before midnight last night. I found out about her from a girl, Lisa Lotte Klose, who works in the Café Arnold. You would have had a copy of my report before the day was out.'

'What was the reason for visiting this, er, Pussy?'

Penrose related what had passed between them and the information he had discovered.

'Tell me Herr Penrose,' Rossmann asked, 'Did you have sexual intercourse with her?'

Inge, who was sat to one side taking notes, jerked her head up and, biting her lip, stared at Penrose. Without glancing at her, Penrose said, 'No I did not Inspector. It cost me one hundred marks for a ten-minute conversation. She did offer a bit of the other for another hundred but, like all good policemen, I declined and left.'

A smile flickered across Rossmann's lips. 'Somebody had sex with her before she died. There were traces of semen but it will not be able to tell us much. Someday, maybe we will be able to analysis it and say with certainty that it belonged to a particular man, but I fear that is many years away. All we can hope for now that the person was a secretor and we can get a blood group. What is your blood group Herr Penrose?'

'Group A. Was there no fingerprint evidence?'

'Hundred of fingerprints. But who do we match them to? Our fingerprint registry was destroyed in the war and has not yet been rebuilt. And tell me. Do you fingerprint your soldiers?'

Jack Adams shook his head, 'No, I'm afraid not Inspector.'

'I will have to take your fingerprints Herr Penrose. There was a perfect set on a tin box near the bed. Did you touch anything while you were in the room?'

'Not a thing Inspector. I hardly went into the room. Stood near the door all the time. The tin box would have been her money box. That's where she put my hundred marks.'

'So that was where she kept her money,' Rossmann said. 'It was empty. The murderer is not only a pervert but also a thief. I thing that will be all for now Herr Penrose.' He turned to Jack Adams. 'Lieutenant. I would like the clothing Herr Penrose was wearing last night and I would like his accommodation searched for any large sums of money.'

Penrose opened his mouth to speak but was stopped by a gesture from Jack Adams, who said to Rossmann, 'Flight Sergeant Baker will take Harry to his accommodation and make the search. With your permission, I would like to go with Fraulein Lang to the scene of the crime.

Penrose lay on his bed in his darkened room. He had been in that position since Flight Sergeant Dick Baker had left after carrying out a search of the room. As night fell, Penrose had not bothered to switch on the room light.

After bringing him from Davidwache, Dick Baker had taken Penrose into the operations room to take his fingerprints. This was done in view of the operations room staff and it soon became general knowledge throughout the Headquarters.

Baker had taken the 200 Reichmarks and £16 in occupation script he had found in Penrose's bedside locker. By chance, the boiler man, whose wife augmented the family income by taking in washing, had not collected Penrose's dirty laundry, so Baker was able to collect the dirty underwear, shirt and suit Penrose had worn the previous night. Before leaving, he had informed Penrose that he was in open arrest and that he was to remain in his room. Penrose had spent the day racking his brains for a solution to what was happening.

A tap on the door followed by it being opened and the room light being switched on. It was the cook sergeant, carrying a tray covered by a white cloth. 'I've brought you something to eat 'Arry. You can't go all day without anyfing.'

'That's good of you Cookie,' Penrose replied, 'but I don't think I could face anything right now.'

The cook sergeant put the tray on the bedside locker, pulled off the cloth to expose a plate of steak and chips and a pot of coffee. 'Come on 'Arry,' he said. 'You've got to keep your strength up to fight this. Nobody believes you did that gel in. You're the straightest bastard in this H Q.'

Penrose smiled as he swung his legs off of the bed. 'Glad you think so Cookie. It's those buggers over at Davidwache who have got to believe it.'

'Your mates are on the job, ain't they?' the cook said. 'They'll look after you. They'll sort it out. The Krauts know fuck all.'

Before Penrose could respond the door opened again and Jones entered the room. 'Hello Harry. What's going on? I've just heard.'

The cook sergeant moved to the door. 'I better get on 'Arry. You get that food inside you.'

Jones laughed as he closed the door. 'Got your own personal batman now Harry. Old Cookie likes you or you've got something on the old bugger. No one else gets personal service. So what's this all about?'

Between mouthfuls of food, Penrose discovered that he was starving, he related all what had happened since he last saw Jones the previous afternoon.

'It's certainly a bugger's muddle Harry,' said Jones. 'But I'm sure Jack Adams and Dick Baker will sort it out. They've known you long enough.' He grinned. 'You didn't do it, did you Harry? You didn't top the old tom?'

'Piss off,' replied Penrose. 'Anyway, how did your job go over at Celle?' he asked. 'Did you get a result?'

Jones shook his head. 'It was a non-starter. I could have had a night in my bed as well as my tea. She wasn't even sure if she was raped or who she was with. It would appear that she was at a hooley in the NAAFI on Saturday night. Too much *Schnapps* went down her throat and to her head. Would appear that the lady has a reputation as a goer. Twice during the party she nipped outside with a couple of blokes for a quickie. No one can remember who took her back to her billet at the end. Anyway, come Sunday she got the idea she was pregnant, and by Monday the idea was a certainty, so she thought the best way to explain it would be to cry rape. Now she'll just have to wait and see.'

The door to the room being opened interrupted Penrose's laughter. Flight Lieutenant Jack Adams entered, followed by Flight Sergeant Baker who was carrying a bundle of clothing, which he threw onto the bed.

'Glad to hear you laughing Harry,' said Adams. 'Now I'll give you something you can really laugh about. You're in the clear.'

Penrose stopped laughing but a smile remained on his face. 'You're not pissing me about Boss?' he asked.

'Gospel truth Harry,' replied Adams. 'Old Rossmann must have a soft spot for you. He had his forensic people working flat out. No stains on your clothing, except for the odd spot of piss on your underpants. By luck, our man was a secretor which showed he was blood group O. Couldn't be any more common but it was not group A like you. Thirdly, your prints didn't match those on the tin.'

'I'll never decry Kraut efficiency again,' said Penrose, shaking his head. 'I'll have to see if I can get Rossmann to relax for a couple of hours so I can buy him a drink And I can't thank you and Dick enough Boss. You must have pulled out all stops.'

Adams shook his head. 'The person you should thank mostly Harry is that bit of stuff of yours. She played a blinder. She wouldn't leave Knocking Shop Alley until she had spoken to every girl who was working in the area last night. It was she who found out from the woman opposite, the one who saw you leaving Pussy's, that she did not see you leave with the patrol. What she was doing at the time was drawing her curtains so she could get down to business with a client.

It was when she opened them, fifteen or twenty minutes later, that she noticed Pussy's curtains were still closed.

.'But your girl Inge spoke to the woman next door, who only came on duty about an hour ago. She had a slack night last night and finished early. But she saw you leave with the patrol and also saw Pussy open again for business after you left. She saw Pussy's next customer, or at least the back of him. Her only description is that he was wearing a blue ski cap and a full length, leather coat, which must have fitted half the men in the street at the time. She didn't notice him leave but remembers that Pussy's curtains were still closed when she called it a night at about 2 am. She assumed that Pussy, who was known as a hard grafter, was still earning her money.'

'Is it possible that she could recognised him again Boss?' Jones asked. 'Those girls know most of the regular punters.'

'She says not Davy,' replied Adams. 'Rossmann has got his men down at the docks to try and find out if anyone fitting the description came through the dock gates. He's also got them swarming on the ships but no end of them could have sailed since it happened.'

'So what happens with me now Boss? Penrose asked.

Adams took Penrose's warrant card from his jacket pocket and gave it to him. 'As far as I'm concerned Harry your back on the job. Me and Dick will get back to Bückeburg and I'll write it up as a negative.' He shook hands with Penrose. 'Good luck Harry.'

Dick Baker shook hands and said, 'Remember what I used to tell you when you worked for me in the Smoke. Always keep a little bit back Harry. It doesn't always pay to let everybody know what your next move is. Take care of yourself mate.'

After the Bückeburg investigators left, Jones said, 'What was Dickie boy on about?'

'When he was my skipper in the Sweeney,' replied Penrose, 'he always said that you should keep all your moves to yourself. Never tell anyone what you're doing until you've got a result. Least of all, the suits upstairs. It will always leak. Seems he wasn't far wrong. Anyway Davy, I'm going to love and leave you. I've got to go and see Inge.'

~ The Hamburg Dossier ~

His knock on the door of the flat in Lattenkamp was answered by Frau Lang. '*Guten Abend Frau Lang. Ist Inge hier?*'

Frau Lang indicated the kitchen where Penrose found Inge sitting at the table. She was still wearing her topcoat and her arms were clutched tightly around her chest. She didn't look at Penrose when he entered. 'Hello sweetheart. I've got a lot to thank you for.'

He went behind her and gently placed his hand on her shoulders. She pulled away from him. 'Don't touch me Harry.'

Penrose looked across at Frau Lang who was still standing in the doorway. She slowly shook her head. He went around the table and sat opposite Inge. He saw that tears were flowing down her cheeks. He reached across for her hands that were now lying on the table. She drew them away. 'What is the matter Inge?' he asked softly.

'I feel so unclean. I don't want you to touch me,' she replied. She started to sob. 'I spent all day with those terrible people. Did you make love with that woman?'

'I didn't think you would have to ask that Inge. No, I didn't,' Penrose replied.

'Then why did you go to see her? And who was the other woman you were in the café with?'

'It's my job Inge. These are the people I have to mix with to do my job.'

She sniffed and then looked him in the eye. 'You mix with these dirty people and then you come back to me in my bed?'

Penrose stared at her for a few moments, then said, 'Look Inge. In this life there are three kinds of people. The good ones and the bad. The third kind are the people like me who have been given the title of policemen. You, the good people, expect us to deal with the bad ones so long as it doesn't encroach on your holier-than-thou lives. But unfortunately police work is not a romance. It's not as you see it sitting in your office, just taking statement or writing reports like the ones you are asked to translate. Sometimes it means getting your hands dirty, mixing with the trash which make up the bad section of the population. Not everybody's cup of tea, but that's my life Inge.'

'Well, I don't want it to be a part of mine,' said Inge. She buried her head in her hand and started to shake. 'Will you please go Harry. I don't want your life to be a part of mine.'

Penrose walked out of the kitchen to the door of the flat. Frau Lang followed him. He turned to her and she cupped his face in her hands. '*Es tut mir leid Harry.* I sorry,' she said hesitantly. 'You good man. I speak Inge.'

Penrose kissed her on the forehead. 'Thank you, *Danke Frau Lang.*' He opened the door and stepped into the cold night.

9

When Penrose entered the Headquarters the following morning he saw that the door to Inge's office was tightly closed. He hesitated in front of it, hand poised over the doorknob, but decided that he would give her a little more time before approaching her. Instead, he knocked on Warrant Officer Lancaster's door.

'Come in Harry. Sit yourself down,' Lancaster said. 'I'm glad they got that nasty business sorted out yesterday.'

'Your not the only one Boss,' Penrose replied. 'Am I still on the job?'

'Don't see any reason why you shouldn't be,' Lancaster said. 'But for Christ sake be careful. This is starting to turn into the biggest can of worms since, oh I can't remember when.'

'Something doesn't seem right Boss. It's as if Chummy has a crystal ball or is able to read my mind,' Penrose said. 'Look, if it's okay with you, I would like to give my briefing at morning prayers a miss and report to you privately.'

Lancaster looked at him before saying, 'What are you saying Harry? Don't you trust some of the investigators in the office?'

'No, it's not that Boss. But you know how word gets out. Passed from mouth to mouth. Talked about over a pint in the canteen. You never know whose listening.'

'All right Harry, as long as you keep me in touch. What's your programme today?'

'I'll go and see Rossmann and see where I go from there.'

As he was leaving the building Penrose went into the Control Room that was manned 24 hours a day for the receipt of prisoners, telephone calls and the dozens of other matters dealt with by any police station.

'Who was on duty Friday evening?' he asked the duty NCO.

'I was Sarge. How can I help.'

'Was there any telephone calls for me?'

'Yes, I remember there was one. Let's have a look at the diary.' The NCO turned back the pages in the Occurrence Book. 'Yes, here it is. 1752 hours. Telephone message for Sergeant Penrose from German national who would not give his name. Text. Meet me at Pier 9 St Pauli-Landungsbrücken at ten o'clock tonight. End of message. I phoned your office but you weren't in. Whoever answered the phone said that you were expected back so I asked him to put the message on your desk.'

Penrose's mind raced. He hadn't gone back to his office on Friday evening but had been at his desk immediately after breakfast on Saturday morning. Except for the blotter, the desk had been clear and there had not been a message on it. 'Can you remember who answered the phone Corp?' he asked.

'No, I can't Sarge. Not offhand. Didn't you get the message?'

'No, I didn't.'

'I hope it wasn't important Sarge.'

'Only a matter of life and death Corp. Only a matter of life and death.'

The *Haupwachmeister* at Davidwache greeted Penrose with a beaming smile. '*Guten Morgen Unteroffizier Penrose. Wie Geht es ihnen?* The Inspector is expecting you. Please to go up.'

My God, thought Penrose as he climbed the stairs, yesterday they were ready to hang me, today I've got the run of the place.

There was also a smile on Rossmann's face as he rose from his desk to greet Penrose. 'Ah! Herr Penrose. How nice to see you.'

As Penrose started, 'Inspector....', he was interrupted by Rossmann. 'Let us not be so formal. You must call me Klaus and I can call you Harry.' Seeing the look of astonishment on Penrose's face, he added, 'Do not be surprised. How do you say it? My bark is worse than my bite. It is the German sense of authority. Anyway, I'm happy that yesterday is behind us.'

'I believe that I've a lot to thank you for Inspect...., er Klaus.'

Rossmann waved his hand in the air. 'Think nothing of it Harry, I was just doing my job.'

'And I'm glad you did Klaus. I was going to ask you out for a drink.'

~ *The Hamburg Dossier* ~

'Much too early for me Harry even though I am a Hamburger. But the Astoria coffee-house is only two doors away. You can buy me a cup of coffee.'

The interior of the coffee-house had a Victorian atmosphere with brown, wooden panelled walls and crimson upholstery. Posters of past plays performed in the nearby Astoria Theatre adorned the walls. Rossmann was warmly greeted by the owner who formally shook Penrose's hand when introduced and said *Grüße Gott'*

An odour of rich coffee wafted from the coffee machine on the counter, a smell that had not tickled Penrose's senses since before the war. The smells of Camp's coffee essence that had replaced the real thing during the war, the recent introduction of freeze dried instant coffee or the ersatz liquid that was passed as coffee in most German cafés could not compete with it. Was it his imagination, wondered Penrose. Coffee that gave off such a smell was unavailable commercially in post-war Germany. His doubts vanished with the first sip from the cup that was placed in front of him. It was very real coffee.

He looked across at Rossmann. 'This is real coffee.'

'But of course,' replied Rossmann. 'This café serves the finest coffee in Hamburg.'

'But where do they get it from?' Penrose asked. 'Nothing like this is imported into the country.'

Rossmann shrugged his shoulders. 'We don't ask. It is none of our business. We only come along and enjoy it.'

Penrose glanced at the owner who was watching him intently. It was obvious that he understood what was being said. He took another sip from the cup then looked up at Rossmann again. In a quiet voice, he said, 'He must be getting it unlawfully. Why are you not doing anything about it?'

Rossmann shook his head. 'No Harry, you are wrong. Under the German law, which I enforce, it is not unlawful for my people to buy coffee or cigarettes offered for sale, if they have the money. It is your people who have made it unlawful for your soldiers to sell to German civilians. It is your soldiers who are committing the crime by selling the stuff, even though it may belong to them, so it is therefore your business. But, as far as the German police are concerned, the German civilians who buy it have not committed an offence.'

'Is that also your policy in regard to penicillin?'

'No Harry. That is different. Medical drugs and medicines, military equipment and food would have been stolen. We also have the offence of receiving stolen goods. Also, in the case of the drugs and medicines, they are more often than not adulterated causing untold harm to those being treated with them. I can show you many hospital wards in this city where the poor, wretched patients are suffering, in some cases dying, after being treated with the stuff. I can assure you Harry that we would pursue those crimes to the bitter end.'

He turned to the café owner and said something in German. The owner took a package from a cupboard behind the bar and brought it to the table. Rossmann handed the package to Penrose and said, 'Please examine it.'

The sealed, bright, red package contained 1lb of coffee beans. The labelling was in English and showed that it had been packed in the United States. There was nothing to indicate that it was from either British or American military sources.

'So Harry, do your food stores issue coffee of this type?'

Penrose shook his head.

'And is it not true that the American forces mark all their stores?'

Penrose nodded. 'But it still does not answer the question. It is not being imported into your economy, so where does it come from?'

Rossmann handed the package back to the owner who returned to his position behind the counter. 'As I said Harry, it is none of our business. But let us enjoy our coffee and talk of what does concern us. How is your investigation going?'

'A little slow yesterday,' Penrose replied, with a sly smile, 'I was otherwise engaged. But I discovered that Winkler telephoned me on Friday evening. He left a message asking me to meet him at Pier 9 Landungsbrüken at 10 pm. So that would put him still alive at that time. I never got the message but somebody else kept the appointment instead.

'Also, in the week before the lad was killed near the hospital, a person purporting to be a policeman visited him. As far as I could establish, it was not anyone from my Headquarters or from the Military Police. But, since this business with the telephone message, I'm not so sure.'

Rossmann leant across the table. 'Last night I had a long chat with the woman who had seen Karen Averbeck, who you call Pussy, alive after you left her room. She saw the next customer talking to Karen. Although she did not see his face, and despite he was wearing clothing that a German would wear, she is convinced that he was not a German. She said that he did not walk like a German, stand like a German or gesture like a German. Don't ask me why or how, but she just had the feeling that he was not German. You must remember that the ladies of Herbertstrasse are experts in the psychology of the male species. As she put it, a little more crudely than I will, if you put a line of men behind a sheet with their members sticking through a hole, she would be able to tell their nationalities.'

Penrose laughed. 'So our only chance of catching him is if he is walking about with his dick hanging out. Have you no leads at all Klaus?'

'We think we may have found his leather coat. A patrol man apprehended one of our well-known drunks trying to sell it to a passer-by on the Reeperbahn yesterday morning. He claimed that the night before he had been sleeping in a doorway in Gerhardstrasse, which is at the far end of Herbertstrasse. He saw, some distance from him, a man take off the coat and drop it on the pavement before getting into a car and driving away.'

Penrose felt his chest tighten. 'What type of car Klaus?'

'A Volkswagen. No other description.'

'The Volkswagen again Klaus. The last time my lad at the hospital was seen alive he was climbing into a Volkswagen. Did you get anything from the coat?'

'Very little. The leather was too wet to develop any fingerprints. Down the lining of one of the pockets was a card from the Tamborin, which is a sex cabaret in Grosse Freiheit. Enquiries there produced nothing. Their cards are found all along the Reeperbahn.'

Penrose signalled to the café owner for two more cups of coffee. Then he looked at Rossmann. 'Pussy told me that Winkler had recently been mixing with the gangsters in Gross Freiheit. Did you find anything at her flat?'

'Just money,' Rossmann replied, with a shake of his head. 'Every type of currency you could imagine. German marks, English pounds, occupation script, dollars. In fact currency that would match every flag of the ships that come up the Elbe. She must have been a busy lady and her trade very cosmopolitan.'

Penrose smiled. 'As Pussy would say Klaus, "Business is business". Look, would you mind if I had a look around the flat? There might be something that that might mean something to me whereas it wouldn't to you.'

Rossmann looked at his watch and then drained his coffee cup. 'Why not? I have a little time. I'll come with you. The flat is only a five-minute walk away.'

Like most of the immediate area adjoining the Reeperbahn, Hopfenstrasse had escaped major bomb damage. The flat, on the second floor of a 19th century tenement, consisted of a living room, bedroom, kitchen and an old fashioned bathroom.

Despite the disturbance made by the police search team, the place was clean. Penrose wondered how Pussy found time for housework between sleeping and business, or did she employ a cleaner; maybe the maid who looked after the business address.

The contents of the drawers of the wall dresser had been stacked on the table. They were mainly bills, correspondence of domestic matters and medical appointments and reports of Pussy's periodic check-ups.

The kitchen did not contain any food or provisions. Penrose did not comment on it but he could not believe that what there was had been removed as evidence. This was a waste not want not country.

The bedroom contained a double bed, a free-standing wardrobe and a chest of drawers. Four of the five drawers contained female clothing. One drawer for working underwear, one for everyday underwear and two others contained a collection of blouses and jumpers. The fifth drawer contained a mixture of male clothing, presumably belonging to the late Willie Winkler. In the wardrobe were a number of dresses and a brown jacket that Penrose recalled having been worn by Willie on a number of occasions. He rummaged through the pockets, not expecting to find anything after the attention of the search team, but at the bottom of the breast pocket his fingers found a crumpled card that he withdrew and palmed into the pocket of his duffel coat.

Rejoining Rossmann in the living room Penrose shook his head and said, 'Nothing of interest here. Where did you find the money?'

Rossmann laughed. 'Where most women would hide it, underneath her knickers.'

They strolled back to Davidwache where they parted after promising to keep in touch. Before driving away, Penrose withdrew the small, red card from his pocket and smoothed it out. It was a card advertising the Tamborin Cabaret. Written, in pencil, across the bottom were the words, *'Der Taucher'*.

Penrose spent the rest of the day at the British Military Hospital trying to find anyone who had seen the policeman who had spoken to McNeil, but with no success. It was late afternoon when he arrived back at Headquarters. As he was approaching the door to Inge's office Warrant Officer Lancaster came out of his.

'Harry. Just the man. I've been waiting for you. Got a rush job on. I want you and Davy Jones to get up to Schleswig. The Control Commission Frontier Guards have caught a Brit, who says he is in the RAF, trying to sneak across the border into Denmark. He was carrying a lot of money, both sterling and US dollars. Might be connected with your job.'

'Right Boss,' replied Penrose. He indicated Inge's door, 'Have I got time to.....'

'You haven't got time for that Harry. Davy's filling up the car. Go and get your overnight bag and get away. I'll see you sometime tomorrow.'

Penrose glanced again at Inge's door before going to join Jones.

10

It was nearly midnight on Friday when Penrose and Jones arrived back at Headquarters from their trip north. The person apprehended by the Control Commission border guards turned out to be a pay clerk stationed at the RAF base on Sylt Island. Believing that his demobilisation date had passed, and that his discharge had been overlooked, he had decided to terminate his service and return to England by way of Denmark. To finance this plan he had emptied the pay office safe of several thousand pounds of disposable currency before jamming the safe to buy time for his disappearance.

Penrose and Jones returned the miscreant to Sylt where they lodged him safely in a cell in the guardroom. The Accounts Officer was aware that one of his clerks was absent from his place of duty but was unaware that his imprest was several thousand pounds light as he had not yet found a locksmith capable of opening his safe. His delight at recovering the money turned to despair when he was told that it would have to be retained as evidence, then to utter misery when the investigators asked how it was possible for a pay clerk to have acquired the key to the safe. Their enquiries revealed both slack working practices and security breaches within the accounts department. When they returned to the mainland they left not only a pay clerk who was certain to see his real demob date pass whilst in the tender care of the Provost Staff at the Glasshouse, but also a dejected Accounts Officer who was uncertain how much longer he would hold his King's Commission.

Penrose asked Jones if he would write the investigation report.

'What are you on then Harry?' replied Jones. 'Off to get your leg over?'

'No Davy. I want to see if I can find Jack Sharp. He's going to put me onto a possible nark. Someone I can use to sniff around the joints on the Reep. The trouble with us doing it is that we always bump into someone who knows us.'

'Yeah, all right,' Jones said. 'Whose this nark then?'

'Someone who Jack has come up against on his anti-vice patrols and who he reckons knows their way around St Pauli.'

'Anyone we know?' asked Jones.

'Haven't got a clue mate. I haven't even got a name yet.'

'Well watch yourself Harry. Don't let this one go the way of the others involved in your case. If you need a hand give us a whistle.'

Just before three o'clock on Saturday afternoon Penrose stood, with Jack Sharp, on the concourse of Hauptbahnhof station looking down onto Platform 9. At the bottom of the stairs a group of women were gathered, awaiting the arrival of their boyfriends.

Exactly at 3.02 pm the military train steamed into the platform. The former State Railway engines and Wagon-Lits rolling stock had been requisitioned for military use on the main lines within the occupation zone and through the Russian zone into Berlin. As the train came to a halt it disgorged a flood of khaki and air force blue which moved towards the foot of the stairs. As each of the waiting ladies saw whom they were expecting, they would wave, shout and finally fling their arms around the necks of the embarrassed boyfriends, oblivious to the raucous catcalls from the crowd passing around them.

'Here comes Tiny.' Sharp said, 'Just passing under the indicator board.'

Penrose looked in the direction that Sharp was pointing and saw a man, a giant of a man, who stood a foot or more above the surrounding flood of humanity. He was so tall that the RAF Regiment flashes on the shoulders of his uniform were clearly visible.

'He's a big bugger Jack,' Penrose said in awe. 'Do you expect me to mess with him? He'd have me for breakfast.'

Sharp laughed. 'Tiny's as good as gold Sarge. He ain't got a vicious bone in his body. He's too big for anyone to want to fuck around with him and he's so placid that you could never rile him.'

'Is that why you patrol boys turn a blind eye to him?'

'Not really. He has helped us out on occasions. If we're having trouble when the piss artists are turning out of Hamburg House we can always rely on Tiny's help if he's about. Once he sides with us the games over.'

As he mounted the stairs, Tiny seemed to grow bigger. Clasp in his right hand was a large suitcase that he swung with ease.

'He must be carrying a load of loot in that case.' Penrose said.

'Wrong. Just a few civvies. Tiny not that stupid to carry the stuff himself.'

'So who does?' a mystified Penrose asked.

'You'll see. Come on, let's follow him'

As they trailed Tiny to the eastern exit of the station into Kirchenalle, Sharp gave Penrose his background. 'Corporal Cyril Chapman known, for obvious reasons, as Tiny. Stationed at Celle with 5126 Squadron, RAF Regiment. Comes to Hamburg most weekends where, for a commission, he does some trading for other members of the squadron. Goods, cameras, watches, nylons, that kind of thing, for cigarettes or tins of coffee.'

Tiny crossed Kirchenalle towards a row of small hotels and bars. He entered the Phoenix Club, a service canteen run by the YMCA, which also had a number of bedrooms where servicemen could stay, with the approval of the military authorities, instead of booking into the army transit camp.

'Tiny always gets a room there,' Sharp said, 'although he rarely sleeps in the place. Just a place to change and hang his hat. He only sleeps there if he has not found a bit of stuff who offers him a share of her bed.'

They entered the reception area of the club where Tiny was booking in. On the right was a refreshment room where a number of the recent train passengers were sat at tables, looking expectantly at the door. Sharp and Penrose slipped inside, found a table in the far corner and ordered tea and cakes from the young waitress.

Tiny appeared at the door of the restaurant and held up six fingers before turning and mounting the stairs past the reception desk. In turn, the former passengers picked up their luggage and followed each other up the stairs, the next one going up after the previous one had returned. Ten people in all went up the stairs.

~ *The Hamburg Dossier* ~

'They're Tiny's mules,' Sharp explained. 'They are going to Room 6. Each are carrying about a thousand cigarettes. They do it for their weekend beer money. Tiny will be out in a little while so I thing you'd better wait outside. He might clock you in here. I'll do a runner cos he knows me.'

Once they were back amongst the crowd at the railway station, Sharp said, 'He'll walk from here to the Alster and along Jungfernstieg. He always walks so he would be aware if someone is following him. Then he will dive into Büschstrasse and go to a first floor flat in the last building on the right.'

'Do you mean Nick the Trader's place?' Penrose asked.

'You know him do you Sarge?'

'I've had one or two dealings with him.'

'Are you going to set Tiny up this weekend Sarge?'

'No Jack. I'm going to let him run for now. I'll find some way of getting in with him and then pounce next week. Softly, softly catchee monkey.'

Sharp indicated with his head across the road. 'He's coming out now. Good luck.'

'Thanks for you help Jack.'

Tiny Chapman had changed into civilian clothes. He was wearing a brown lumber jacket, flannel trousers and brown, suede brothel creepers. He was carrying his suitcase but not with the ease that he had done so on the station platform. Because he was aware of where Tiny was going, Penrose allowed him to get about one hundred yards ahead before following him. When he turned into Büschstrasse Penrose found a doorway on the other side of the road and waited.

Dusk was falling when Tiny emerged from Büschstrasse. He no longer had his suitcase. Hands in pockets, he ambled around the corner to Hamburg House where he went to the first floor restaurant. Penrose found a table on the opposite side of the room, and seeing that Tiny was ordering a meal, he signalled a waiter and did the same.

Tiny took his time over his meal which he rounded off with two glasses of beer. From time to time people would stop at his table and pass the time of day but it became apparent that he was not expecting to meet anyone there. At about half past seven he rose from his chair and left the restaurant and the building. He strolled along Drehbahn, occasionally acknowledging the shadowy figures touting for cigarettes. Despite there being few pedestrians on the almost deserted streets, Penrose was able to take advantage of the darkness to close the gap between them. Tiny walked the mile or so to Zeughausmarkt and entered the bar of the Seamen's Mission.

Penrose waited before he went into the club. It was crowded but it was easy to pick out Tiny who was standing at the bar with a group of seaman. The Chaplain, the Reverend Peter Andrews, smiled when he saw Penrose and moved across the room towards him, but stopped when Penrose gave him a slight shake of the head. Penrose saw that Tiny was paying for a round of drinks and then slip something into his pocket that had been handed to him by one of the seamen.

Tiny left the bar after an hour. Penrose delayed his departure as long as he dared without fear of losing him. When he stepped into Zeughausmarkt he saw the unmistakable figure pass alongside the English Church and duck into a low doorway about fifty yards further down the street.

Above the door was a sign declaring the place to be the Canadian Bar. Penrose found a dark doorway on the opposite side of the road where he stood watch for about a quarter of an hour to ensure that Tiny was not just paying a brief visit. When he was sure that Tiny was there to stay Penrose made his move.

The door opened directly in a small, dimly lit bar-room. On the right of the entrance was a L-shaped, zinc-topped bar that stretched about three-quarters the width of the room. Opposite was a door leading to a kitchen. In the top, left-hand corner was a large, oval table. On the left of the entrance was an archway that gave access to a second room that had brighter lights. Behind the bar was a short, stocky man wearing a white apron. Another man, wearing a full-length leather coat and a fedora, was leaning on the short arm of the bar, a glass of beer in front of him. Through the archway, Tiny could be seen, sitting at a table with two women. But it was the oval table that intrigued Penrose. Around it were six noisy men. They were wearing black sombreros, black bolero jackets and flared trousers, all trimmed with silver lace. They would not have been out of place in a Mexican cantina.

Penrose climbed onto a bar stool, ordered a glass of beer and returned his attention to the crowd in the corner. On the table was a large, glass boot containing beer. It was placed in front of one of the men who drank as much of the beer as he could, to the raucous comments of his companions, before passing it to the next man. As the beer diminished so the racket got louder. Penrose then realised that drinking from the glass boot was the same principle as the English yard of ale. Air entering the foot of the boot could cause a blowback of the beer. The trick was to start drinking from the boot with the toe pointing towards you, then, whilst drinking, rotate the boot until the toe was pointing upwards. After drinking your fill, the boot had to be rotated back as it was lowered. The person who caused a blowback had to refill the boot.

Penrose became aware of someone behind him. The leather-coated man at the corner of the bar leant close to his ear and whispered, 'You have cigarettes for sale?'

Penrose shook his head. Just then Tiny did what Penrose had been waiting for. He rose from the table and went into the toilet. Penrose followed. As he stood next to Tiny at the urinal he realised just how big he was. Although Penrose was over six foot tall, when he and Tiny did what all men do when they meet in those circumstances; they look at each other and nod; he had to peer upwards at Tiny.

Penrose decided to break the ice. 'Who are the Cisco Kids out there then?'

Tiny smiled. 'That's the Guild of Carpenters. They hold their monthly meeting here. They make a lot of noise but they're harmless.'

'And what about the guy stood at the bar? He's not SIB is he? He wanted to know if I had any fags to sell and I didn't know whether to or not.'

'Oh, that's Albert. He does a bit of buying. He's all right,' replied Tiny. He then added, 'Have you got some you want to sell?'

'I've got two hundred,' Penrose said, 'but I wasn't sure about him. I ain't been here long.'

'Tell you what,' Tiny said, 'come and join me and the girls I'm with for a drink and I'll get rid of your fags for you.'

The women were introduced as Christine, who was sitting by Tiny, and Elsa who patted the chair beside her, indicating that Penrose should sit there. Both were in their early 20s and heavily made-up. Elsa's skirt was pulled halfway up her thighs revealing a shapely pair of legs which she drew attention to by crossing one over the other. Penrose introduced himself as Harry.

After Tiny had disposed of his cigarettes, Penrose ordered a round of drinks from the old waiter who was patently standing by the centre wall, out of sight of the first room.

'Where're you stationed then Harry?' Tiny asked.

'Uetersen. M T driver.'

'How long you been in BAFO then?

Penrose offered his packet of cigarettes around. 'About a month. This is my first run into town. I don't know how I ended up in here.' He offered a light to Elsa who grasped his hand to guide it to her cigarette and kept hold of it. Penrose went on, 'I wandered up from the docks where I was having a shufti at the ships. It looked a bit quite and I thought the town patrol might not come here, so I came in for a quick one.'

'You don't have girlfriend?' Elsa asked, pushing Penrose's hand onto her bare thigh.

Penrose shook his head. 'I haven't been here long enough.'

'I'll be your girlfriend,' Elsa replied, squeezing his hand tightly and pushing it further along her thigh, under the hem of her dress.

Tiny winked across the table at Penrose. 'You'll have to ask when she can fit you in Harry,' he said with a laugh, 'She's got a boyfriend on every ship and a few waiting in the wings for when the fleet's out.'

With a toss of her head, Christine said, 'She got lots of boyfriend because she is too much sexy.' She illustrated her meaning by pushing her thumb between the first and second finger of her right hand.

'Not true,' Elsa replied. 'Me *Jungfrau*. Wergin.' She turned to Penrose and continued. 'You feel.' She shoved his hand up to the top of her legs where he found that, like stockings, she also did not wear any underwear. She smiled broadly whilst moving her lower body suggestively. 'You like?' she asked.

Penrose had to act the innocent. He pulled his hand away and, feigning embarrassment, said, 'Very nice, but we've only just met.'

The evening past quickly. The general banter was interspersed with sexual suggestions by both Elsa and Christine. Elsa, having given up trying to replace Penrose's resistant hand, had switched her attack to caressing his thigh. He had to defend himself against her persistent attempts to unbutton his fly.

Soon eleven o'clock, the curfew hour, approached. Penrose decided to leave, much to Tiny's disappointment. 'I was wondering if you fancied a creep down the Reep Harry?' he said.

'Not tonight Tiny,' Penrose replied. 'I've got an early morning job to do and I want to get to Hamburg House to catch the liberty truck.'

As Penrose stood up, the door of the bar opened and two Royal Military Police Lance Corporals entered. Penrose glanced at his watch and saw that it was passed eleven o'clock. The police patrol moved to their table.

'Are you a member of His Majesty's Forces?' one of them asked Tiny.

'Merchant Navy.' Tiny replied.

'Can I see your shore leave pass?'

Tiny took a buff coloured form from his pocket which he handed to the policeman.

'What ship are you from?'

'As it says on the pass,' Tiny replied. 'The *British Grassmere*.'

The policeman handed the pass back to Tiny and turned to Penrose. 'What about you?' he asked.

Penrose shrugged his shoulders. 'I'm in the Air Force.'

A smile appeared on the policeman face as he glanced at his colleague. 'Right. Let's go outside.'

~ The Hamburg Dossier ~

As Penrose followed the policemen to the door, he glanced back at Tiny. 'See you next trip then Tiny,' he said, giving him a wave.

Outside, on the pavement, the police said, 'You know it is after curfew and that you are committing an offence by being on the streets at this time? Can I see your identity card?'

Penrose produced his warrant card. 'Sergeant Penrose, RAF SIB. I'm on a job.'

The smug look on the policemen's faces disappeared as they looked at each other. The one who had been doing the talking said, 'Sorry Sarge. I hope we haven't buggered up anything.'

'Don't worry about it Corp', Penrose said with a smile. 'You did me a favour. Now if you'll give me a lift to a RAF Police patrol I promise to tell Staff Sarg'nt Reader how good you were.'

11

Penrose was nursing the mother and father of hangovers when he entered the Headquarters on Monday morning. A quiet Sunday lunchtime drink in the mess had turned into an all day and night session and he could not remember going to bed.

He opened the door to Inge's office and stopped short. Behind the desk was a middle-aged man who looked up, smiled and politely said, 'Can I help you Sir?'

Penrose looked around the office. 'Where is Inge?'

'Fräulein Lang has transferred to another post. I am her replacement. Heinz Dittmar.'

'Where has she gone to?' Penrose asked.

'I really don't know Sir. I was just ordered to report here.'

Penrose crossed the corridor to Warrant Officer Lancaster's office. 'What's happened to Inge Boss?'

'Haven't got a clue Harry. Control Commission Admin rang me on Friday to say that she had requested a transfer and that they would be replacing her. Thought you might know.'

'She was a bit pissed off on Wednesday night after seeing the dirty side of police work, but I didn't think she was so upset that she wanted to leave. Any idea where she's gone Boss?'

'Haven't got a clue Harry. They didn't tell me anything.'

Penrose pulled up outside the house at Lattenkamp. A middle-aged women, who Penrose recognised as an occupant of one of the rooms, answered the door. She stared at Penrose before saying, '*Bitte? Was wollen Sie?*'

'Fraulein Lang,' replied Penrose.

The woman broke into a string of German that was too fast for Penrose to follow. He interrupted her flow by raising his hand. '*Langsam. Ich verstehe nicht.* No understand.'

An elderly man appeared behind the woman. '*Fraulein Lang, nicht heir,*' he said. 'She go.'

Penrose pushed passed them and opened the kitchen door. It was empty of furniture. Sitting on the floor, in front of the stove, was a young woman and two children who stared at him, expressions of fear showing on their faces. Penrose turned and went to the room at the end of the hall and found it empty.
Penrose rounded on the old man. 'Where did they go?'
The man shook his head. *'Ich weiss nicht.'*

The reception area of the Control Commission Administration office at the rear of the Rathaus was crowded with people seeking employment or permits to carry out some act as required by the hundred and one regulations to which the occupied population were subjected. Fighting his way through the crowd thronging the counter, Penrose managed to collar one of the harassed clerks who said that she would get one of the administrators to come and see him. After kicking his heels for ten minutes, Penrose saw a tall man looking at him from the top of stairs. The man beckoned to him to go up.
After introducing himself, the man asked Penrose what he could do for him.
'I'm trying to get in contact with Inge Lang who used to work in our Headquarters. I've been round to her home but she appears to have moved.'
The administrator tugged his right ear and peered at Penrose over his spectacles. 'I don't know if I can give you that information old chap. She particularly asked that her whereabouts should not be revealed. I could get a message to her tomorrow.'
'Shit,' replied Penrose. 'That will be too late. I've got a court case this afternoon and I can't find a bunch of statements that Inge was translating. I've just got to have them before two o'clock.'
The man rubbed his nose, deep in thought. Finally he said, 'Okay. You didn't hear this from me. She is working at the Legal Services Department out at Schenefeld.'
Legal Services were housed in a large, imposing villa; the type of property that would befit the Judge Advocate and the barristers from leading legal practices and now commissioned into Army and Air

Force. It stood in its own grounds, screened by a row of trees bordering the drive from the wrought iron gates that were guarded by a watchman.

Penrose parked up in a secluded spot where he had a view of the gates and settled down for a long wait. It was four o'clock in the afternoon before Inge emerged, but not on foot, as Penrose had hoped, but as the passenger in an army staff car being driven by an army captain. Inge, in the front passenger seat, was turned towards the driver, laughing at something he had said. Penrose's hand moved towards the ignition key but he never turned it. Forget it, he thought, I don't want to embarrass her. He watched the car drive off into the distance.

Jones looked up from his desk as Penrose entered the investigators' office. 'The Warrant's looking for you Harry. He's been tearing his hair out all afternoon. Where the hell have you been?'

Penrose shrugged his shoulders, left the office and tapped on Warrant Officer Lancaster's door.

'Come'

Penrose entered, to be greeted by a Warrant Officer with a face like thunder. 'Where the fuck have you been all day?'

'I was trying to track down Inge, Boss.'

Lancaster's face turned puce. 'Tracking down Inge. Jesus Christ. You're in the middle of a murder inquiry. The men upstairs wanted a briefing on your progress, which I couldn't give them, and you come in here and tell me that you have spent the day running after a bit of skirt. That's not good enough Harry.'

Penrose was sensible enough to look contrite before saying, 'It was stupid of me Boss. I know that now. But you know how it is? I had to find out if her leaving was the result of anything I had done.'

Lancaster calmed down. 'I didn't expect it of you Harry. You are my most experience investigator. If you were a regular, instead of just on secondment, you would have a crown above your three stripes and would be knocking on the door for your Warrant. You might even be under consideration for a commission as you are a bloody sight better that most of them we call our masters. But you go and do a bloody stupid thing like this. Accept it Harry, it's over. It might have been good while it lasted, but it's over.' Lancaster leant back in his chair and crossed his arms. 'In all my years I've never run after a bus or a woman as I knew another one would be coming along later. Get yourself one of the women you are always chatting with and screw yourself silly. But most of all get me a result on this fucking murder. Get out.'

12

The music from the cabaret below vibrated around the upstairs room of Der Tamborin, where The Diver sat at a small table with his two henchmen, drinking cognac of a suspect distillation.

'So the stuff is on its way, Jonny?' The Diver said to the heavily built German on his right.

'*Ja Taucher*. The chemist here,' indicating the third man, 'cut it three to one and we moved it out last night. To Hanover, some to Frankfurt and the rest to Berlin into the Russian Zone.'

'Is there any left in Hamburg?' The Diver asked. 'I don't want any of it around here. They may well be getting a bit close.'

The two Germans looked at each other. 'Just a little *Taucher*' Jonny said. 'We owed a small amount to Karl-Heinz Necker from the last consignment he paid for which was a bit light. It was not enough for him to spread it all over town. It will not be noticed.'

'I hope not,' The Diver replied. 'That fucking Penrose is like a ferret. I don't want anything around that he can get his teeth into.'

Jonny shrugged. 'So why let him try? Why not take care of him? Feed him to the fishes like his nosy friend.'

'You've got to be fucking crazy.' The Diver said. 'If anything happened to him that was not an accident, they would close this town down. There would be more police running around than fleas on a dog's back. Not only military police but old Rossmann, who seems to have developed a liking for Penrose, would flood the area with his men and tear it upside-down. You wouldn't be able to spit let alone do a bit of thievery. We'll just have keep an eye on the situation and arrange an accident if necessary. So when do we get the money?'

'It should be all in by the end of this week,' Jonny replied with a smile.

'And you'll keep mine in my account?' The Diver asked, rising from his chair.

'Of course *Taucher*. Are you going to see Lilli? She said she was expecting you tonight.'

'I'll pop over there later. I've got a bit of business to do first'.

Going down the stairs The Diver had to squeeze between two naked girls who were sat on the stairs, smoking, while awaiting their cue to go on-stage. As he passed, one slid her hand up his leg and groped his crotch. 'Going early *Taucher?*'

The Diver turned and tweaked her right nipple. 'Got to darling. Got to do a bit of business.'

The girl laughed. 'Better you do a bit of business with me,' she said, quickly exposing herself by opening and closing her thighs.

'That's exactly where my business is sweetheart,' The Diver said with a grin. 'The Elbe Tunnel.'

It was nearly eleven o'clock when Penrose left the Seamen's Mission where he had spent an hour talking to the Reverend Peter Andrews. He had discovered that Tiny Chapman was a regular visitor to the Mission where he was friendly with a lot of the crew members of the ships that regularly docked in Hamburg. It was from one or another of these friends that he would obtain a shore leave pass that would give him immunity if he was stopped by a military patrol.

Zeughausmarkt was shrouded in fog that had come up from the river. The lights of the surrounding bars, which normally illuminated the triangle, now took on a ghostly appearance. The mournful hooting of the sirens of passing ships added to the eeriness. From one of the surrounding streets, muted by the fog, came a rendering of the *Wehmacht* paratroopers march, the *Horst Wessel* song. Penrose smiled to himself. They never give up he thought. We've only just finished kicking their backsides.

He smelt food cooking. Through the mist, near the English Church, he saw what looked like a lighted brazier. Approaching, he saw a man, standing at the rear of a van, turning a row of sausages on top of the hot coals.

'*Guten Abend,*' said Penrose. '*Was est das?*' pointing towards the cooking food.

'*Wurst,*' replied the man. Then, hesitantly, 'Sausage. Cherman sausage. Good *essen.* Food'

'Where did you get them?' asked Penrose, hoping that the man would understand him

'From my friend who has a farm. You want? *Schoen. Gut essen.*'

The smell of the food had caused Penrose's mouth to water. 'I'll try one.' He bit into the hot sausage served on a hunk of bread with a dollop of mustard. It was delightful. After swallowing his first bite, he waved the sausage at the man. 'This is bloody good.'

'*Ja. Est gut.* Before the *Krieg*, er war, *Wurst* on every street. Me now *kom heir* everyday.'

A girlish giggle made Penrose aware that someone was behind him. He turned and saw Lisa Lotte Klose. 'Mr Harry, his English is as bad as your German. I guess that is how you understand each other.'

'What are you doing sneaking up on me?' asked Penrose.

'I not sneaking up on you, I waiting for you. I saw you go into the sailors' bar so I wait.' A smile lit up her face. 'Will you buy me a drink?'

'Sure,' replied Penrose. As he turned in the direction of the Café Arnold Lisa stopped him by linking her arm in his. 'Not there.' She pulled him in the direction of the Café Koch.

'*Auf Wiedersehen,*' said the sausage seller.

The entrance to the Café Koch led onto a mezzanine that overlooked the bar situated in the basement, a large, unattractive room. A dance floor took up most of the floor space. There was a bar at one end of the room and a small stage, on which the three-piece band performed, at the other. On the other two sides were tables surrounded by banquettes.

Penrose and Lisa descended the steep staircase and found an empty table. When Lisa shed her shapeless raincoat, Penrose saw that she was wearing a tight, red sweater and a black, pencil skirt that emphasised her firm, high breasts and slim figure. Joining him on the same bench, she sat very close to him.

With the waiter hovering behind him, Penrose asked, 'What would you like to drink?'

Lisa smiled. 'A real drink this time. I no on commission in here.'

~ The Hamburg Dossier ~

Penrose ordered a bottle of cognac before turning back to her. 'So, you're not working tonight?'

Her face took on a serious expression. 'Mr Harry. I am not a proper business girl. You think I like what I do? I have to do it so that I can live. So I have four or five boyfriends I go with when they come to Hamburg. They look after me, give me money, so that I don't have to go with all sailors, just drink with them. None of my boyfriends are here now.'

Penrose lit two cigarettes to cover his embarrassment. He handed one to her and then said, 'So what do you have to tell me that is so important that you hung around for an hour outside the Seamen's Mission?'

Lisa looked around to ensure that there was no one nearby taking an interest in them. She brought her lips close to his ear and whispered, 'There is penicillin in Hamburg.'

Penrose's eyes darted around the room before asking, 'Where?'

'Doctor Rick in Peterstrasse. He looks after the girls around here and those who are sick have been told to go and see him tomorrow.

Penrose raised his glass to her. *'Prost.'* They touched glasses before sipping their brandy. 'How sure are you of this?' Penrose asked.

'Very sure. The girls very happy because when they are sick they no earn money.'

'So why are you telling me this? You know what I will do. Then the penicillin will not be available to the girls.'

'I am doing it because I know that penicillin will not be good. The girls think they are better but they will not be. They will have to pay plenty money for something that is not good. That is not correct.'

'And what about you Lisa? Do you need treatment?'

Lisa blushed nearly as red as her sweater. 'No. I am clean.'

Penrose re-filled their glasses from the bottle before him. 'Then why don't you quit and get a proper job. You sound like you are educated.'

'It is not possible. I come from the east; a little town called Zwickau. My father was killed in Russia. I lived with my mother. I was at college when the Ruskies came. It was a very bad time. One night seven of them came to my house. They kill my mother, but first they...' Tears appeared in her eyes. 'My mother had pushed me out of the back door and I hide in the woodshed. After the soldiers had gone, I see what they had done to my mother. Then I ran. For many days I walked through the forest. Then I come to a village where the people tell me I am in American Zone. Slowly, slowly I come here. First Frankfurt, then Hanover and then here. I cannot get work because I have the wrong papers. Only papers for Russians. If I try to get work I will be sent back to Russians.'

Penrose knew of the problems of stateless persons and the policy of repatriation, and he wished that there was something he could do for her, but he bit his tongue. 'What were you studying at college?' he asked instead.

Lisa wiped her eyes and a smile lit up her pretty face. 'I was designing clothes. One day I will have my own shop selling my clothes and make a lot of money.' She nodded to herself. 'Yes, that is what is going to happen.' She turned and looked into Penrose's face. 'So Mr Harry, what about you? Why you on your own tonight and not with that good girl of yours?'

In order to collect his thoughts, Penrose picked up the bottle of brandy to pour more drinks and noticed that half of the contents was already gone. 'To tell the truth Lisa, it's over. There is no girl now, good or otherwise.'

'Lisa's smile faded into a look of compassion. 'Oh! I am sorry Mr Harry. What happened? Did you have a fight?'

'I don't really want to talk about it Lisa. Just say that she decided that she did not want to be involved with a policeman.' Penrose gave her a quick smile. 'Come on. Let's have a bit of a dance.'

They joined the other dancers on the dance floor. Lisa moved up close against him, closed her eyes and laid her head on his shoulder. He became aware of the heady perfume she was wearing and the softness of her body. He realised that he was becoming aroused. Lisa also felt it. Without opening her eyes, she giggled and pressed herself tighter against him. In an effort to take his mind off of what was happening, Penrose gazed around the room. Looking over the railings of the mezzanine were two members of an RAF Police patrol. One was staring hard at Penrose who recognised him as Corporal Lofty Wilson, his adversary from the encounter in Herbertstrasse. Unable to resist it, Penrose smiled up at Wilson, winked and nodded his head. Wilson glared back, said something to his partner, who also looked at Penrose before they turned on their heels and left.

Back at their table, Lisa draped Penrose's arm around her shoulders and cuddled up to him. She pulled his head down to hers and kissed him deeply. 'I think you must come back to my house tonight and I will make you happy again,' she said.

The fog had become more dense when the left the Café Koch. There was still a smell of cooking. 'Do you want a sausage?' Penrose asked.

Lisa giggled. 'Not a cooked one.'

'How do we get to your place? I don't have a car with me tonight and the U-Bahn has stopped running.'

Lisa tightened her arm around him. 'We walk, it is not far. I live near the Michel.'

Arms around each other, they strolled between the bomb rubble towards St Michael's church. For once the fog obscured the well-known landmark. They rounded the church until they came to a terrace of old, 5-storey buildings that stood like a sentinel amongst the devastation. Taking his hand, Lisa led him up ten flights of darkened stairs to the top of one of the houses and unlocked a door. They stepped into a small kitchen that led off to a bathroom at one end.

'Do you want a drink or anything?' Lisa asked.

Penrose shook his head.

'Nor do I.' said Lisa. 'Let us go to bed.'

The second door in the kitchen led into the bedroom. When Lisa switched on a bedside light it revealed that the roof sloped down at one wall which showed that they were in the roof space of the house. The furniture consisted of a bed, slightly wider than a single one, a divan, two upright chairs, a dressing table and a single wardrobe, all of which had seen better days. A small rug was the only covering on the wooden floorboards.

Lisa took off her sweater and skirt to reveal a white brassiere and minute panties, which certainly had not been obtained in Germany, or even England, and were most probably of American origin. Her dusky skin contrasted with the white underwear. She adopted a pose, hands clasped behind her head and one leg slightly bent. 'You like?' she asked with a smile.

Penrose found that his mouth had gone dry so he could only nod.

Lisa giggled. She brought her arms down so the they hung away from her sides. 'So help me with the rest and you will see a little more.'

She stood perfectly still while Penrose, with trembling hands, reached around her and unhook the clip of the brassiere which remained balanced on her breasts until he pulled it away. Her breasts had no sag; perfect orbs tipped by large, dark, almost black, aureoles, in the centre of which were pert, erect nipples. Penrose took one into his mouth and sucked hard whilst Lisa cupped the back of his head, pulling him closer. Sinking to his knees, he hooked his thumbs into the waistband of the panties and slowly drew them down. A neatly trimmed, jet-black nest covered her vulva.

She pulled away and slipped under the duvet where she watched Penrose get undressed. When he joined her, she wrapped her arms around his neck, hooked one of her legs around his thigh, and then kissed him, her tongue probing deeply into his mouth. Penrose caressed the side of her body, from armpit to the back of her knee. When he stiffened, Lisa ground her crotch into his. He pushed her onto her back, caressed her breasts before moving his hand down her body. She opened her legs to allow him access. Her found that she was wet, ready to receive him. Lisa grasped his erect manhood and guided him towards her. As Penrose slid his body on top of her, he heard a noise.

Looking over his shoulder, he saw a small door, which gave access to the eaves of the roof slowly opening. A small, old, ugly face popped out followed by a small, deformed body of a hunchback. The man was wearing a dirty shirt, an old pair of trousers and carrying a tattered overcoat. As he moved towards the bedroom door he glanced towards the pair in bed, gave a faint grin, and said, *'Morgen Lisa, Mein Herr'* before disappearing into the kitchen.

Lisa broke into peals of laughter.

'Who the bloody hell was that?' Penrose asked.

'That my landlord, Manfred. He sleep in the roof. I thought he would have gone to work by now. He must be late. He cleans up at the Fish Market. Come on. He has gone now. Get back to what you were doing.'

'I don't know if I can.' said Penrose, shaking his head. 'Does he do that often?'

'He doesn't take any notice.' replied Lisa. 'He is nice old man.' Pulling Penrose back on top of her, Lisa said, 'And I know that you can do what you were doing before if I help you.'

And he could.

13

Morning prayers had started when Penrose entered the Investigators' Office. The investigator holding the floor stopped what he was saying as the rest turned to see who was entering.

'To what do we owe this pleasure Harry?' Warrant Officer Lancaster asked sarcastically. 'I thought that you were going to give these meetings a miss.'

'I've got a lead on some of the penicillin Boss. A local pox doctor has got some. I need a couple of guy to spin his drum.' Penrose looked around the room. 'I'd like Davy and one of the mobile patrols to come with me.'

Jones rose from his desk and put on his jacket. 'Where are we going Harry?'

'Peterstrasse. That's just behind the Café Arnold.' He looked at Warrant Officer Lancaster. 'If it's a positive Boss, I plan to bring the good doctor back here for a little chat before we hand him over to the Krauts. Can you field any enquiries that might be made about his whereabouts so I have the time to get as much out of him as I can.'

'No problem Harry. You just get the bugger in here and let me worry about the rest. I'll give the mobile patrol Flight Sergeant a bell so he can have a couple of his guys standing by when you're ready to go.'

Peterstrasse was a small side street of large houses converted into flats and small offices. Dr Manfred Rick ran his practice in two small rooms of a building situated halfway along the street. In the small waiting room, three women were sitting, two of whom Penrose recognised as patrons of the Café Arnold. Their smiles of recognition faded as Penrose, followed by Jones, crossed to the door leading to the consulting room and throw it open.

In the room was a desk, a filing cabinet, medicine cupboard, an old fashion ice chest and a gynaecological examining table on which lay a woman, her raised legs clamped by stirrups, being examined by the doctor.

Dr Rick jumped to his feet while the poor, unfortunate, forgotten female attempted to cover her modesty and. at the same time, frantically trying to disengage herself from the restraining stirrups.

Rick was in his middle 30s. A tall, blonde, slim man, with the looks of the arrogant Aryan so loved by Hitler. During the war he had served as a Medical Officer in the Waffen-SS. It had been strongly suspected that he had been on the staff of Dr Mengele but the War Crimes Commission failed to find any evidence to support the suspicion. He was subsequently cleared by the de-nazification tribunal and allowed to start a civilian practice.

'What is the meaning of this outrage?' Rick said, in precise English.

'Military Police,' replied Penrose. 'We have reason to believe that you are in possession of stolen drugs and we intend to search these premises.'

As Jones crossed the room towards the ice chest, Penrose went to the aid of the still struggling woman and, with an apologetic smile, freed her captive legs and assisted her to her feet. Her face scarlet, she brushed down the skirt of her dress, snatched up her discarded panties and dashed out of the examination room into the waiting room.

On the top shelf of the ice chest were rows of glass phials containing a colourless liquid. Some of the phials were plain while others had a batch number etched on them.

'What are those?' Penrose asked Rick.

'Medication that I prescribe for the treatment of my patients.'

'What type of medication?' asked Penrose.

Rick tossed his head. 'I do not have to tell you anything.'

'In that case,' Penrose replied, 'I will take you to Sierichstrasse where we will continue this conversation.'

He called the two uniformed patrolmen from the waiting room and told them to collect all the medication they could find, patient's records and any other paperwork and transport it to Headquarters.

He then went into the waiting room where the four bemused women were still sitting. He told them that Dr Rick would not be available for some time, if ever again, and advised them to seek medical advice elsewhere. After some protest, they left the office, two of them in tears.

The interview room at Sierichstrasse was situated in the basement. Windowless, no sound could be heard from the outside. Jones was leaning against the wall near the entrance door while Penrose and Rick were seated, facing each other across a table. On the table between them were two of the phials taken from Rick's office; one marked with the batch number, the other blank.

'So Dr Rick,' Penrose began, 'what is the contents of these phials?'

Rick pursed his lips before shouting, 'I am a respected physician in this city. You cannot treat me like this. I demand to see the German authorities.'

Penrose remained silent, looking at Rick. Then he pointed his finger at him and said, slowly, 'Rick, you are nothing but a fucking pox doctor. I can keep you here as long as I wish and treat you how I like. Then, maybe, I'll hand you to the German authorities. I am sure they will be very interested in what you have to say. Now, do those phials contain penicillin?'

'Yes,' Risk replied, abruptly.

'Where did you get it from?' Penrose asked.

'It was supplied to me by an agent who obtained it from a Swiss pharmaceutical company.'

'Is this stuff pure or has it been adulterated?'

Rick bristled. 'Are you accusing me of treating my patients with adulterated drugs? That is a slander to my professional reputation.'

'Do you have any documentation to prove you obtained it lawfully?'

Rick sneered. 'I did have, but you have taken everything from my office. Only you can now say if the paperwork still exists.'

Penrose shook his head. 'You are a liar Rick. That does not come from Switzerland. The batch number shows that it was manufactured in England and it was also part of a consignment stolen from the British Military Hospital a couple of weeks ago. So, where did you get it from?'

Rick raised his chin and remained silent.

Penrose persisted. 'Where did you get it from?'

Rick's eyes hardened. 'I have told you, you stupid *Englander*. I will tell you no more. Prove otherwise, if you can.'

Penrose remained silent, looking at Rick across the table. Then, abruptly, he stood up and left the room.

Rick stared at the closed door, then looked at Jones. 'Where has he gone?'

'I don't know,' Jones replied. 'You must have pissed him off.'

A smile formed on Rick's lips. 'I think he gives up very easily.'

Jones shook his head. 'I don't think so. You've just made him mad. I hate to think what will happen when he comes back.'

Rick laughed. 'So now we play the good cop, bad cop. We too have seen the movies. You become my friend and I confess all to you.'

Jones slowly took out a packet of cigarettes, lit one and blew a stream of smoke towards the ceiling. 'Look squire, I don't give a fuck if you tell me anything or not. I couldn't care less where you got that stuff from. For all I know, you might have pinched it from the hospital yourself. It's no skin off my nose. I'll still get my pay at the end of the week if you tell me or not. But him,' Jones nodded towards the close door, 'he's a whole different kettle of fish. If he'd had been on your side he would have been in the Gestapo. He would have been the baddest bastard of the lot. He'll find out where you got it from, so just let's wait until he comes back.

The next ten minutes passed in silence. Jones leaning against the wall, chain-smoking, whilst Rick stared at the table. From time to time a look of concern formed on his face. Suddenly, the door opened to admit Penrose. A second man wearing a white coat and carrying a covered, chrome kidney bowl accompanied him.

Penrose crossed to the table and picked up the phials, one in each hand and placed them behind his back. 'Eenie, meenie, minor, mo. Which shall we have.' He brought his hands back to his front, looked at both phials before putting the marked one into his pocket and held out the unmarked one to the man in the white coat. 'That one I think Doc.'

The man in the white coat took it. He removed a hypodermic syringe from under the cover of the kidney bowl, inserted the needle through the rubber cover of the phial and drew up some of the contents. Then, remembering the hospital films he had seen, the investigator posing as a doctor made great play of expelling the air from the syringe. Rick, whose eyes were transfixed on the syringe, failed to see Penrose make his move. His wrists were grasped and he was hauled across the table. Penrose, holding Rick's arms hard against the edge of the table so that he could not rise, called to Jones, 'Get his strides down Davy'. Jones quickly unbuckled Rick's belt and pulled his trousers down to his ankles and stood on them to prevent any movement of the legs. Rick was helpless, spread-eagled across the table.

'Right Doc.' Penrose said. 'Give him a jab in the arse.'

Rick screamed. 'No, please no. Don't put that stuff into me.'

Penrose leant towards him. 'What's up Rick? The stuff is good. Remember your professional reputation. It won't hurt you. Just a sore arse, but it might clear up any pimples you might have.'

Tears were running down Rick's face as he strained against Penrose's grip. 'No, please. You are right. It is not good stuff.'

'Who did you get it from?'

'Let me up and I will tell you.'

'Not a chance Rick. You stay there until you answer all my questions. I may still want that needle stuck into you. Who did you get it from?'

'From Karl-Heinz Necker. He has supplied me before.'

'And you knew it was adulterated?'

'Not at first. But later I found out.'

'But you still used it on your patients?'

'Yes.'

Penrose released his wrists and pushed him back onto the chair where he attempted to pull up his trousers. He looked a picture of misery.

'Where can I find this Karl-Heinz Necker?' Penrose asked.

'He lives in Neuerweg, in Baumwall. I am not sure which number, it is in the middle and there is a street light outside the building.'

While Penrose made a note of what he had been told, Rick began to regain his control. 'So Sergeant,' he said to Penrose, 'I have told you everything. Am I now free to go?'

Penrose felt his temper rising. He looked hard at Rick. 'You think you should go? You piece of shit. You have been pumping that crap into those young girls and now you think you are free to go.'

'It rid them of their symptoms' Rick replied.

'But it didn't cure them,' Penrose retorted. 'They just thought they were cured and they went on their merry ways spreading pox and the clap to all and sundry. No mate, you're not free to go. You wanted to see the German authorities. Well, you'll get your wish. I know a Police Inspector who will want a long chat with you. Meanwhile, you remain here.'

Later, in the investigators' office, Penrose and Jones were frantically searching the directories to locate Neuerweg. They summoned one of the patrol sergeants who brought the maps used by the mobile patrols.

'To be quite honest Harry,' the patrol sergeant said, 'that area, Baumwall, is completely devastated. Nothing but a pile of rubble. I know there are people living there but I don't know one street from the other. I think your best bet is to have a word with the German police to actually pinpoint it.'

'Does that area come under Davidswache?' Penrose asked Jones.

'I guess so Harry.' Jones replied. 'Look. Davidswache must have some street maps from before the war. Why don't I nip over there and see if they can roughly pinpoint the area of Neuerweg. It shouldn't take me more than half an hour.'

'Okay Davy you do that. I'll sort things out here while you're away. Be as quick as you can.'

'Right,' replied Jones, leaving the office.

Penrose slumped into his chair and lit a cigarette. He ran his encounter with Dr Rick through his mind. The interview had not been conducted strictly in accordance with Judges Rules, but are they ever? London villains expected the occasional smack around the head during interview as par for the course. It helped to focus the mind and refresh the memory. He wondered if the German police had any rules for interrogation. If you would believe the propaganda of the wartime films, their approach was 'Ve haff vays of making you talk'.

His mind shifted to the broken bodies of McNeal, Willie and Pussy. A wry smile played on his lips. He had never realised before how compatible the last two had been named. At last there might be a break-through in solving their murders. If that break-through had been achieved by threatening Rick with a syringe loaded with nothing more lethal than distilled water, so be it. The end might just justify the means.

14

It was early afternoon before Penrose and Jones got to Neuerweg. Jones had taken over an hour to return with the information from Davidswache. While he was away, Penrose had reported his intentions to Warrant Officer Lancaster only to be told that the Commanding Officer wanted a verbal briefing on the interrogation of Dr Rick. But the Commanding Officer was also the Wine Member of the Officers' Mess and he was at a meeting with the Mess Manager discussing the replenishment of the cellar, leaving Penrose and Jones to kick their heels until lunchtime.

At the briefing, the Commanding Officer thought it prudent that Rick should be handed to the German authorities as soon as possible, so Penrose and Jones had taken him to Davidswache. There, Penrose had briefed Inspector Rossmann on Rick's involvement and of his intention of arresting Karl-Heinz Necker. Rossmann suggested that he and one of his officers should accompany Penrose to Neuerweg, not only to overcome any language barrier that might occur, but also that Necker might be relevant in his investigation into the murder of Willie Winkler.

Neuerweg, and the area surrounding it, was a scene of devastation. Without the help of the German police, Penrose would not have been able to identify the track between the mounds of rubble as once having been a street. Furthermore, he was amazed that any of the piles of bricks could be habitable.

Standing alone was a light standard that had somehow survived the onslaught of the bombs. Nearby, steps, which had been cleared of any obstruction, led down to a basement area where a door stood ajar.

Penrose, his pistol in hand, cautiously pushed the door fully open. It led into a stone passage, so dark that the far end could not be seen. On the left was an open door from which light flickered. Penrose poked his head around the door frame and saw that the room had once been a scullery. On one wall was a stone basin and draining board. Against the opposite wall was a small table and two, upright chairs. On the table, an oil lamp burned giving a low light to the rest of the room. In the centre of the floor was a body of a man, lying face down with a dark pool, which could have been blood, spreading from his head.

Penrose turned to Rossmann, who was immediately behind him. 'We have another body Klaus. We are going to need some light in here.'

While Jones and Rossmann's officer went back to their respective cars for flash lights, Penrose and Rossmann peered through the gloom at the body. 'I fear that is the man we have come to talk to, Harry,' Rossmann said. 'But I don't think he is going to tell us too much.'

When the flash lights arrived, Penrose and Rossmann entered the room, careful to avoid disturbing anything underfoot, leaving Jones and the German officer to search the remainder of the basement.

Rossmann played his light along the body. It was clad in a shirt, a pair of trousers and a pair of surprisingly good shoes. He was obviously dead. At the base of the skull was a small, gunshot wound that had been inflicted so close that flash and powder burns were apparent on the surrounding blonde hair. Grasping the hair at the top of the skull, Rossmann lifted the head to reveal a massive exit wound that had obliterated most of the facial feature. 'Even his mother would have trouble recognising him,' Rossmann said, as he gently lowered the head to its original position.

A jacket was hanging on the back of one of the chairs. From its inside pocket Rossmann took a wallet and extracted a civilian identity card. 'This is your Karl-Heinz Necker,' he said.

'Come here Harry,' Jones called to Penrose from the passage.

He was standing at the door to the next room along the passage. This room contained a double bed, a chest of drawers and a wardrobe. The German police officer was crouched at the far side of the bed. When he stood up his torch revealed the body of a seated woman, her back resting in the corner of the room. She had a gunshot wound in the centre of her face, the bullet having passed through the palm of her right hand before entering the face. It was apparent that she had been hiding behind the bed and had tried to protect her face with her hand at the time she was shot.

'What about the two rooms on the other side, Davy?' Penrose asked.

'Empty,' replied Jones. 'It looks like they had been occupied but whoever was living there have made a quick exit.'

'So Klaus,' Penrose said, still staring at the body of the woman, 'its looks like the tide has turned again and the shit is floating back to you.'

Before leaving the room, Penrose played his light around it. Amongst the clutter on the top of the chest of drawers was a red card from the Tamborin cabaret.

Rossmann had joined Penrose and Jones in their car from which they watched the activity around the abode of the late Karl-Heinz Necker. In the background was the noise of a portable generator that was supplying lighting by which Rossmann's medical examiner and scenes of crime men were carrying out their tasks in the building. It was nearly two hours since they had discovered the bodies. Still not in possession of any hard facts, their conversation was conjectural.

They had agreed that, without any evidence of a struggle, Necker had been shot in the back of his head as he led someone, possibly known to him, into the room. The female had tried to hide but was hunted down and eliminated because she could identify the murderer.

'But what was the motive Harry?' Rossmann asked. 'Was it connected with your arrest of Rick? Did they know that he would name Necker and that the trail would lead back to the suppliers?

Penrose shook his head. 'God knows Klaus,' he replied. 'We only pulled Rick mid-morning and kept him under wraps until we delivered him to you at Davidswache. Only us knew about it.'

'What about the four tarts who were in Rick's office?' Jones asked. 'Could they have let the cat out of the bag?'

Penrose thought for a while before replying. 'I don't think so. The only place they would have opened their mouths would have been in the Arnold, which doesn't open until midday. We were at Neuerweg at, when was it, about two o'clock, so it doesn't give much time for the word to get around; to reach the ears of the big boys, and for them to put the wheels in motion.'

'Well, what about the person who gave you the information last night?' Jones asked. 'Was it your new snout or someone else?'

In order to gain time whilst he put his thoughts into order, Penrose reached into his pocket for his cigarettes. He did not want to involve Lisa, as he was certain that she would not have spoken to anyone else after giving him the information. Anyway, she was still in a deep sleep when he had left her that morning. 'My snout is not in town at the moment. No, last night I overheard the girls in the Arnold chattering about Rick having penicillin. Anyway, if it was a set-up, why bother giving us Rick? They could have just taken him out instead of Necker. No. I think that us pulling Rick throw them into a panic Somehow, they found out and decided to go for the next link in the chain.'

'Who is they, Harry?' Rossmann asked. 'It does not appear to be your *Taucher* unless he has changed his style. If it had been him I think he would have used his rope rather than risking the noise of two gunshots.'

The emergence of the medical examiner from the ruin brought their conversation to an end. Getting out of the car, they waited for the doctor as he picked his way through the fallen bricks.

In consideration of Penrose and Jones, Rossmann addressed the doctor in English. 'So Doctor, what do you have?'

'Both deaths were caused by gunshot wounds,' replied the doctor, in English. 'In both cases death would have been instantaneous and occurred not more than fours hours ago.'

Penrose instinctively looked at his watch and saw that it was now three minutes after four o'clock.

The doctor continued, 'I have arranged for the bodies to be removed to the mortuary where I will carry out a full autopsy, but I fear that we will learn little else.'

They stood aside to allow the two stretcher containing the corpses to be carried to the ambulance, before making their way back along the track to the building where the scenes of crime men were packing their bags.

Rossmann spoke to them in German, translating their answers for the benefit of Penrose and Jones.

There had been little of evidential value in either of the rooms. In the bedroom they had found a 9-mm cartridge case under the bed which was of German manufacture and made during the war. Papers had identified the female as Irma Stubbe, aged 24 years.

'It looks like this is your problem Klaus,' Penrose said. 'I don't think there is much more Davy and I can do here. I'll pop into your office in the next couple of days to see if you have come up with anything.'

After shaking hands all round, Penrose and Jones made their way back to their car. With Jones driving, Penrose was deep in thought. Who had got to Necker, and why? Was it connected to the earlier arrest of Dr. Rick? Could Lisa have inadvertently, or otherwise, opened her mouth? He became aware of Jones talking to him.

'So what's going on Harry. It seems as if someone knows our every move. Who the bloody hell is it Harry?'

'Penrose shook his head. 'I wish I knew Davy. I wish I know.'

After briefing the Warrant Officer, and then completing a progress report, the clock in Michaeliskirch was striking eight as Penrose parked in the shadow of the church. He cautiously made his way up the ten flights of dark stairs to Lisa's door.

It was some minutes before the door was opened to his knock. Lisa, who was wearing a dressing gown, did not invite him in. She glanced quickly at the closed bedroom door behind her before saying, 'I can't see you now Harry. Meet me on Saturday night.'

Penrose stopped her attempt to close the door. 'Lisa, did you tell anyone about Doctor Rick?'

'No. I will talk to you on Saturday night.'

'I want an answer now Lisa. Did you say anything to anybody?'

The door to the bedroom opened and a middle-aged man came into the kitchen. He was barefooted and wearing just a pair of dark trousers and a white shirt. He looked at Penrose while he said, 'Is there any trouble Lisa?'

Before Lisa could reply, Penrose held up his warrant card and said, 'Police business. Who may you be?'

'First Officer Jackson of the *SS China Trader*,' the man replied.

'Then I have no business with you,' Penrose replied. Looking back at Lisa, he said. 'I will talk with you another time *Fräulein* Klose. Goodnight to you.'

As he turned to descend the second flight of stairs, Lisa and Jackson were still watching him. There was a look of anguish on Lisa's face.

15

Wherever you are in the world, thought Penrose, a wet Saturday afternoon is always miserable. Idly sipping a glass of beer, he gazed through the window of the Alsterpavillion at the rain pelting down on Jungfernstieg. He found it hard to imagine that the drab, grey scene before him had once been one of the most fashionable shopping streets in Europe. Somehow, he could not picture it thronged with elegantly dressed women on the arms of smart, arrogant *Wehmacht* officers; a vibrant street filled with movement, laughter, chatter and, maybe, music.

Because of the weather, he had decided not to pick up Tiny Chapman at the railway station. Instead he would let the mountain come to Muhammad. Tiny would pass the Alsterpavillion on his way to Büschstrasse and he would not be easily missed in the near deserted street.

Penrose's chain of thought drifted to the reason he was going to use Tiny. Five killings, all seemingly connected, but nether he or Rossmann were any nearer to solving them than they were after the first, the death of Winkler. The only witnesses were the victims themselves. The killer, or killers, seemed to be aware of this, always one step ahead to eliminate the next link in the chain that might hold the key to unlocking the answer.

Rossmann had confirmed that a 9-mm bullet fired from the same weapon had killed both Karl-Heinz Necker and Irma Stubbe. The absence of any evidence of a struggle suggested that Necker had admitted the killer to his room and had not been troubled by turning his back on the killer before being shot in the back of the head. It was apparent that Irma Stubbe was killed only because she could identify the killer. Not that she was involved in Necker's activities, just being at the wrong place at the wrong time. She had tried to protect herself by hiding in a darkened bedroom, but the killer had known she was there. There, she had placed her hand in front of her face in the futile hope that it would protect her from the fatal bullet.

~ *The Hamburg Dossier* ~

Rossmann had learnt very little about Necker. A small-time crook, he had been an independent operator not affiliated to the larger gangs and had made a living buying and selling stolen goods. One piece of information that had raised Penrose's interest was that Necker was a former submariner, serving in U-boats throughout the war and had still kept in contact with former colleagues. Thinking laterally, Penrose made the connection of submarines to diving and submariners to divers. Could the Diver come from amongst one of them?

Rossmann was convinced that Dr Rick's only involvement had been buying the adulterated penicillin from Necker. It had amused Rossmann that throughout the interview Rick had protested that he was only in his predicament because Penrose had wanted to stick a hypodermic in his backside. All he had wanted in life was to help the poor, unfortunate females that inhabited the dockside bars.

Penrose could not bring himself to believe that Lisa Lotte Klose had talked about Dr Rick's imminent arrest. When he had left her that morning she had still been fast asleep and looked like she would stay that way for the rest of the morning. Further more, Penrose had discovered that the *SS China Trader* had docked at six o'clock that morning and it was hard to believe that the ship's Mate would not have been ashore later than noon to meet Lotte. He might have even found her still in bed. No, the leak was from someone else. But who? He would have to find the four females who had been at Rick's surgery.

Although he was muffled against the weather under the hood of a duffel coat, the unmistakable figure of Tiny Chapman passed the windows of the Alsterpavillion, lugging his large suitcase. Penrose watched him until he turned right into Büschstrasse before lighting a cigarette. He would let Tiny settle at his destination before confronting him.

In response to Penrose ringing the bell, the door to the second floor flat was opened by Nick the Trader's helper cum bodyguard. As Penrose was known to him, he nodded towards the door of the living room.

~ *The Hamburg Dossier* ~

The curtains to the windows of the room were drawn tight. The centre light was pulled down on its pulley lead to about three feet above a table, illuminating the tabletop but leaving the rest of the room in semi-darkness. Arranged on the table were Nick's wares; cameras, cigarette lighters, electric shavers, perfume and, what every young woman in Britain would give not only her eye-teeth for but in some cases herself, packets of nylon stockings.

Like a spider hovering in the centre of his web, Nick sat, hunched, at the far side of the table, A cigarette dangled from the corner of his mouth set in a expressionless face. His eyes gave no flicker of recognition or welcome.

Tiny was seated to one side in the outer darkness. His open suitcase was on the floor in front of him, crammed with cartons of cigarettes of various brands.

Without a change of expression, Nick said, '*Guten Tag* Sergeant.'

Tiny had broken into a smile. 'Hello Harry. It hasn't taken you long to find this...' He paused, a look of concern clouding his face. 'He called you Sergeant. You told me you were a corporal.' He paused again, concern changing to alarm. 'Oh Christ. Don't tell me. You're SIB.'

Penrose nodded.

'So you buggers have got me at last,' Tiny continued. 'So what happens now? Are you going to arrest me?'

Penrose shook his head. 'No Tiny. I'm not going to arrest you. I'm going to buy you a drink.'

Puzzlement replaced the expression of alarm. 'What's your game Sergeant?' Tiny asked.

'No game Tiny. And it's still Harry.' Penrose replied. 'Just get on with your business as if I wasn't here. Then we can go and have that drink.'

Nick had been watching the exchange between the two, his cold eyes flicking from one to the other. Now he indicated a chair where Penrose should sit and turned his attention to Tiny. Penrose watched as Tiny handed Nick a list and the bartering began. Nick scribbled numbers against the items on the list and totted up the total. Tiny's cigarettes were counted. The numbers needed to settle the list were stacked away before Tiny was handed a bundle of currency for the remainder.

'I'll pick the stuff up tomorrow as usual Nick,' Tiny said. He looked at Penrose before adding, 'That's if I'm still about.'

Penrose led Tiny to his parked car and drove to the Seamen's' Mission. There he bought two pints of beer at the bar before indicating that Tiny should follow him into the Chaplain's office where the Reverend Andrews was working at his desk. After passing the time of day, Andrews rose and said, 'I'll leave you gents to it. I'll put the finishing touches to my sermon later.'

After the Chaplain had left, Tiny stared at Penrose. 'What the fuck going on Harry?'

Penrose smiled. 'Language Tiny. Remember where you are.' He raised his beer glass to Tiny. 'Cheers.' Tiny did not respond. Penrose continued. 'The thing is Tiny, I need someone like you. Someone who knows his way around this town. In return, I'll look out for you. You won't need to scavenge for seaman's shore leave passes to stay out after curfew.'

Tiny took a sip from his glass. 'That's not the way the game is played. Most of the police patrols know who I am. But by producing a shore leave pass I cover their arses. Anyway, what do you want me to do?'

Penrose told him about the series of murders, the Diver and possible connection to the Tamborin Club before saying, 'You see Tiny I want someone who can sniff around the Tamborin, and other dives, and see what they can pick up without anyone suspecting they are connected to the police.'

Tiny thought for a moment. 'I don't mind giving it a go but how do I contact you?'

'We could meet when you get off the train on Saturday afternoons,' Penrose replied.

'No need for that,' Tiny replied. 'I'm just starting ten days local leave and after that our squadron starts a three month tour of guard

~ *The Hamburg Dossier* ~

duty at the Equipment Depot here. Out in Altona. I'll be in town for the next three and half months.'

'Couldn't be better,' Penrose replied. 'We can arrange regular meetings at different places. If a meeting is needed urgently, I'll give you my telephone number. Just ring it and say "Tiny" and I'll meet you two hours later at the top of Michel.'

A ship's siren made the room vibrate. 'What the fuck is that?' Penrose said.

This time it was Tiny's turn to laugh. 'Language Harry. Remember where you are. Don't you know what that is? That's the coffee run. Come on, I'll show you.'

The rain had stopped. They walked up the knoll next to the Mission, went around the large, square plinth of Bismarck's statue from where they had a view of the river. On the far side, a large, white liner was being manoeuvred alongside a dock in one of the tributaries.

'The *SS St Louis*,' Tiny said. 'Docks every three weeks from the States. Brings in the Yanks' supplies and rotates their troops.'

'So the girls will be working for the Yankee dollar tonight,' Penrose remarked.

'Not a hope,' Tiny replied. 'The boys will be in luck, but not the girls. Ninety percent of the crew of that ship are queer. Not interested in the girls.'

'So what was the remark about the coffee run?' Penrose asked.

'Let's get a little closer.'

They walked down the hill onto the U-bahn station, which overlooked Landungsbrücken where a number of small boats were plying for hire. Two panel vans drew up at the jetties. The driver of the first van opened the rear doors of both vans to allow ten young women to emerge. All the women were wearing baggy dresses.

'I know that bugger,' Penrose said. 'That's the owner of the Astoria coffee-house. What are they up to Tiny?'

'Going to get his supply of coffee.' Tiny replied.

The coffee house owner and the women trooped down one of the slipways and boarded a small boat, leaving the second driver with the vans. The boat pulled out into the river and headed for the *SS St Louis*.

'It will take them about half an hour or so.' Tiny said. 'There's a small bar next to the station entrance. We might as well have a beer while we're waiting.'

The bar was no more than a hole in the wall containing a zinc-topped bar and two tables. There were no other customers so the sullen bartender returned to a book he was reading after drawing them two glasses of beer. The small window of the bar gave a clear view of the two vans on the other side of the road.

'So what's the SP on this caper?' Penrose asked.

'The girls are so say going to meet their so say boyfriends on the ship.' Tiny replied.

'But you said that the majority of the crew were poofters,' Penrose said.

'That's right. I did say, "so say boyfriends". Being a poof doesn't mean that they are not in the market for a bit of business. The coffee they bring will give them something to spend on their boyfriends while they are here. You'll see a bit of difference in the women when they come back.' Tiny looked at his watch. 'While we're waiting let's talk a bit more about this other business.'

Over the next half an hour they discussed the means by which Tiny would obtain any information and how he should contact Penrose on a regular basis. Penrose emphasised that Tiny should in no way put himself at risk as it was apparent that the people they were dealing with could be very ruthless.

Dusk was falling as the second driver alighted from his van and opened the rear doors of both vans. The small boat edged its way to the jetty and was tied up. The coffee house owner, his ten mules and three very effeminate men disembarked and walked up the slipway. Each of the women now appeared to be heavily pregnant.

'The crafty bastard!' Penrose hissed.

Tiny laughed. 'There you are Harry. In about ten minutes they will all give birth to a healthy ten pounder called Coffee Beans. Your mate there has really got his little racket tied up. No Customs officers and a dropsy to the harbour police to be somewhere else.'

As Penrose watched the women climbing into the vans while the coffee shop owner made his farewells to the three seamen, he wondered if Rossmann was as innocent as he claimed about the origins of the coffee sold in the Astoria. It was something to keep in mind and use later, if necessary.

They strolled back over the knoll to the Seamen's Club.

'I'll have to pop in to find a Shore Leave Pass for the weekend.' Tiny said. 'Are you coming in for a quick one?'

'No.,' Penrose replied, 'I've got a couple of calls to make. I'll meet you back here at midday tomorrow. Take it easy tonight and don't do anything stupid.'

'Don't worry about me Harry,' Tiny said, with a laugh as he turned to go into the bar. 'I'm too much of a coward to stick my neck out.'

Penrose drove to the Military Police Headquarters where he found Terry Reader propping up the bar in the Sergeants' Mess. 'Jesus Christ Harry, are you still at it?' Reader greeted him, with a smile. 'Don't you ever forget the job and relax?'

'Wish I could Terry,' Penrose replied, 'but the powers that be are on my back over this job. I've got to come up some answers soon.'

Reader ordered a pint of beer for Penrose before asking, 'So how is it coming along?'

'Bloody awful Terry. It's one step forward and two back. I guess you heard about the shootings over at Neuerweg? It seems as if some bastard knows what I'm thinking and is one step ahead of me.'

'Yeah, I read it in the daily crime brief. Do you reckon that was connected to your Diver thing?'

'It's too much of a coincidence for it not to be. I get Necker's name from a pox doctor who is using some of the stolen penicillin and a couple of hours later he has a bullet in his head. Have we now got a Kraut connection or has The Diver changed his MO?'

Reader took a swallow of beer whilst he pondered on the question. 'Just because Necker and his girlfriend were shot with a German

~ *The Hamburg Dossier* ~

weapon doesn't mean that the killer was a German. I would bet you that half the squaddies in the Zone have got a war souvenir stashed in their kit. Lugers, Mausers, Walters are ten a penny All of them nine millimetre. You can pick them up anywhere. So why wouldn't your Diver have a shooter?'

Penrose shook his head. 'It doesn't feel right. I'm not saying that The Diver is not connected with these two murders but I don't think he is the shooter. I think he is supplying the intelligence to a gang. Where and when to hit and helping in the planning. He has to have a German connection to distribute the stuff. Somehow he discovered that the pox doctor had been lifted, knew he would lead us to Necker and had warned whoever he is working with.'

'What makes you so certain that this Diver is a Brit Harry?' Reader asked. 'All you've got is the opinion of a tom in Herbertstrasse who saw him going into Pussy's place and Pussy herself who said that your nark had told her he was. Why didn't Willie tell you himself?'

'I think he was going to on the night he got knocked off. He had left a message for me to meet him. I didn't get the message but somebody else did. Then you've got the guy who was wandering around the hospital posing as a policeman. No German would have been able to have done that. No, I'm beginning to think that I have got to start looking nearer to home.'

Reader looked at him in disbelief. 'Are you saying that one of your lot is involved. For Christ's sake Harry, tread carefully.'

'Or one of yours,' Penrose said. 'That's why I've popped into see you.' He looked around to ensure that he was not being overheard. 'I've thrown a bit of bait out. I've got a man out on the ground, someone to shake the trees and see what falls out.'

'Who?' Reader asked.

Penrose shook his head. 'I'm not going to say. But I have given him your name in case he is picked up by one of your patrols. I've told him to ask for you. Then you can contact me to check him out. Will you do me that favour Terry?'

Reader stared at Penrose before slowly nodding his head. 'Just as long as you don't drop me in the shit Harry. I've known you long

~ 112 ~

enough to think that you won't. But watch your bloody back Harry, and that of your man. I can't help thinking that you are dealing with a bunch of bad bastards.'

16

It was nearly eleven o'clock when Tiny Chapman ambled along the bottom of the Reeperbahn and turned right into Grosse Freiheit. Literally meaning Great Freedom, the narrow, cobbled, side street was a part of old St Pauli. In years to come it would be synonymous with the Star Club and the Fab Four, but now it was a dingy street containing the Tabu, Safari and Tamborin cabarets and Hamburg's only baroque Catholic church.

Tiny had spent the proceeding three hours drinking in the Canadian Bar where, between fighting off the sexual advances of both Christine and Elsa, he had been turning over in his mind whether to undertake what Penrose had asked him to do. Eventually, his curiosity, and the prospect of a little danger, had won.

The shaven-headed doormen outside of the three cabarets watched Tiny approach before going into their spiel. 'Come inside Tommy Very sexy girls.' 'This club better,' from across the road. 'Our girls more sexy.'

Tiny stopped in front of the Tamborin. 'Just look inside,' the doorman said, opening the door halfway. 'All girls naked. Very best jig-jig.' Placing his hand in the middle of Tiny's back, the doorman propelled him inside.

Tiny entered a large, low-lit room with a bar at one end and a small stage and dance area at the other. Between the two were twenty or so small, round tables. On each table was an old fashioned telephone and a small pedestal holding a printed number. Along the length of the internal wall were a number of alcoves containing banquettes. At each alcove were draped curtains, some of which had been drawn, making the alcove a private place. On the stage was the obligatory, three-piece band which was playing a reasonable rendering of Glenn Miller's "Moonlight Serenade" to which, under the glare of a spotlight, a naked, willowy blonde was attempting a seductive gyration whilst, at the same time, keeping her attributions in full view.

Tiny took a seat at the bar and ordered a beer. Turning his back to the bar, he surveyed the clientele. About three-quarters of the tables were occupied, either by couples, unaccompanied men or two or three women. The women wore figure-hugging, full-length dresses with a frontal split to the top of their thighs. Waiters were strategically placed around the room but were not doing any business as, in a polite silence, all eyes were on the performer. All except one. Standing by curtained doorway, next to the stage, was a bull-necked thug whose unblinking eyes were boring through the gloom, directly at Tiny.

The spotlight snapped off and the dancer disappeared through the curtained doorway to a ripple of applause. The waiters sprang into action, circulating amongst the tables gathering orders. The telephones began to ring on the tables occupied by the single men. As they listened to the caller, their eyes were scanning the surrounding tables trying to identify who was offering their company. Occasionally a couple would move into one of the unoccupied alcoves, drawing the curtains as they entered.

Tiny heard a telephone on the bar behind him ring and the bartender muttering into it. A minute or two later, the bartender moved towards Tiny as he was mopping the zinc-topped bar. 'Mien Herr,' he murmured behind Tiny's back, 'if you wish the company of a young lady you will have to sit at one of the tables. The ladies are not allowed to come to the bar.'

Tiny turned. 'Okay mate. I'm just checking out the talent before I make my move. I'll sit down in a little while.'

A roll of drums and the dimming of the house lights heralded the next cabaret act. Two naked women stepped into the spotlight, one blonde and the other brunette. The band started a rendering of Blue Velvet as the women moved towards each other. Their act could not be called a dance, more sensuous fondling in time to the music.

Tiny became aware of someone climbing onto the barstool beside him. A whiff of expensive perfume told him that it was a women. He waited until the cabaret act had ended before turning back to the bar and inspecting the person sitting alongside him. She was a blonde with deep blue eyes set in an impeccably made-up face. She gazed intently back at Tiny before breaking into a smile which revealed a set a perfect white teeth. She too was clad in a tight evening dress, but, unlike the others in the club, her dress did not have the frontal slit.

Tiny winked at her. 'I'd like to ask you if you would like a drink,' he said, 'but the barman tells me that the ladies are not allowed to drink at the bar.'

She laughed. 'That is true,' she said, 'but that rule does not apply to me.'

'What makes you different?' Tiny asked.

'Because I am the boss's daughter,' she replied. 'My name is Lilli.'

'In that case it should be you buying one for me' Tiny said, with a laugh. He indicated to the barman to serve her a drink. 'No doubt he will know what you have.'

The barman set a stemmed glass containing a golden liquid in front of her that she sipped before replacing it on the bar. 'Thank you. What do I call you?'

'My name is Tiny. I can't get over you speaking perfect English.'

'That's the product of your English public school system,' Lilli replied.

'Interesting,' Tiny said. 'How did that come about?'

'Before the war my grandfather was the Naval Attaché in London. I had to live with him because my father, who was also in the navy, was always at sea and my mother was dead. So grandfather sent me to one of your public schools.'

'And was your father also a naval officer?' Tiny asked.

Lilli laughed. 'No, not Johnny Gross. He was a black sheep. He never made it to an officer. He was what the Americans call a top non-com. He was a coxswain on a U-boat. His friends say that Big Johnny was the best-damned diver in the Navy. He could take a submarine to the bottom in minutes.'

Tiny stiffened, the smile fading from his lips. Lilli noticed the change. 'Is there anything wrong?' she asked, with a look of concern.

Tiny recovered his composure. 'No, nothing.' Rubbing his chest, he said, 'Just a bit of heartburn. Too much beer I guess.'

Lilli smiled. 'Good. So what about you Tiny? You are so big that you must be a policeman.'
Tiny laughed and shook his head. 'Nothing like that. I've got no time for them. I'm just an ordinary soldier. The most exciting thing I do is guard duty.'
'And where do you do this exciting thing?' Lilli asked.
'At the Equipment Depot in Altona.'
'Is that the big warehouse next to the racecourse where all the trucks are parked? They say there are many fine things in the warehouses. Things that can make you rich.' She chuckled. 'Maybe you can take me in there and let me help myself.'
Tiny smiled as he shook his head. He took hold of her hand. 'If it was up to me Lilli, a lovely girl like you could have everything that's stored there. But it's not as easy as that. I just can't let you walk in there. It would take a bit of planning.'
The doorman came into the club and whispered to one of the waiters. He in turn came over to Lilli and whispered in her ear. She slipped off of her barstool and pulled Tiny by he hand. 'Come,' she said. 'The military police are in the street and might come in here.'
She led him behind the bar and through a door into a storeroom. 'We will be safe here until they leave.' She reached up to wrap her arms around his neck but her face only came up the middle of his chest. '*Mein Gott* you are so big.' She looked around the room before pushing him towards a wooden crate and forcing him to sit down. 'Now you are like a normal man.' She pushed his knees apart and moved close to him, her arms around his neck. Nuzzling his ear, she whispered, 'So when are you going to take me to your warehouse.'
Tiny's wandering hands had discovered that the dress was the only garment she was wearing. He grasped her waist, his massive hands practically encircling it. He gently pushed her backwards and looked into her eyes. 'I said it would take some planning. Tell me what you want and we can then sort something out. But it would have to be worth my while.'
There was a tap on the door. The barman stuck his head into the room and nodded. 'They have gone.' Lilli said. 'Let us go back in.'

'I better get out of here,' Tiny said. 'The crafty bastards might still be hanging around. Can't we go to your place or a hotel or something.'
Lilli pulled his face towards hers and kissed him. 'Not tonight Tiny. My boyfriend is coming to see me. But he will not be here next week.'
'So when can I see you again?' Tiny asked.
'Any night next week. I'm here every night.'
'Is there a back way out?' Tiny asked.
Lilli led him to a door that opened onto an alley. Tiny grasped her under her arms and effortlessly lifted her up so their faces met. He kissed her before gently lowering her to the ground, 'See you next week kid,' he said before slipping away into the night.

In the office above the club The Diver sat silently as he listened to Lilli relating what she had learnt about Tiny.
'So,' 'Big' Johnny Gross asked, when she had finished, 'do you think we will have an in to the depot?'
'Of course papa,' Lilli replied. 'I'll have him eating out of my hand. We'll get into the warehouse if he thinks it will get him into my knickers. All we have to decide is what to go for.'
'Motor vehicles and spare parts,' The Diver said. 'There are so many of them there that they will not be missed.' He turned to Lilli. 'You work on your soldier boy and get as much information as you can so that we can set up the job. Promise him anything but just keep your knickers on. Remember, you belong to me.'

17

At the time that Tiny was leaving the Tamborin, Penrose was sitting in his car, parked across the road from the Café Arnold. He was deep in thought, cigarette in his left hand whilst his right was slowly rubbing the murder case file laying on the passenger seat next to him.

After leaving Terry Reader he had gone back to his office where for two hours he had poured over the file searching for something he might have overlooked; that something that might just point to the solution. That something had been nagging at the back of his mind but, despite reading and re-reading the file, he could not bring it to the fore and identify the something that was bothering him. Finally, realising that his thoughts were going around in circles, he closed the file. As he went to lock the file in his desk drawer, he hesitated. Instead of putting it in the drawer, he just locked the drawer and left the office carrying the file with him. As he passed the Duty Room on his way out of the building he bade farewell to the Duty Corporal who, not lifting his eyes from the Hank Jansen paperback he was reading, just raised a hand in acknowledgement.

A tap on the window of the car brought Penrose back to reality. It was the sausage seller. Penrose wound the window down. 'You want *Wurst?*' the sausage seller asked, indicating his stall behind the car.

Penrose shook his head. *'Nein danke. Ich möchte ein trinken haben.'*

The sausage seller stood upright. Before turning back to his stall, he shook his head and said, 'German still bad. *Fräulein* no teach. More *sprechen, klein jig-jig.'*

Penrose chuckled as he slipped the file under the driving seat before getting out of the car and locking it. Crossing the road, he pushed through the velvet curtains into the Café Arnold. There didn't seem to be the usual Saturday night crowd. Adjusting his eyes to the gloom, he saw Lisa in her usual booth at the rear of the café. She was staring intently at him. Face expressionless, her eyes didn't leave him as he made his way towards her. As he squeezed onto the bench beside her, she dropped her gaze to her hands resting on the edge of the table. She remained silent.

~ *The Hamburg Dossier* ~

'So, is jolly Jack Tar back on the high seas then?' Penrose asked.

He saw tears welling up in her downcast eyes and a mixture of pity and shame surged through him. He grasped her hand and turned her towards him. 'Oh, I'm sorry Lisa. It was only a joke. I didn't mean to upset you.' He pulled her towards him and kissed her tears before taking out his handkerchief and wiping them dry. 'Come on sweetheart. Cheer up and give us a smile.'

A trace of an uncertain smile touched Lisa's lips. 'I no think you like me any more Mr Harry.' she said in a quiet voice. 'You know why I have to see that man. I tell you all about it. It is better if I be with you. I show you that before.'

Penrose gently touched her cheek. 'Of course I understand Lisa.' he said. 'In another place at another time you wouldn't have to do what you do. And I like you Lisa whatever you do. I like you a lot. So come on, cheer up and let's have a drink.'

Herman the waiter had been hovering a short distance away, a look of uncertainty on his face, as if he was wondering whether to interrupt what appeared a lovers' tiff. Penrose signalled to him to bring two drinks.

'You not angry with me?' Lisa asked. 'When you come to my house you were very angry. You call me *Fräulein* Klose. That sound very angry.'

'I was just being official,' Penrose replied. 'I didn't want to cause you any trouble with your boyfriend.'

'He not my boyfriend,' Lisa said, grasping Penrose's hand. 'You my boyfriend, he only business.'

Penrose smiled. 'Business is business and love is bullshit.' he said.

'You are not bullshit,' Lisa stated, in a whisper.

Whilst Herman fussed around changing the ashtray after serving the drinks, Penrose studied the customers in the bar. It was apparent that there were more men than women sitting at the tables, which was unusual.

'It seems very quiet tonight.' he said to Lisa, 'Where are all the girls?'

'They have gone away They all very frightened of what is happening.'

I am looking for the girls who were at Doctor Pick's. I'm sure I have seen them in here before. Do you know who they were?'

Lisa bit her lip. 'I know two of them who were there. Pia Langer and Ingrid Müller. They have both gone to Bremerhaven.'

'Gone to work for the Yankee dollar eh?' Penrose said. 'How did you know they were in Pick's office?'

Lisa looked startled. 'Ingrid tell me. She say she leave Hamburg so she no killed like that girl Irma.'

'Irma? Irma Stubbe?' Penrose casually asked. 'Did you know her?'

Lisa hesitated for a moment. 'I see her sometimes. For a long time she leave here and work at the Tamborin cabaret.'

The Tamborin again, thought Penrose. 'What about her boyfriend?' he asked. 'Karl-Heinz Necker, did you know him?'

Lisa shook her head. 'I no know him. Everyone say he was a big gangster. I stay away from them.'

Penrose grasped both of Lisa's upper arms and looked deep into her eyes. 'Lisa,' he said, 'tell me the truth. Did you tell anyone that you had told me about Doctor Pick?'

Lisa's eyes again became watery. 'No Harry. I tell you before. I no speak about it.'

'Hello! hello!, hello! What's this? A lovers' quarrel or can anyone join in?' Penrose looked up and saw a smiling Davy Jones approaching the table. 'Thought that was your car outside Harry. As I haven't seen you for a couple of day I thought I'd pop in and say hello.' He looked at Lisa. 'Whose this lovely lady then? Is she your new ...,' he tapped the side of his nose with his forefinger, ' or just a bit of the other to help you get over Inge?'

'Neither,' Penrose replied. 'This is Lisa, a friend of mine. Do you want a drink?'

Jones ignored the question, looking hard at Lisa. 'Do I know you? I think I've seen you around somewhere.'

Lisa shook her head. 'I don't think so.'

'Do you want a drink?' Penrose asked Jones again.

Jones shook his head. 'Not for me Harry. I've been to see my *schatz*. I've had enough booze, and the other, for tonight. I'm on my way back to the mess. Are you coming back tonight or are ?'. He looked at Lisa and gave her a wink with a shake of his head.

'I haven't made my mind up yet,' Penrose replied.

Jones started to turn away. All right mate. I guess I'll see you Monday morning.' With a wave of his hand, he walked out of the bar.

Lisa watched him go before turning to Penrose. 'Is that your friend? I think I have seen him before but I no remember.'

The night passed quickly. Half the lights in the bar were switched off as Herman went from table to table, totting up the drink tabs and collecting what was owed.

'Are you coming to my house Harry?' Lisa asked. 'I want you to.'

'As long as we don't have Manfred creeping around as we're doing the business,' Penrose replied. 'He puts me off my stroke.'

Lisa laughed. 'He will not be there. Tonight he work all night at the *Fischmarkt.*'

She clutched his arm as they left the bar. The sausage seller was standing by Penrose's car. As they approached he spoke to Lisa in German, too fast for Penrose to catch the drift.

'He say a man was trying to get into your car,' Lisa translated.

'When?' Penrose asked.

'*Zwei Minuten.*' the sausage seller said. 'I see, I shout, he run.'

'Ask him what he looked like?' Penrose said to Lisa.

Lisa had a short conversation with the sausage seller before turning to Penrose. 'He cannot say what he look like. It was too quick. The man run there.' She indicated the direction of the knoll beside the Seamen's Bar.

An inspection of the car showed that the locks had not been forced and the murder file was still beneath the driving seat. Penrose thanked the sausage seller as he and Lisa got into the car.

The Diver stopped his car in the shadows of *Michaeliskirche* and watched, across the bomb rubble, as Penrose parked his car outside of Lisa's apartment block. He watched them enter the building and waited three or four minutes until he saw a light come on in a skylight at the top, before driving away.

18

Penrose awoke, wondering what the time was. The skylight above him framed a watery sunlit sky. He studied it for a while before letting his gaze move along the heavy timber beams that supported the sloping roof.

Lisa was sound asleep, her head resting on his shoulder and her left arm and leg straddled across his body. His left arm was trapped under her so he was unable to see the face of his watch. After getting into bed they had made love slowly at first and then, at Lisa's instigation, with increasing urgency before they both dropped off to sleep.

He looked down at her face framed by jet-black hair. She looked so young. Too young to have had to experience the trauma of the past two years. As much as he hated to disturb her, the call of nature was so pressing that he pulled his arm from beneath her before padding through the kitchen into the bathroom.

Wide-awake, she watched him return and climb back into bed. Without speaking, she pressed her lips into the side of his neck, letting her free hand move up and down his body. Penrose glanced at his watch and saw that it was quarter to eleven. He did not have to meet Tiny until noon. He responded to her caresses and soon they were making love, Lisa with the same urgency that she had shown the night before.

When it was over and they lay in each other's arms. Penrose propped himself up on his elbow and looked down at Lisa. 'What did you mean last night when you said that I wasn't bullshit?' he asked.

Lisa stared at him before answering. 'Don't you know? Can't you see? I love you Harry. *Ich liebe dich.* Even with your bad German you should understand that.'

Penrose drew her towards him and held her tight. His mind was in a whirl. 'Lisa, oh Lisa,' he whispered. 'This is crazy. We both know that nothing can come of this.'

Lisa lifted her head and looked at him. Tears were welling up in her eyes. 'Why?' she asked. 'Is it because you still love that good girl of yours?'

Penrose shook his head before kissing her tears. 'No sweetheart. That's history. But you know the regulations. We shouldn't even be seeing each other. As far as the army is concerned the non-fraternization rule still applies.'

Lisa pulled away, turned and lay looking the other way. 'So the army says that British soldiers can fuck German girls but not marry them.' she said, bitterly.

Penrose stroked her hair. 'It's not that at all Lisa. One day the rules will change and there will be no problem. But I will have gone back to England before that comes about.'

'Then you can come back and get me?' Lisa asked, her voice softening.

'We'll see sweetheart.' replied Penrose. 'Look, I've got to go out and do a bit of business. Only for an hour or so. When I get back we'll go out to find some food.'

'I've got food here Harry. My friend, who you call Jolly Jack, brought me plenty from his ship. Do you want me to make you something?'

'No. I don't want to take your food Lisa. I'll have a bite at the Seamen's Club.'

There is definitely a touch of spring in the air, thought Penrose as he left Lisa's building. He decided to leave his car where it was and walk the few hundred yards to the Seamen's Club. As he made his way along the deserted roads between the piles of rubble that had once housed people and businesses he again tried to imagine the horror of those nights that had produced the devastation all around him.

His thoughts moved to Lisa. Love had never been on the agenda. He had hoped that she would be a means to an end. That her knowledge of the local happenings might just give him a lead to help untangle his case. Love was an additional complication he didn't need.

The Reverend Peter Andrews was standing in the hallway of the Seamen's Club when Penrose entered.

'Hello Harry,' he greeted Penrose. 'I'm afraid that you are a little late for morning service again,' he added with a laugh. 'Your friend is in the restaurant. Do you want to use my office?'

'No thanks Peter,' Penrose replied. 'I'll go in and have something to eat if you have anything.'

'Food aplenty Harry. The *St Louis* docked yesterday and its Chief Steward, a good churchgoer I might add, sent over ample supplies so that his lads would not go hungry whilst they were enjoying their run ashore.'

'Hope he included a few bags of coffee with the loaves and fishes,' Penrose said, with a straight face.

'Of course he did,' Andrews said. Looking perplexed, he added, 'Why do you ask?'

'Nothing Peter,' Penrose replied. 'Just a joke. I'll tell you it someday.'

Tiny was sat at a table in the far corner of the restaurant with a large plate of ham and eggs in front of him. Seeing Penrose he waved him over before putting a forkful of food into his mouth. Penrose signalled to one of the two waitresses and ordered the same before joining Tiny.

'Looks like you've got an appetite Tiny' Penrose said. 'Have you had your leg over all night or something?'

Tiny swallowed what he was chewing 'That's bugger all to do with you. I don't remember that my personal life was included in our deal. But if you are interested, yes, I did see a friend who offered me a bed for the night. Nothing for free with her so I got my money's worth.'

They exchanged small talk until the waitress brought Penrose's meal. After she had retreated to the other side of the room Penrose asked, 'How did the business go last night? Did you get anywhere?'

'Not a lot. I got chatted up by the boss's daughter. Her name's Lilli. Got a lovely pair of tits. I think she was sounding me out. Wanted to know if I was a policeman.'

'I hope you convinced her otherwise,' Penrose said.

~ The Hamburg Dossier ~

'Yeah. I told her I was a guard at the Equipment Depot. That really got her going. She would have creamed her knickers if she had been wearing any.'

'How do you know she wasn't?' Penrose asked with a laugh.

'I've already told you Harry that my personal life is my own. Whether she was wearing knickers or not is not going to help you with your case. As soon as I mentioned the Depot she was all over me. Wanted to know if I could get her into the place.'

'Did she say why she would want to get in there?' Penrose asked.

'I don't think it was for herself. More like her old man. He's called Jonny Gross. I've never seen him but have heard whispers about him from Nick the Trader. As well as owning the Tamborin he's also a big wheel in the black market. Deals in anything. But I ain't told you the best bit. She said that her old man's nickname is Diver.'

The forkful of food that Penrose was lifting to his mouth stopped halfway from the plate. He looked in amazement at Tiny. 'Are you sure? Did you understand her correctly?'

'Harry, that woman speaks better English than you do. Educated in England. Roedean or somewhere. She said that Jonny Gross's mates call him Diver.'

'Jesus H Christ,' Penrose swore, pushing his plate to one side. 'Do you know what this means?' Without waiting for an answer, he continued, 'It means that I've been on the wrong track. I always thought The Diver was a Brit. Did she say anything else?'

'No really Harry. The bloody Redcaps decided to pay the place a visit, so she dragged me into a back room.'

'And that's where your brains dropped to your bollocks and you found she was not wearing any knickers?'

'Eh, let me remind you again about my personal life. No, she said her boyfriend was coming. I don't know who he is. But he's away next week and she said I could see her any evening.'

Penrose sat silently, thoughts whirling around in his head. Finally he looked up. 'I've got to have a looksee at this Gross character. What do you think my chances are of not being recognised if I go to the Tamborin with you?'

~ *The Hamburg Dossier* ~

Tiny threw his head back and stared at the ceiling while he thought. 'You might get away with it Harry. Don't take this the wrong way, but you are a bit faceless in this town. I thought I knew all you guys but I had never seen you before. Admittedly it is the uniform police I know, not the SIB. It's dark in the Tamborin, and it is the other end of the Reep. If you have not done any business in the clubs at that end you might be okay. You know the girls generally keep to the places where they do business and not try to muscle into other places where they would not be welcome, so the chances of any of them having seen you is remote. I reckon you should go for it.'

'Right mate, I don't know when but for the next couple of day be in here about ten o'clock at night and I'll meet you. Another thing. I know you're on leave, but if you come to any arrangement with this bird and a visit to the Equipment depot, you might have to go back on duty. Okay? Now let's go and have a pint.'

From the viewing platform of *Michel* tower The Diver watched Penrose walk back to Lisa's building. He cursed under his breath. As Penrose's car was still parked outside the building he had assumed that Penrose was still inside. Now the wait would have to be extended until he left again.

It was nearly dusk when Penrose and Lisa came out and drove away in the car. Descending the tower, The Diver walked slowly to the tenement. Quietly, he climbed the stairs, stopping on each landing and listening for sounds at every door. It didn't take long to force the cheap latch bolt lock securing Lisa's door. The Diver glanced around the sparely furnished kitchen, deciding that what he was seeking would not be there, before moving into the bedroom. Switching on the light, he moved to the dressing table on which were a scattering of bottles and tubes of cosmetics. The four drawers contained items of glamorous underwear, mostly of American manufacture, and pieces of outer apparel.

Glancing into the mirror, he saw the reflection of a small, ugly face peering at him from behind a partly opened door leading to the eaves. Manfred drew the door closed as The Diver turned and crossed the room, but did not have the strength to hold the door shut when The Diver pulled on the outer handle.

The Diver grabbed Manfred by his shirt-front before slamming him back against the doorpost. Manfred collapsed to the floor and lifted his hands defensively in front of his face.

'Bitte mein Herr. Bitte. Bitte,' he said, terrified.

The Diver easily pulled him to his feet, turned him around and slid his right arm across Manfred's throat. Locking his hand into the crook of his left elbow, he placed the palm of his left hand onto the back of Manfred's head, then he easily lifted the little man clear of the floor. There was a sharp crack as he increased pressure on the back of the head and Manfred's whimpering ceased.

It was nearly midnight when Penrose and Lisa climbed the stairs to her room. As they started on the last flight they saw that the door to the flat was ajar.

'Would Manfred go out and leave the door open?' Penrose whispered.

Lisa shook her head.

Pushing her back down to the landing, Penrose quietly crept back up the stairs. Slowly pushing he door open he saw, by the faint moonlight filtering through the skylight, the silhouette of a man framed in the open bedroom door. Hurling himself across the kitchen and into the bedroom, Penrose made a grab but the figure swung away from him and then, like a pendulum, swung back, colliding with his chest. Penrose reached for the light switch. The dim light showed the naked, deformed body of Manfred suspended, by a rope around his neck, from one of the roof beams.

19

Penrose and Lisa waited in his car outside of her apartment building for Inspector Rossmann's to come and talk to them. As there was still no effective civil telephone system in Hamburg, Penrose had had to drive to Davidswache to report the finding of Manfred's body. The Medical Examiner and forensic staff were already working in the flat, while other detectives were interviewing the other occupants of the building, but Penrose had decided not to become involved in the preliminary investigation.

It was gone one o'clock before Rossmann arrived. After a quick word with Penrose, he had disappeared into the building. When he emerged he indicated that Penrose should join him in his car.

'So Harry, another night, another death. My men tell me that the deceased is the landlord of the young lady sitting in your car.'

'That's correct. She is Lisa Klose. I only knew the landlord as Manfred. You will have to ask her what his surname was.'

'We are aware of it. His name was Haller. But what do we have? Murder or suicide?'

Penrose shook his head. 'I don't think there is much doubt about it. It's murder and we don't need three guesses to come up with the killer.'

'So you think this is another victim of *Der Taucher?* Then why that old man and why is he naked.?'

'I'm not trying to teach you to suck eggs Klaus, but the poor little bastard was hanging about two feet off the floor. There was no sign of anything he could have stood on to tie the rope around the beam before kicking it away. Why him? I think he was not the intended victim, he just happened to be in the wrong place at the wrong time. I think the murderer was leaving a message for me. And why was he naked? Because the person who did it is a twisted bastard. Remember what he did to Pussy when he killed her. He wanted to humiliate the old man. Would you like to be seen naked if you had an ugly deformed body like his?'

~ 130 ~

'You say he was not the intended victim Harry. So who was? Was it you or the young lady in your car?'

'I don't know Klaus,' Penrose replied shaking his head. 'I have spent a couple of nights with her and we have been seen out and about together. Maybe somebody thinks that's a bit dangerous; that she is telling me things they would rather she didn't.' He paused in thought for a few seconds before continuing. 'I don't think they would be stupid enough to make a play for me.'

Rossmann nodded. 'Look Harry,' he said, 'we still have a lot of work to do here. Would you bring *Fräulein* Klose to my office later this morning so that statements can be taken from you both?'

'Will do.' Penrose replied. He hesitated. 'There is just one little problem.'

'And that is?' Rossmann asked.

'I realise that she cannot return to the flat up stairs until you have finished there.' Penrose replied. 'But she has nowhere else to go.'

'Then you must take to the town authorities Harry and arrange temporary accommodation.'

'That's the problem Klaus. She doesn't have papers for the British Zone.'

'There is nothing I can do about that Harry. It is something she will have to sort out.'

Penrose looked at him, a half smile on his lips. 'Klaus, a few days ago you lectured me on the rights of German civilians to buy and sell coffee. You said that there was no law against them doing such trade. I won't argue with you, but I bet that if I should study the Occupation Regulations issued by my political masters I might prove you wrong. If you are prepared to overlook something like that for the well-being of your people, why are you not prepared to stop a young German girl being returned to the Russian Zone where unspeakable horrors might await her?'

Rossmann sat silent before taking a notebook from his pocket. He wrote something on a page, signed it, tore out the page and handed it to Penrose. 'Take this to Davidswache and give it to the *Wachmeister*. I still have the keys to Karen Averbeck's apartment. We have finished there but I have been unable to trace any next of kin to hand the keys to. Let *Fräulein* Klose use the place until she can return here, Now let us take her upstairs so that she can collect some of her clothing.'

It was just after half past seven when Penrose arrived back at his room in the mess. Lisa had been apprehensive about staying in Pussy's apartment and had insisted that Penrose remain with her for the remainder of the night. Before leaving he had instructed her to keep the door locked until he returned for her later in the morning.

Penrose had the feeling that someone had been in his room. Nothing appeared to be missing, but one or two things, both on the dresser top and in the drawers, were not as he had left them. There was no sign of forced entry so, if someone had been in the room, entry had been effected by means of a key. As with all door keys, a duplicate to his room was held in the control room.

When Penrose entered the investigators' office the place was in an uproar. Everyone seemed to be talking over each other. Davy Jones, seeing Penrose enter the room, came across to him,

'What the fuck's going on Davy?' Penrose asked.

'Some bastard has had a go at the desk drawers over the weekend.'

Penrose went to his desk where he saw that the locked drawer had been forced open. 'Who was Duty NCO last night?' he asked Jones who had followed him across the room.

'Your mate, Lofty Wilson. Someone has gone over to his billet to haul his arse back here. I can't understand what the person was looking for. It's not as we keep anything of value in the drawers. None of the lads reckon that there is anything missing.'

Before Penrose could answer Warrant Officer Lancaster bounced into the room. 'Okay, simmer down. Shut the noise up,' he shouted above the din. Once the chatter had subsided he continued, 'They also had a go at the filing cabinets in the Collator's office. The only thing that appears to be missing is...' He turned to Penrose, 'that file of yours on the murders Harry.'

'It's not missing Boss' replied Penrose, lifting the file in the air. 'It has been with me as I've been working on it all weekend.' He decided not to say anything about the possible intruder in his room or that he had kept the file in his car. He also decided not to mention anything about Manfred's death until he could have a quiet word with Lancaster.

A uniformed sergeant entered the office with Lofty Wilson and a second corporal in tow. 'Corporal Wilson was Duty NCO from yesterday morning until this morning and Corporal Woods was on duty until yesterday morning, Sir,' he said to Lancaster. 'But neither of them say they know anything about this.'

'Who came into the Headquarters whilst you were on duty yesterday?' Lancaster asked Wilson.

'There was a bit of traffic Sir, but I can't remember who offhand. But I certainly didn't see anyone who shouldn't be here.'

He looked at Woods. 'What about you?'

'No one came in while I was on duty Sir.' Woods replied.

Penrose looked across at Woods. 'Bollocks,' he said. 'I was in here for a couple of hours on Saturday evening. You even gave me a wave when I left but you were too engrossed in your book to look at me.'

Corporal Woods' face went red and he looked down at the floor. Wilson gave Penrose a look of hate.

'Right.' Lancaster said to the two corporals, ' Go and wait outside my office. We'll have a little chat when I've finished here.'

Morning prayers took a shorter time than normal and Penrose followed Lancaster to his office. The two corporals were standing in the corridor, Woods was still gazing at the floor whilst Wilson stared defiantly at Penrose.

'We've got another problem Boss.' Penrose said after closing the office door. 'There's another body.'

Lancaster raised his eyebrows. 'Oh Christ!' he said. 'Who now?'

'The landlord of a bit of stuff I've been cultivating,' replied Penrose. 'I found him hanging from a beam in her room last night. It might look like suicide but I don't think it was. I'm seeing Rossmann later this morning when I might learn a bit more.'

'So how did he become involved?' Lancaster asked.

'Wrong place, wrong time Boss. I thing he caught someone turning over this bird's drum. Someone who was looking for something I might have left there.'

'Had you left anything there Harry?'

Penrose shook his head. 'No. But somebody might have thought I did. I think they were looking for the same thing in my desk drawer. The rest of the lad's drawers were done as a cover up.'

'You still think there is an inside connection Harry?' Lancaster asked.

'I just can't shake that feeling Boss.' Penrose laid his file on Lancaster's desk. 'I've put a progress report in it for you. Can I ask you to keep the file in your safe when you've finished and not put it back in the Collator's office? I'll get it back from you later.'

It was early afternoon when Penrose finished giving his statement to the German investigators at Davidswache. Whilst Lisa was finishing her statement, Penrose went along the corridor to Rossmann's office.

'Come in Harry,' Rossmann said when Penrose entered after tapping on the door.

'Please take a seat.'

Rossmann shuffled some papers around on his desk before looking up at Penrose. 'So Harry, it would appear that you were correct. It was not suicide. The marks on the neck were post-mortem Death was not due to strangulation but from a broken neck.' He ran his finger down the paper in front of him before continuing. 'The Medical Examiner says that the break was caused by applied pressure. Pressure applied by a very strong person or someone skilled in the art of killing that way.'

Penrose shrugged his shoulders. 'That would include most of the male population of Hamburg, both German and British. Anyone who had been in the army would have had some unarmed combat training. Did forensics come up with anything?'

'Plenty of fingerprints Harry. Yours, we do have your prints on record, as you will recall, those belonging to the deceased, small ones that no doubt belong to *Fräulein* Klose. We shall see. But also many others which we may or may not match.'

'No doubt the owners of those are spread out across the seven seas.' Penrose said.

'The rope around the neck was similar to that which killed Winkler,' Rossmann continued, 'so it looks like one of your people is involved.'

'Oh! Come on Klaus. Just because the rope is of the type used in British kitbags doesn't prove that the perpetrator was a British squaddie,' Penrose said. 'There must be no end of them, used for all kinds of things, around the city. There are Germans working in all the military stores and it doesn't take much to stuff a bit of rope in a pocket.' Penrose took out a packet of cigarettes then returned them to his pocket when he remembered that Rossmann didn't smoke. 'Klaus,' he asked, 'do you know anything about a Jonny Gross?'

'He is known to us.' Rossmann replied impassively.

'Have you ever pulled him in and asked him what he knows about this affair?'

For the first time Penrose saw a look of discomfort appear on Rossmann's normally calm expression. Avoiding Penrose's eyes, Rossmann said, 'We have no reason to question *Herr* Gross. There is nothing to connect him to any of this matter.'

'Good God Klaus', Penrose exploded. 'He's the biggest crook in town. Nothing goes down without him being involved. Even if he is not connected you can bet a pound to a pinch of shit that he knows about it.'

Rossmann had regained his composure. 'I repeat Harry. We have no reason to question him.'

Penrose was framing another cutting remark when the office door opened and Rossmann's subordinate entered. After a short conversation, Rossmann turned to Penrose and said, 'We have finished with *Fraulein* Klose and she is waiting for you in the reception.'

Penrose nodded, rose from his chair and left Rossmann's office. Neither of them bid the other farewell. Penrose's thoughts were troubled.

After taking Lisa back to the Hopfenstrasse apartment where he warned her not to answer the door to anyone before he returned later, Penrose drove to Büschstrasse. Still worried by Rossmann attitude and his refusal to interview Jonny Gross, he hoped that he might find answers from Nick the Trader.

Nick the Trader was a man of mystery. Before the war he had been the owner of a large import and export business. At the outbreak of war, realising that his dockside warehouses could become bombing targets, he had moved most of his stock away from the city to a large family farm. During the war he had never been drafted, claiming to have medical evidence that he was unfit for military service. At the end of hostilities he found that his hidden stock, mostly cameras, watches, cigarette lighters, writing implements and electrical goods, were of no value to the general population whose only interest was those commodities that would sustain life. He soon realised that his customers could be found amongst the occupying servicemen. Trading his stock for cigarettes, he soon branched out into other lines. Buying jewellery and other treasures from local civilians, he slowly expanded his range of goods. He made an American contact who supplied him with perfume and nylon stockings, which the British soldiers snapped up as presents for their girlfriends back home. He was also a mine of information of what was happening in the town. He would impart this information to the Service police in exchange for them turning a blind eye to his activities. Nothing happened without Nick knowing about it.

Nick was sitting in his darkened room, in his usual chair behind the table on which samples of his wares were displayed. Cigarette hanging from the corner of his mouth, his hooded eyes watched Penrose being shown into the room by one of his minders. As always, the spider and web came to Penrose's mind.

Expressionless, he greeted Penrose and indicated that he should sit on a chair opposite him. After exchanging small talk for some minutes while the duty minder served coffee, real coffee, Nick looked Penrose up and down. 'So Sergeant, I can see that you are not here for trade, so how can I be of service?'

'Jonny Gross Nick. What do you know about him?'

'Ah. Big Jonny.' Nick shrugged his shoulders and took another cigarette from the packet on the table in front of him. Lighting it from the stub of the last one, he placed it in his mouth and wriggled his lips until it was firmly set in the corner. 'What can I tell you about him Sergeant? He is the number one gangster in the town. He has ...., how do you say it..., his finger in all of the pies.'

'I guess you know about the consignment of penicillin that was stolen from the British hospital. Was he involved in that?'

Nick nodded. 'But of course. Only Big Jonny could have pulled that off.'

'So where can I find the drugs Nick?'

'They have gone Sergeant. All over Germany. There was only a little in Hamburg. Karl-Heinz Necker had that and I think that you found most of it.'

'You know about that?'

'Of course Sergeant. Everybody does. We had a big laugh when we hear that you wanted to stick it in Dr Pick's arse. He is very mad about that.'

'Was Gross involved in the murders of Necker and his girlfriend?'

Nick stared at Penrose for nearly a minute before shrugging his shoulders. 'Of course. If he did not do them himself, he gave the order. He is a big problem for you Sergeant. I know that there are other murders you are looking at.'

'Are you saying that he is involved in the other murders?'

Nick slowly nodded his head. 'Somewhere Sergeant. He is involved somewhere.'

Penrose thought for a moment before making up his mind to ask his next question. 'What do you know about an Inspector Rossmann Nick?'

Nick's lips parted slighted, a gesture that might be taken as a smile. 'Honest Klaus.' he said.

Is he honest?' Penrose asked.

'He is..., how do you say it?' Nick pushed out his hand horizontally in front of him, 'He is straight down the middle. He is an honest policeman.'

'If he is so honest Nick, why won't he go after Gross?' asked Penrose.

After pulling out another cigarette, Nick pushed the packet across the table to Penrose. 'Politics Sergeant. Look, we lost the war and you now occupy our country. Your Control Commission now makes the rules and runs this city. But it is impossible for them to do it without the help of a German administration. There still has to be a police force, trams and trains must run, electricity supplies and a telephone network must be restored and not forgetting the recruiting for the of the German Labour Corps that you need to carry out work to restore some kind of order. And who is this German administration?' Nick asked, pointing his finger across the table at Penrose. 'The same administration that was running the city before you people arrived.

'Now let's talk about Klaus Rossmann,' Nick went on. 'That man should be the police chief. But, after all the years he has been a policeman he is still only an Inspector. Why?' Nick slapped the palm of his hand on the table. 'Because he is not corrupt. He would not dance to the tune when the Nazis were in power, so he did not get promotion. But now he has a problem. Unlike thousands of other people, he has a job. He is earning money and able to provide food for his family. But he knows he could easily be out of a job and scraping amongst the bomb rubble like a lot of others. He is still not corrupt but he has to do as he is told.'

'But ....', Penrose began, wondering where this was leading, only to be hushed by Nick's raised finger.

'Let us go back to Jonny Gross. His family name is von Grosse. An aristocrat. His father was an Admiral. I don't know if he is still alive. His uncle is *Graff* von Grosse, what you call a Count. All have friends in high places and some of those friends are in the *Rathaus,* the Town

~ The Hamburg Dossier ~

Hall. They look after Jonny and he looks after them in turn. Supplies them with food and women if they want them. So that is Honest Klaus' problem.'

'Are you saying that Klaus is prevented from making a move against Gross? Penrose asked.

'Sergeant, you have superiors. Would you proceed if those superiors told you not to?'

Penrose didn't answer. He leant back in his chair and studied the ceiling. Nick watched him in silence as he exchanged his cigarette stub for a fresh one. After some minutes Penrose nodded his head, his mind made up. 'Looks like I'll have to go after the bastard myself,' he said.

'I warn you Sergeant, go slowly slowly. Jonny Gross can be dangerous.' After a slight hesitation, he continued, 'Look at who he does business with.'

As Penrose rose to leave, Nick gave one of his rare smiles. 'Tell me Sergeant. My friend Tiny. Have you got him in jail?'

'No Nick. He is still ducking and diving. No doubt you will get a visit from him soon.'

'Good. You see his suitcase is still here. Come again if I can be of more help.'

As Penrose left the flat he had a feeling that Nick knew more than he had let on.

20

Although criminal investigators will deny it, in the majority of enquiries brought to a successful conclusion there is always an element of luck. This luck can often come from the most unlikely source.

After leaving Nick the Trader. Penrose decided to go on the scrounge at the Equipment Depot. A former industrial site situated in Altona, the dozen or so warehouses had been surrounded by a barbed wire fence, which was patrolled by armed guards. Across the road, opposite the Equipment Depot, a former racecourse had been utilised as vehicle park containing not only row upon row of British and German military vehicles but also hundreds of requisitioned civilian cars and trucks.

Showing his warrant card to the uninterested sentry on the gate, Penrose made his way to the Depot Warrant Officer's office. They were old friends, a friendship forged by the number of times Penrose had been called to the Depot to look into the continual loss of stores that seemed to vanish into thin air.

Warrant Officer Bride was sitting at his desk when Penrose entered his office. 'Fuck me Harry, you must be psychic. I was just thinking about you,' Bride said. 'What are you doing here?'

'Just a social call Jack,' Penrose replied.

'Don't give me that bollocks Harry, You either know something or you want something.'

Penrose laughed. 'You're right Jack. I'm on the scrounge. I want a lock.'

'Lock? What kind of lock? Rimlock? Yale lock? Deadlock? Padlock? Picklock? Fetlock? Forelock? Flintlock? There are all kinds of locks Harry.'

'I want something to fix a bloody door you old fool.' Penrose replied. 'Something that's easy to fit. I'll also want a screwdriver, some screws and a couple of heavy bolts.

'Are you sure that's all?' Bride asked sarcastically. Without waiting for an answer, he shouted, 'JOHNSON.'

~ *The Hamburg Dossier* ~

A young airman poked his head around the door. 'Make Sarg'nt Penrose a cup of char and then go and get me a rim lock, a screwdriver, some screws and a couple of heavy bolts.'

As Penrose sipped his tea whilst they waited for Johnson to return, he said, 'Why were you thinking of me Jack? You're not that way, are you?'

'Piss off Penrose. You wouldn't stand a chance if you and me were the last persons alive.' He turned to the window and nodded towards the vehicle park. 'No, it's that bloody lot out there.'

Penrose followed Bride's gaze then looked back at him. 'So?'

Bride was still staring out of the window. 'It looks like we are losing a few.'

'How can you tell?' Penrose asked. 'That would be like having a slice off of a cut loaf.'

'I've been sent a gang of Pioneer Corp lads who I'm using to tidy up that lot out there. Their Corporal seems to be on the ball. Used to be in the car trade or something before the war. He reported to me that he thought the occasional vehicle was going missing.'

'Do you want me to have a word with him Jack?'

'Might as well Harry being as you're here,' Bride replied. ' 'ARRIS,' he yelled.

A second young airman poked his head around the office door. 'Nip over the road and get Izzy Finkelstein over here,' Bride ordered.

Penrose stiffened. Izzy Finkelstein? There can't be two people with that name, Penrose thought, but it can't be him. Impossible. He kept his thoughts to himself, exchanging small talk with Bride whilst they waited for the Pioneer Corporal to present himself.

Penrose didn't turn around when a tap came on the office door and someone entered behind him.

'How can I be of service Sir?' a sycophantic voice asked.

Penrose knew the voice and could imagine the speaker rubbing his hand together as he spoke. Penrose turned and looked at the man behind him. 'Hello Izzy.'

Izzy was tall and thin with a swarthy complexion, black oily hair and a pencil moustache. If he had been dressed in a drape suit and a

~ The Hamburg Dossier ~

fedora rather than a uniform there would have been no mistaking what he was, a typical spiv. As he stared at Penrose the colour drained from his face. 'Fuck my old boots. Mister Penrose. What are you doing here?' he uttered.

'More to the point Izzy, what the fuck are you doing here?' Penrose replied. 'I thought you had been banged up in the Scrubs for that petrol coupon fiddle a couple of years back.'

'I was Mister Penrose. I was. Three years I got. But the beak called me back and offered to drop the bird if I joined the Kate Karney. As I fancied my liberty, here I am.'

'And no doubt with your liberty went the opportunity to do a bit of villainy.'

'I'm a changed man Mister Penrose. Honest.'

'Honest? I doubt if you could even spell the word Izzy.' Penrose said. 'You're so bloody crooked that you couldn't lay straight in bed.'

Bride was following the exchange with an amazed look on his face. 'Do you know Corporal Finkelstein Harry?' he asked.

'Know him? I've nicked him more times than I care to remember Jack. Putting him in charge of those vehicles over there is like putting the fox in charge of the chicken coop. Cars and anything to do with them are like money in the bank to old Izzy here.'

'Come on Mister Penrose, that's a bit strong.' Izzy murmured.

'I'll tell you what's a bit strong Izzy. You've been nicking the vehicles over there, then reporting them missing to cover your arse. That's been the story of your life. So do you want to tell me about it and what you've done with them?'

'That's a bloody lie Mister Penrose. Anyway, what's it to do with you? This isn't London and you're out of you're manor. I'm in the army so there's nothing you can do to me.'

Penrose smiled. 'That's your second mistake Izzy,' he said, with a smirk. 'It just so happens that at the moment I am a Sergeant in the RAF SIB so, under Kings Rules and Regulations I can do what the fuck I please with you. But I'm not going to. Instead I'm going to hand you over to a nice friend of mine. He's a Staff Sergeant SIB in the Corps of Military Police. If you don't tell him all you know he'll put you where the crows won't shit on you. You'll find that the 'Scrubs was a picnic compared to Shepton Mallet Military Prison.'

Opened mouthed, Izzy watched Penrose pick up the telephone receiver on Bride's desk.

It was late evening when Penrose arrived at the Military Police Headquarters. After waiting for Terry Reader to arrive at the Equipment Depot, who arrested Izzy and his men and had them conveyed to his headquarters to be interviewed, Penrose had collected Lisa and returned her to her flat. There he secured the door with the new lock and bolts and instructed her to stay inside until he returned. Then he had met up with Tiny at the Seamen's Mission to cancel their planned visit to the Tamborin and arranged to meet him the following evening.

Terry Reader was in his office, writing up his notes. He looked up and smiled when Penrose entered. 'Good one Harry!' he said. 'Old Izzy certainly doesn't like you.'

'Gave you a full and frank confession I hope Terry" Penrose replied.

'Eventually, after ranting on how you were the most bent copper ever to join the Flying Squad. Reckoned that every time you had dealing with him you fitted him up'

Fitted him up,' Penrose exclaimed. 'There was no need to fit him up. He was the most inept villain that walked the streets. If he didn't leave his signature with every stroke he tried to pull he would shout his mouth off about it when he pissed the proceeds up against the wall. At times we knew what he was about before he knew himself. Anyway, what's the S P?'

Reader took a cigarette from his packet before tossing it across the desk to Penrose. 'They're all in on it but it was one of his men that broke first. Told one of my Sergeants that he had been giving this bird one and she had put it to him that she had a friend that would be interested in taking a few vehicles off his hand. He put it to Izzy who planned and arranged the whole thing.'

'I'll bet you that Izzy denied everything,' Penrose said.

'Of course he did Harry, but you have not heard the half of it yet. Seems that the woman this young soldier was having it off with was Irma Stubbe. He met her in the Tamborin, and the money man was Karl-Heinz Necker.'

Penrose sat very still. 'Go on,' he said.

'Remembering our chat the last time we met,' Reader continued, 'I decided that I would have a go at Izzy myself. As soon as I entered the interview room he began to protest his innocence. I said, "I'm not here to talk about stolen cars Izzy but about a more serious matter. So before I ask you about the murders of Irma Stubbe and Karl-Heinz Necker I am going to caution you." I thought he was going to fall off of the chair. Suddenly you became his best friend. Said I should talk to you, as you knew that violence was not his forte. He quickly admitted that he had been involved in the vehicle caper but it was the young lad that did the dealing with Stubbe and Necker. He claimed that he didn't even know they were dead because the young lad had been on jankers for the last ten days and had not had the chance to get out of camp to see her.'

'So what was happening to the vehicles?' Penrose asked.

'They would take a convey of them out on a road test and dump a couple of them at a farm out Elmshorn way. Izzy's job was to lose the paper work. We are going to raid the place in the morning. Do you want to came along for the ride?'

'Try and stop me,' Penrose replied. 'Meanwhile, do you mind if I have a few words with Izzy?'

'Be my guest,' Reader said. 'Let's go down to the cell block,'

Izzy Finkelstein was the picture of misery, sitting on the edge of the cell's bed and staring blankly at the opposite wall. When he saw Penrose and Reader enter the cell his eyes took on a look of appealing hope.

'It's like old times Izzy,' Penrose said. 'You and I chatting in a cell. How many times have we done this together?'

'As God's my maker Mister Penrose, I don't know anything about any murder. You know that I'm not a violent man, I'm too much of a coward. You've got to help me, please tell the Staff that I don't get involved in violence.'

'Nothing to do with me Izzy,' Penrose replied. 'This is between you and Staff Sergeant Reader and whether he believes you or not on that score.'

The look of hope faded as Izzy looked down at the floor.

Penrose continued, 'But let us see how truthful you are. Tell me about the nicking of the vehicles, and don't give me any bullshit.'

Izzy licked his lips. 'When me and my squad started working in the vehicle park we got talking about how nobody seemed to know how many vehicles were there and how easy it would be to half inch a few. Even the keys were left in the ignitions, although a lot of the batteries were flat. Then a couple of months ago young Smudger Smith had a word with me. He said that he was shagging this girl Irma and she said she had a contact that would take a few of them off of our hands.'

Penrose smiled. 'How many times had you heard that Izzy? I bet it was music to your ears.'

'Yeah,' Izzy replied. 'You know I'm easily tempted Mister Penrose. It seemed an easy way to make a bob or two. Anyway, so we all had a talk and came up with the idea that we should start charging the batteries and then taking the vehicles out on a road test. If we took out a convoy of them we could then lose a couple and it wouldn't be noticed when we came back.'

'And, how many did you ... er ... lose?' Penrose asked.

'I don't know Mister Penrose, Twenty or thirty or so.'

'How much did you get for them Izzy?'

'Depended on what they wanted. But it was around ten thousand marks each.'

'A hundred quid each Izzy!' Penrose exclaimed. 'What were you running, a charity or something?'

'Well you know what it is Mister Penrose. The money ain't no bloody good anyway. All we wanted was a few bob to go on the piss with.'

Penrose looked at Reader and shook his head. 'So were you paid on delivery?'

'No. Young Smudger would collect the money, bring it back and then we would have a divi up.'

'Who did you deliver the vehicles to?'

'No-one. We took them to this farm in the sticks, a run-down old place and left them in a shed. We never saw anyone there but I think there was someone in the farmhouse looking through the window.'

Penrose thought for a while. 'Right Izzy, if this was a doodle of a job, easy money, why did you mention to Mister Bride that you thought vehicles were going missing?' he asked.

'Well, he started coming to the vehicle park and looking around. I thought he had noticed something, that he was suspicious. So I thought if I said something to him he wouldn't suspect me and the lads.'

'You never change Izzy.' Penrose said, with a laugh. 'What you was doing was covering your arse. Not worrying about the lads. You are the most inept bastard I know. If you had kept your bloody mouth shut, you and I and Staff Reader wouldn't have been here now. Your mouth has always dropped you in the shit and it always will. If brains were dynamite you wouldn't have enough to blow your head off.'

Izzy sat with his mouth open as the penny dropped. Before he could say anything, Penrose put his face close to his. 'While you're in a confessing mood, did you also top Irma and Karl-Heinz Necker to ensure that your arse was really covered?' Penrose asked, in a harsh voice.

Izzy sat back sharply, tears appearing in his eyes. 'No Mister Penrose. I had nothing to do with that. What are you going to do with me?'

Penrose shook his head. 'Nothing Izzy. I'm not going to do anything with you. That's up to Staff Reader here.'

Izzy turned and looked at Reader. The unasked question hovering on his lips.

'I'm going to take you for a ride Izzy.' Reader said. Izzy blanched. 'Tomorrow you are coming for a ride in the country with me and show me where this farm is.'

21

Penrose caught Warrant Officer Lancaster before morning prayers and updated him on his progress.

'Any chance of taking Davy with me this morning Boss? His German is much better than mine and I don't know if Terry Reader has anyone who is pretty fluent.'

'Too late Harry.' Lancaster replied. 'He was Duty Investigator last night and got called out to Sylt. That Accounts Officer you had dealings with a few weeks back was found swinging from a rope in his room last evening.'

'Jesus!' exclaimed Penrose, shaking his head. 'I knew he was a worried man but I didn't think he would go as far as that. Still, I guess that's one less court martial I have to worry about before I finish my time here.'

'An officer and a gentleman taking the honourable way out. Falling on his sword.' Lancaster mused. 'You'll just have to make use of the *Deutsch* you know. You seemed to have got by with it in the past.'

Terry Reader was waiting in is car when Penrose arrived at the Military Police Headquarters. In the rear seat, beside one of Reader's sergeants, sat a subdued Izzy Finkelstein.

'On your own Harry?' Reader asked, after Penrose had parked his car and climbed into the passenger seat beside Reader.

'Afraid so. I had hoped to bring Davy Jones with me but he has been called away, so I might as well travel with you.' He turned to the sergeant in the back seat. '*Sprechen Sie Deutsch* Sarge?'

The sergeant grinned. '*Klien,*' he replied, 'just enough to order a beer. Even though my name's Jerry.'

Penrose let out a laugh. 'Well, it looks like we might just be in the shit. We will just have to muddle along between us Terry.' he said.

As they drove out of the courtyard a Jeep containing two uniformed Military Policemen fell in behind them. In less than an hour they had left the city and had passed through the small town of Pinneberg.

As they approached the turning to the former German airfield of Uetersen, Izzy indicated a narrow road on the right and told Reader to take it. The ground on either side of the road was fens and a stand of pine trees, in the far distance, was ahead. Beyond the trees they drove through a small hamlet of ten or twelve houses. Their passing was observed by most of the inhabitants who either came out of their doors or leant out of upstairs windows. About a mile further on the road ended before a large, rundown farm complex. An arched entrance gave access to a farmyard enclosed on all sides. To the left was a rambling farmhouse, ahead, a number of byres and to the right a large shed shuttered by tall, wooden doors.

'That's where we left the vehicles Mister Penrose,' Izzy said, pointing towards the shed.

Telling Izzy to remain where he was, Penrose, Reader and Jerry got out of the car and walked towards the shed doors. Pulling the doors open, they entered. The shed was empty. Traces of oil on the floor showed that vehicles had been parked in there. 'Looks like the horse has bolted.' Reader said. 'I wonder if there is anyone in the house?'

'I thought I saw a movement at one of the downstairs windows as we drove in Boss,' Jerry replied, 'but I can't understand why nobody has come out to see what we're up to.'

'Then we'll have to find out,' Reader said. 'Jerry, get the uniformed lads to have a good shufti in the shed and the other barns, then join Harry and me in the house.'

Penrose and Reader walked over to the farmhouse where Penrose hammered on the door. There was no reply. Reader worked the latch and pushed on the door. It opened inwards. They entered a large, stone-floored kitchen. The centre was taken up by a long, refectory table surrounded by heavy Black Forest styled chairs. A large oak dresser, on which were displayed china plates stood against the wall opposite the entrance. Beneath the window was a large, stone sink with draining boards at either end. On the third wall was a black, kitchen range on which a number of blackened pots were simmering. A pair of Gothic, oak armchairs were in front of the range, in which sat a very old man and woman, hands clasped on their laps and their eyes downcast.

'*Guten Tag.*' Penrose said.

The old man lifted his head and looked at him but he didn't reply. Instead, a look of fear crossed the old man's wrinkled face and his hand began to tremble.

'*Sprechen Sie Englisch?*' Penrose asked.

The old man gave a slight shake of his head.

Penrose tried again. '*Ist jemand hier, der Englisch spricht?*'

Again the old man gave a slight shake of his head. No one there spoke English.

Penrose looked at Reader and raised his eyebrows. Turning again to the old man, he said, '*Wie heissen Sie?*'

'Walter Temmen,' the old man answered in a trembling voice. He nodded towards the old women. '*Meine Frau.*'

Penrose looked pleadingly at Reader. 'Can you put your twopenn'orth in?'

Reader just shrugged his shoulders Penrose looked at the sergeant who had just entered the building. 'Jerry?'

Jerry grinned. 'I could ask them for a beer, or a cup of tea at a push.'

Penrose started to laugh. 'Looks like we're up the creek,' he said. 'We will have to get an interpreter up here. We can hardly take these two poor old buggers in for questioning. I doubt if they would survive the journey even if we could heave them into the back of the jeep.'

'May I be of some help?'

The three of them turned towards the direction from where the voice had come. In the doorway stood a burly man in a green uniform.

'Who are you?' Penrose asked.

'My name is Mett, Dieter Mett. I am the *Waldmeister,* the forester here.'

'And you speak English?' Penrose asked.

'Enough. I trained in the American Forest Service long before the war. I still remember some English.'

'Who are these people?' Penrose asked, pointing to the old couple.

'They are the janitors, the caretakers. The farm is no longer in use,' Mett replied.

'We want to ask them about cars and lorries being brought here and who has taken them away.'

Mett pulled out a chair from the table and sat himself close to the old man. He quietly spoke in German to the couple, obviously calming their fears. Soon they began to respond to his questions; occasionally giving frightened glances towards the three policemen.

After about ten minutes Mett turned back to the policemen. 'They know that automobiles come and go from here, but they were instructed to stay inside when anything was happening. They were not allowed to see who brought them or who collected them or to go into the storage shed. They did as they were told, as they were frightened that they would be sent away from this place, or worse.'

'Who owns this place?' Reader asked.

'This belongs to *Graff* von Grosse.' Mett replied. 'But the *Graff* has not been here for many years. He lives in the south.'

'So who gives them their instructions?' Reader asked.

After a further conversation with the old couple, Mett said, 'One of the men who works for the *Graff's* nephew would bring them some food and a little money. He would warn them not to see what was happening. The nephew is a businessman in Hamburg They do not know where.'

'What about the people down in the village?' Penrose asked. 'Would they be able to tell us anything?'

Mett shook his head. 'I don't think so. They are all retainers and hope to work on this farm again someday. They would be like the three wise monkeys, see, hear and speak nothing.'

'Well what about you? You saw us here and soon put in an appearance. Haven't you seen anything?'

Mett gave a slight smile. 'I live on the other edge of the wood. I do not come around this side very often. I just happened to be on this side when I saw you drive pass. I came to see what was happening.'

As they drove back through the hamlet all the doors and window were tightly shut and the placed seemed deserted. 'That bloody wood chopper knows more than he is saying,' Penrose mused. 'I bet he is the head shed around this place and has told the locals to keep their heads down. But at least we're got a connection with Jonny Gross. If it's Okay with you Terry, I'll handle that end.'

When they arrived back at the Military Police HQ, Izzy said, 'What's going to happen to me Mister Penrose?'

'I don't give a shit Izzy,' Penrose replied. 'That up to Staff Reader and, as I've said, I hope he puts you where the crows can't shit on you for a bloody long time. In a few weeks I'll be back on the streets of London and you'll be one less bloody crook I'll have to worry my head about. Just enjoy you stretch Izzy.'

Before he got into his car, Penrose watch a downcast Izzy being led into the Headquarters.

22

After meeting Tiny at the Seamen's Bar where he told him that he intended to go into the Tamborin later that night, and that Tiny should be there as backup just in case of trouble, Penrose drove to Lisa's flat.

He was pleased that she had taken his advice. She had to unbolted her door when she let him in and put the bolts back in place after he had entered. Once she had locked the door she threw her arms around his neck and kissed him deeply before dragging him into her bedroom.

'Are we going out tonight Harry?' she asked. 'It is so long since you took me out.'

'It will have to be later on *Schatz*,' Penrose replied, 'I have a bit of business that I have to do first.'

'Business. Always business,' Lisa said, with a mock pout on her lips. 'When have you got to do this business? I have missed you so much.'

'I'll have to go out in a couple of hours or so, but I will only be a short time,' Penrose replied.

'In two hours we can have lots of short times and I feel so sexy,' Lisa said, pulling off Penrose's tie. 'Let us go to bed for those couple of hours.'

After they had made love, Lisa cuddled up to Penrose. 'Harry,' she whispered, 'I have a problem we must talk about.'

Penrose's heart gave a leap. 'What?' he asked, tightly.

Lisa jumped out of bed and disappeared into what had been Manfred's room. He heard a couple of thumps and a dragging sound. Lisa's delectable bottom appeared in the doorway. She was bend double, dragging a wooden box that she pulled to the side of the bed. 'I have found this,' she said.

'What's in it? It sounded heavy enough,' Penrose said, leaning over the side of the bed.

Lisa lifted the lid. Inside were bundles of various currencies, marks, dollars, guilders, and pounds, which Lisa pulled out and dumped on the bed. This exposed a collection of pieces of jewellery that she scooped up and dropped on top of the money. At the bottom of the box was a layer of small gold ingots, each imprinted with the Nazi eagle holding the swastika in its talons.

'Where the hell did that come from?' Penrose asked.

'I found it far back in the roof. What am I going to do with it?' Lisa asked.

'It's a racing certainty that Manfred didn't earn that sweeping up in the *Fischmarkt*,' Penrose said with a laugh. 'Was he into anything that might have been a bit dodgy?'

'I think he did some business with some of the crews on the ships, but I don't know what. But what am I going to do with it?'

'I guess you will have to hand it over to his family,' Penrose said.

'He did not have a family Harry. All were killed in the fire-storm in 1944.'

'Well in that case Lisa, although as a policeman I shouldn't say it, I think you are a rich woman. When things get back to normal and the banks start operating again, deposit the money. Sell the jewellery piece by piece and I guess you can find a market for the gold. That just might be the start of the clothing business you are hankering for.'

Lisa picked up a piece of jewellery, a diamond encrusted leopard on a heavy, gold chain, and hung it around her neck. 'This I will not sell. It will be my lucky mascot.'

The sight of the naked Lisa, only adorned by the jewelled leopard, aroused Penrose who pulled her onto the bed where they made love again, surrounded by a small fortune in bank notes and jewellery.

It was nearly midnight when Penrose entered the Tamborin. He found an empty side table that gave him a view of all the room. About three-quarters of the table were occupied. Most of the men were obviously seamen. Tiny was sitting in one of the alcoves with a very attractive women who Penrose assume was Lilli Gross. He ordered a beer from a passing waiter, but before it was brought to him the telephone on his table rang. Picking up the receiver, he heard a very seductive voice. 'You like that I come and sit with you and you buy me a drink?'

His eyes searched the room but he was unable to identify who was making the call.

'Hello. Can you hear me? Buy me a drink and I give you a happy time.'

'No thank you,' Penrose replied 'I'm waiting for someone.'

A sharp laugh was followed by, 'Are you a queer boy?' before the connection was broken.

Penrose saw an elderly, overweight brunette, sitting near the dance floor, replacing the receiver on her table and flashing a look of contempt across at him. He silently thanked his lucky stars.

With a roll of the drums, the house lights dimmed and a floodlight was directed on the curtained archway at the side of the stage. Nothing happened. The drummer, concern showing on his face, looked at the other two members of the band before repeating the drum roll. Still nothing happened except the sound of an argument coming from backstage.

The noise brought Jonny Gross out of his office. He saw one of his heavies pushing a naked girl towards the entrance to the stage while she resisted, protesting loudly.

'What the fuck's going on?' Gross asked.

'This bitch won't go out on stage Boss,' the heavy replied.

Gross came down the stairs into the backstage area. He grasped the girl's face between his fingers and thumb. 'What the fuck's up with you? Get out there and do what you're paid to do.'

The girl shook her head and pointed to the curtained doorway. 'That English policeman is out there.' she said, struggling to speak.

Gross released her chin. 'What English policeman?'

'The one that came to Dr Rick's office. He is looking for me.'

'Show me,' Gross said, guiding her by the arm to the curtained opening. Through a chink in the curtain she pointed out Penrose.

As the drums rolled for the third time, he pointed to one of girls watching from the dressing room. 'Get out there.' Turning to the first girl, he led her to the bottom of the stairs. 'So why do you think he would recognise you? I was told that he only spoke to all of you briefly in the waiting room.'

'He saw more of me than that. I was the one who was stuck on the doctor's table with my legs in the air. It was him that got my feet out of the clamps and helped me to stand up. I'm sure he would remember what he saw.'

Gross smiled. 'I always thought that one looked very much like another. Okay, you don't need to go on again until I have got rid of him.'

As the floodlight died around the artistic pose of the dancer and the house lights rose, Penrose became aware of Gross approaching his table. He had never met Gross but there was no mistaking the description he had been given. The name Big Jonny did him justice. He was not as tall as Tiny but the build was enormous. Penrose wondered if he had put on weight since leaving the German Navy or, if not, how he had been able to get through the hatches of his submarine. Gross pulled out the chair opposite Penrose and sat down. Penrose glanced over towards Tiny and gave him a slight shake of his head.

'So Mister Penrose,' Gross said, 'we meet at last.' There was a slight trace of an American accent that all Germans seem to have when speaking English.

Penrose gave him a blank stare. 'Why should I be interested in meeting you?'

'Because Mister Penrose you are very interested in me, asking questions about me and causing me a fucking lot of problems. So, if you want to know about me, just ask.'

'Okay.' Penrose replied. 'Let's talk about Karl-Heinz Necker, Irma Stubbe, Gerhard Winkler, Pussy Averbeck and last, but not least, Manfred Haller. Where would you like to start?'

Gross looked blank. 'Who? I have never heard of any of them.'

Penrose slowly lit a cigarette. 'Well, Necker seems to know you, or did. I was out at your farm, up Elmshorn way. You know, the place where Necker used to store things.'

'That farm is not mine. It is part of the estate of my uncle, which I'm sure you know. I haven't been there since I was a child, So I don't know if this Necker did or did not store things there.'

Penrose knew that he was not going to get anything out of Gross so he decided to rile him, to rattle his cage. 'Do you know what Jonny boy? I don't like you. I think you're an arsehole. I think that I should see about putting this den of iniquity out of bounds.'

Gross' face went deep red and his left eye twitched. Then he gave a short laugh. 'Put your board up outside if you wish.' He waved his arm around the room. 'Do you see any British soldiers in here. They have not got enough money to use my place. Your out of bounds will not apply to the seaman and I don't need your English soldiers.' He paused and leant across the table. Lowering his voice to a harsh whisper, he said, 'But you Mister Penrose. Tread very carefully or you might come to some harm. This can be a very nasty town. And do not forget the lovely Lisa. Tell her to take care. It must be terrible living in a house where a man was found hanging.' He stood up and signalled a hovering waiter. *'Bringen Herr Penrose ein trinken."* Then, looking at Penrose, 'Have a drink on me and then fuck off out of my club.'

He walked back to the curtained entrance by stage, followed by the girl who had been sitting with Tiny. The telephone on Penrose's table rang. He instinctively glanced towards the overweight brunette but she had managed to snare a punter. Picking up the receiver, he heard Tiny's voice. 'You all right Harry?'

'Fine Tiny. You just keep your head down.'

Penrose replaced the receiver as the waiter placed a stein of beer in front of him. He pushed it back towards the waiter. 'Take this to Fat Jonny with my compliments and tell him to stick it up his arse,' he said.

He rose from the table and walked out of the Tamborin.

Penrose had not intended to go back to Lisa's place that night, but now he felt uneasy about her being alone. He found that she was still naked, except for the jewelled leopard around her neck. The money was still on her bed, now neatly stacked, and it was apparent that she had been counting it.

She threw her arms around his neck. 'Harry, you have been a long time. I was waiting for you. Are you going to stay?'

'I am tonight sweetheart. Tomorrow I will have to find another place for you.' A look of concern crossed her face. 'It will only be for a short time.' he continued. 'I promise that in a few days everything will be over.'

'Okay,' Lisa giggled. She swept the money onto the floor and scrambled into bed, 'Quick, get into bed. Let us make a short time here.'

When Lilli returned to the table she took hold of Tiny's hand and pulled him to his feet. 'My father has gone home, we can go upstairs now.'

'Upstairs?' Tiny asked. 'What's upstairs?'

'My room is up there. That is where I live. You keep wanting to know where I sleep, now you will find out.'

As the passed through the backstage area towards the stairs the next performer came out of the dressing room. She leered at Tiny. '*Wo ist der Taucher Lilli?*'

'*Arbeiten.*' Lilli replied. '*Seien Sie still.*' Lilli looked at Tiny but he gave no indication that he had understood the exchange, that the Diver was working and that the other girl should remain silent.

The dancer apologised with '*Verzeihung*' and hurried to the stage entrance.

Lilli's room was at the rear of the building, along a low-lit corridor. A thick carpet covered the floor and the furniture was of heavy oak that had once adored a better home. The bed was an ornately carved four-poster.

'I must go for a pee-pee.' Lilli said with a smile. 'The bathroom is two doors back.'

Tiny wandered around the room peering at the clutter on the tops of the dressing tables. Tucked behind one of the bottles of perfume he saw a familiar sheet of cardboard. It was a military cigarette ration card. He was holding it when Lilli returned to the room. 'You should not be looking at that,' she said, taking the card from him. 'It belongs to my boyfriend.'

'Just curious,' Tiny remarked casually. But he had seen a name and, more importantly, the stamp of the unit where it was issued.

'So,' Lilli said, undoing his trouser belt, 'let me see if you live up to your name or if, as I hope, it is a lie.'

23

It was mid-morning before Tiny got back to his room in the Phoenix Club. He had intended to leave Lilli earlier but she had been insatiable and had resisted his departure. He had had very little sleep; dropping off after a bout of lovemaking only to be awoken by Lilli's frantic attempts to arouse him, she being ready for another sally. He smiled as he recalled her use of English public school idioms during her throes of passion; "spiffing", "super", "smashing".

But he had information that he had to get to Harry Penrose. Leaving the Phoenix Club he crossed the road to the main railway station and entered the Military Railway Travel Office, The Sergeant Major on duty was known to Tiny. They had often met when the Sergeant Major acted as Conductor on the military trains.

'Hello Tiny. What are you up to?' the Sergeant Major asked.

'I was wondering if I could use your telephone Sir.'

'As long as it is an official call Tiny.'

'It's to the RAF Police.'

'What? You going to turn yourself in Tiny?' the Sergeant major said with a laugh, lifting the telephone onto the counter.

'Hoping to get myself out of the shit more likely,' Tiny replied with a wink.

As he waited for the Military Exchange operator to connect him, Tiny began to realise the enormity of what he was doing. When his call was answered he spoke agitatedly, only pausing briefly to listen to the answers.

'Is Sergeant Penrose there? ... When will he be back? ... Can I leave a message? ... Tell him Tiny called. I have got a name for him. I will meet him at the usual place. I will be there at twelve o'clock but will wait until he comes. ...... He knows where it is.'

Tiny returned to is room. The bed looked very tempting but he knew that he had to get to St Michaelis church. Resisting the temptation of the bed, he headed for the shower.

Penrose had left Lisa's flat early after warning her to remain inside with the door locked. He had wanted to brief Warrant Officer Lancaster before morning prayers and then to go and discuss the developments with Inspector Rossmann in the hope that he would bring Gross in for questioning.

After briefing the Warrant Officer, Penrose broached the subject of putting Lisa in a place of safety.

'What have you got in mind Harry?'

'I was thinking that we might lodge her in one of the WAAF blocks for a few days Boss.'

Lancaster hissed as he took in a breath through his teeth. 'I don't think the powers that be would be happy with that.'

'Can't you convince them she is a material witness or something Boss? That she needs protecting.'

'The trouble is Harry that she's also on the game. Not only might the girls object but just think what would happen if their mummies and daddies heard about it. Letters to their MPs. Questions asked in the House. They'd have our guts for garters.'

'Can't you give it a try anyway Boss?' Penrose asked pleadingly.

'I'll see what I can do Harry, but don't hold your breath. So, what's your next move?'

'I'm popping over to Davidswache to see Klaus Rossmann. See if I can persuade him to take some action. I should be back before lunch. When are you expecting Davy back?'

'He left Sylt this morning so should be back by dinnertime or soon after.'

'Right Boss, I'm away,' Penrose said turning to leave the office. 'I'll see you in a while.'

When Penrose arrived at Davidswatche the duty *Haupwachmeister* told him that Inspector Rossmann had been called away but that he was expected to return within a hour or so. Rose decided rather than going back to his office he would await Rossmann's return by having a decent cup of coffee in the Astoria Coffee House.

~ *The Hamburg Dossier* ~

Tiny looked around the deserted viewing platform of the tower of Michaeliskirche. It had only just gone half past eleven so he had not really expected Harry Penrose be there yet. He wandered over to the safety railing overlooking the distant St Pauli and lit a cigarette. Standing against the rail was a precarious position because, where with a person of normal height the guardrail would be waist high, with Tiny it was halfway down his thighs. But heights did not bother Tiny who had once trained as a paratrooper.

He heard the door to the stairs open and turned, expecting to see Penrose. It was just another sightseeing soldier, camera strung around his neck. Tiny turned back to the view and lit another cigarette.

The Diver circled the viewing platform stopping occasionally to take a photograph. As he passed behind Tiny he violently shoved him in the middle of his back. Tiny lurched forward, frantically grabbing for the railing, but he was beyond the point of equilibrium. His feet were slipping backwards on the marble floor and the rail was out of his reach. As he tipped further forward, the Diver grasped hold of his legs and pulled them upwards. Tiny began to fall. He fell two thirds of the 271-foot drop before a sound came from his lips. Not a scream, more like a high pitched wail. An elderly nun, who was entering the church to carry out her daily devotions, looked up at the noise and saw a man hurtling down towards her. It was the last sound she heard and the last sight she saw.

The Diver ran down the tower steps and the length the nave where he scrambled through a broken window, out onto a pile of bomb rubble. Hidden from the front of the church, he ran to where his car was parked.

At the same time as Tiny had entered Michaelskirche, Rossmann returned to Davidswache. He greeted Penrose, who was sitting in the Watch Office, with a firm handshake and invited him up to his office.

'It is good to see you again Harry.' Rossmann said. 'I was hoping that our last meeting was not going to spoil our friendship.'

'Not at all Klaus I only wish that at the time I knew of the pressures you were under. I didn't appreciate your situation.'

'And so it seems that you have been asking questions.' Rossmann said with a smile.

Penrose nodded. 'I also had a run in with Jonny Gross last night.'

'I am aware of that.' Rossmann replied. 'That is the reason I was out of the office. I was called to the German administration who told me to make you lay off Herr Gross.'

'And?' Penrose asked.

' I told them that I did not have any authority or jurisdiction over you. That you would carry out your investigations in any way you wished and that you were under no obligation to inform me of what you were doing.'

'I bet they didn't tell you that Gross made an implied threat against me and Lisa Klose,' Penrose said. 'I don't care about myself, I'm big and ugly enough to look after myself, but it is Lisa I'm worried about. I am trying to get her into a safe house, but if I can't, is there anyway you could give her protection?'

'If the safety of a German citizen is at risk Harry, that is something I have to deal with. I'll have one of my men have a word with Gross. I will give you my personal guarantee that she will come to no harm.'

'Good. So Klaus, how is the Manfred Haller investigation coming along. Do you have any leads?'

'Ah! Manfred the man of mystery. He would have had many enemies,' Rossmann exclaimed.

'What? That poor little crippled bastard?' Penrose said. 'I can't imagine him antagonising anyone. A fart of wind would have blown him over.'

'Looks deceive Harry,' Rossmann replied. 'I remember him before the war. Although he might have looked helpless, he was the best cat burglar and jewel thief in Hamburg. I had many dealings with him. He could climb the side of a building like a fly. I had many dealings with him. He could have upset any number of people, but, with all our records having been destroyed, we are having to rely on what any of us can remember about him.'

'Had he been active lately?' Penrose asked.

'Not that we can tell, but he was always creeping around in the night so only God knows what he was up to.'

Penrose shook his head. 'I still think that it was the Diver that killed him. Any of his enemies that wanted to do him harm wouldn't have gone to the length of stripping off his clothing and then stringing him up on a beam.'

The internal telephone on desk rang. 'Excuse me.' Rossmann said, picking up the receiver.

Penrose wandered over to the window and gazed down on the Reeperbahn, thinking about the stash in Manfred's room and his former profession. . He was aware that Rossmann, after listening, started his reply with *'Du lieber Gott...'* followed by some sharp questions. Penrose turned when he heard the phone being replaced. Rossmann's face was ashen.

'Harry, you had better come with me. There has been a terrible accident at Michaeliskirche and they think it involves a British soldier.'

Two German police cars had blocked off either end of the small, cobbled street in front of Michaeliskirke. On the steps of the church was a heap covered by a bloodstained, white tablecloth, with a priest standing nearby. Four German policemen were talking to a small group of people gathered at the doorway of a Bierkeller opposite the entrance of the church. One of the policemen approach Rossmann and they fell into a lengthy conversation which Penrose could not follow.

When they had finished talking Rossmann turned to Harry. 'It seem that a man, who they believe to be a British soldier, fell from the top of the tower and landed on a woman, a nun. The people in the bar heard the noise and came out and saw the two bodies. No one else came out of the church. Two of the policemen have searched the church and, apart from the priest, who was in his office in the crypt, there was no-one in the tower or the naive.'

'What makes them think that the man is British?' Penrose asked.

'He was a very big man and was dressed like your soldiers do when they are not in uniform,' Rossmann replied.

The word 'big' sent an icy shudder through Penrose. 'Well, we better have a look,' he said walking over to the gruesome bundle.

Penrose lifted the sheet. Tiny was dead but, as his fall had been broken by the woman beneath him, there was very little body damage and his features were recognisable. Most of the blood was from the nun who had virtually exploded having taken the full force of a 300lb man falling at terminal velocity.

Penrose let the sheet drop. 'I know the man Klaus. His name is Corporal Cyril Chapman. He was most probably here to meet me.' Penrose glanced down at the sheet. 'Something that might interest you. Last night he was in Gross' club with Gross' daughter. He was working for me.'

'Are you suggesting that Gross might be involved Harry?' Rossmann asked.

'I can tell you that Chapman would not have committed suicide and that he was too careful for his fall to have been an accident. That only leaves one other possibility, he was pushed. I think we have another murder... no, ... two murders on our hands.'

'But, there was nobody else in the building Harry.'

'Nobody else was seen to come out Klaus but I bet that when we have a look round we will find that there are other ways of leaving the building.'

Penrose found that the Bierkeller had a working telephone so was able to arrange for Tiny's body to be collected and taken to the Military Hospital. Rossmann arranged for the removal of the nun.

They went to the viewing platform where they found scuff marks on the marble floor at the place where Tiny must have gone over the railings. When interviewed, the priest, an old man, did recall hearing someone running in the naive before the police found him in his office, but, because of his age, he had not bothered to investigate. A search of the naive revealed the broken window through which the Diver had made his escape.

~ *The Hamburg Dossier* ~

It was late afternoon when Penrose arrived back at his Headquarters. After leaving Rossmann at Michaeliskirche he had gone to the Military Hospital where he had collected Tiny's personal effects and had arranged with Lt. Col. Belfour, the pathologist, to be present at the autopsy on the following day.

After spending an hour briefing Warrant Officer Lancaster, he went to the investigators' room to start the inevitable paperwork. Davy Jones, who was working at his desk, looked up as Penrose entered.

'Hello Harry. You look a bit pissed off,' Jones greeted him.

'Give me a chance to grab a fag and get my head together and I'll tell you,' Penrose said. 'Anyway, when did you get back?'

'Just after one,' Jones replied.

'What? Did you take the scenic route or something?' Penrose asked with a laugh.

'No. The bloody car was playing up. I had to stop and do some running repairs.'

'You want to have a word with the Motor Transport Officer Davy. It's time they pensioned off that bloody old beetle of yours and gave you something better. If you had been here a couple of days ago I could have introduced to a man who could have done something for you.'

'It's not worth it Harry. It will do me for the little time we've left here. What man are you talking about?'

'Izzy Finkelstein. He was doing a nice little racket in cars at the Equipment Depot.'

'Izzy?' a perplexed Jones asked. 'Not our Izzy Finkelstein of the motor trade fame?'

Penrose nodded. 'The very one.'

'What the hell was he doing here? The last we heard he was banged up.'

'You ain't going to believe this Davy. Some benevolent judge thought spending some time in the army could rehabilitate him.'

'Bloody do-gooders. Where is he now?'

'I left him to the tender mercy of Terry Reader.'

'He'll certainly rehabilitate him,' Jones said with a laugh. 'So what's pissing you off mate?'

'My man's dead. Killed,' Penrose replied.

Jones stared at Penrose, his mouth open. 'You don't mean your er...'

Penrose nodded.

'How?' Jones asked.

'Some bastard tipped him over Michel's Tower.'

'Bloody hell,' Jones said in a quiet voice. 'Any leads?'

Penrose shook his head. 'Nothing definite, but I would put money on it that Jonny Gross was involved somewhere. Last night my man was in his club with a bint who I reckon was Gross' daughter.' He paused to light another cigarette. 'I can't understand why he was at Michel unless he had discovered something and was waiting for me.' Penrose drew hard on his cigarette before continuing. 'But we didn't have an arranged meet. If he wanted to meet me urgently he should have phoned me or left a message here. But the Boss tells me that no one had been in the office all morning. They are all out on jobs.'

A knock came on the office door and Corporal Bill Sharp poked his in. 'All right to come in Sarge?'

Penrose nodded.

'Is that right what I've heard about Tiny Chapman?' Sharp asked.

'Penrose nodded again.

'The poor bastard,' Sharp murmured.

'Is that who your man was Harry, Tiny Chapman?' Jones asked in a surprised voice. 'I didn't know that you knew him.'

'Bill here put me onto him. He was doing a bit of digging for me. Anyway, how did you know him?'

'He was always ducking and diving around my end of the Reeperbahn,' Jones replied. 'In fact, I had a whisper that he was beginning a tour of guard duty at the Equipment Depot and was putting it around that he was open for orders.'

Bill Sharp shook his head, 'No. That wasn't Tiny's style. I've known him since I was posted here. A fiddle with fags and Nick the Trader, yes, but Tiny wasn't into nicking equipment. I think you've got it wrong Sarge.'

'It doesn't matter a rat's arse what he did or didn't do. The poor bastard's dead,' Penrose said with passion. 'I want the fucker who done him in. I'm going to lift Jonny Gross tonight whether Rossmann likes it or not.' He looked at Bill Sharp. 'Bill, I'll arrange for you and some of your boys as backup. I'm going to squeeze that fat bastard until he tells me everything he knows.'

'Whoa. Don't go off at half-cock Harry,' Jones said. 'Even if you go into Gross' place mob-handed it could be a bloodbath with the heavies he's got hanging around the place. Let's be a bit more supple. Let me have a sniff around tonight and see if I can find out where he lives, then we can lift him when he goes home tomorrow night.'

Penrose thought for a while then said to Sharp. 'Will you be all right for tomorrow night Bill?' Sharp nodded.

'Okay,' Penrose said. 'Tomorrow night it is. See what you can find out Davy.'

24

A worried look on his face, Warrant Officer Lancaster tapped a pencil on his desktop. 'Are you sure about this Harry?' he asked Penrose who was sitting in the corner of his office.

For nearly an hour he had been listening to Penrose who had been briefing him on the happening of the previous day and his plans for arresting Jonny Gross.

'I've never been more certain of anything in my life Boss,' Penrose said. 'Davy found out that he has a drum in Altona, Blücherstrasse. Well, it's more of a love nest really. He has a big spread at Bargteheide, way out on the way to Lübeck, so during the week he shacks up in Blücherstrasse. It's where he lodges his dancers and hostesses as he calls them. So he is always okay for a bit of the other with any of them who have not grabbed a punter for the night.'

'Are you saying it's a brothel?'

'Call it what you like Boss.' Penrose laughed. 'We aren't planning to go in there. We are going to lift him when he gets out of his car which he parks on the road in front of the house.'

'Doesn't he have a minder with him when he goes home?'

Penrose shook his head. 'Not that arrogant bastard. He thinks he's fireproof in St Pauli and Altona.'

Lancaster thought for a while. 'Do you reckon that you, Davy and a couple of the uniform lads can pull it off?'

'A piece of piss Boss. Element of surprise. A bit of Flying Squad tactics. We'll have him tucked up before he know what's hit him.'

'And what about Rossmann? Are you going to let him in on it? From what you told me, there's sure to be a cartload of shit going to fall on his head.'

Penrose brushed back his hair, a grimace on his face. 'I don't know Boss. Can I be sure that he won't say anything? I don't want this to go tits up. What do you think?'

'To be forewarned is to be forearmed Harry. He's done you a favour or two. You say that you've got to go and see him today so why don't you feel him out?'

~ The Hamburg Dossier ~

'I'll think about it Boss,' Penrose said, rising from his chair. 'I've got to get over to the hospital. The pathologist is expecting me.'

The mortuary, like most hospital mortuaries, was tucked away at the rear of the complex. Penrose entered the square, white tiled room, with sinks and working tops lining the walls. A zinc autopsy examination table took up the centre where Lt. Col. Belfour and a male nurse were at work.

'Ah! Sergeant,' Belfour said, looking up from what he was doing, 'I had to start without you as I have a busy day ahead of me.' With a chuckle, he added, 'They seem to be dropping like flies. Must be the time of the year.'

Penrose looked at Tiny's remains. The Y-incision had been made and some of the internal organs had been excised and were in chrome dishes on the nearby worktop. In death, Tiny still looked huge, his feet protruding six inches over the end of the table. Penrose wondered how a man who looked so indestructible in life could be reduced to the cadaver before him.

Belfour bend back over the corpse. 'The external examination showed no apparent injuries inflicted before death, all the injuries are post-mortem. Most of his bones are broken and his major organs ruptured, which is conducive with him falling from a great height. I hate to think of the damage to the poor lady that he fell on.'

'Is there any possibility that he had a heart attack or a blackout before he fell Sir?' Penrose asked.

'We have yet to excise the brain, then we will make detailed examinations of the organs, but his medical records indicate that he was a healthy young man with no adverse history. In the case of a heart attack or blackout I would have expected him to collapse backwards onto the floor. I think that he either jumped, or was pushed, off of the tower. I will let you have my report in a day or two.'

Seeing Belfour's assistant picking up the small circular saw, Penrose decided that it was time to leave. As he went out of the door he heard the whine of the saw as it circled Tiny's skull. He was glad he was leaving.

~ *The Hamburg Dossier* ~

At Penrose's invitation, he and Rossmann were sipping coffee at a table in the Astoria Coffee House because he was uncertain where their conversation might lead and he was uncomfortable that it might be overheard in Davidswache. Rossmann was telling him of his investigators' progress, or lack of it, on the incident at Michaeliskirche.

'There is no doubt about the cause of death of the unfortunate nun Harry. I am afraid that she was not a pleasant sight. Her Sisters in Christ will have to say their prayers over a closed coffin.'

'What about Jonny Gross?' Penrose asked. 'Has he been spoken to?'

'*Ja*. I did that myself. He denied threatening, or even that he knows a Lisa Klose. He admitted that he had spoken to you two nights ago but said that it was only a friendly chat and that he had bought you a drink. He said that he could not recall seeing your friend, *Herr* Chapman, in the club, claiming that the only customers who are brought to his attention are those that are causing trouble. There was no trouble in the club that night.'

'The lying bastard. Did you talk with his daughter, Lilli?'

'Yes. She denied knowing Chapman. Also, she said that she did not see you in the club. She said that she was working in the office all evening and did not go into the bar until closing time when she collected the takings from the bar and the waiters.'

'They're all lying Klaus. There's a bloody conspiracy.'

'I agree. We intend to return there tonight and question all of the people who work there.'

Penrose took a sip of his coffee then looked at Rossmann. 'Can I ask you to delay that for twenty four hours Klaus?'

'May I ask why?' Rossmann asked in an impassive tone.

Penrose chewed his bottom lip while he searched his pockets for his cigarettes.

'Is there something you are not telling me Harry?' Rossmann asked.

Penrose sighed, then looked straight into Rossmann's eyes. 'Klaus, I think we trust one another but I am going to ask you to extend that trust even though it might cause you problems.' Concern showed on

Rossmann's face as Penrose continued. 'I intent to pick Gross up for interrogation tonight. I wasn't going to tell you so that, if necessary, you could truthfully say that you had no knowledge of the arrest. But I want everything in the Tamborin to be normal tonight so that Gross is off of his guard. So I'm asking you, lay off of him or his women tonight.'

Rossmann stared at Penrose before turning and ordering two more coffees from the owner behind the counter. He turned back to face Penrose. 'Harry, no-one more than I would like to see Gross arrested but I have not got enough evidence to do so. With you, as one of the occupation police, it is different. Do it. I can find something else for my men to do tonight. This conversation never took place.'

Before returning to his office Penrose decided to call on Lisa to ensure that she was all right. She unlocked the door wearing her nightdress and it was apparent from her appearance that she had only just woken up. The fact that she was wearing a nightdress told Penrose that she had most probably been sleeping alone and that he would not find anyone else in her bed.

'Where were you last night Harry?' Lisa asked, after bringing two cups of coffee from the kitchen.

'Busy sweetheart. I have to work sometimes you know. Anyway, are you okay? No-body giving you any trouble?'

Lisa shrugged her shoulders. 'No,' she replied with a shake of her head. 'Why should anyone give me trouble? I have lots of friends.'

Penrose detected a tone of annoyance in her reply. He gazed at a woollen dress and a pile of silken underwear that had been tossed onto the back of a chair 'Did you go out last night?'

'Yes. I went to the Café Arnold to see if you would come in but you didn't. There I see my friends and they tell me truth.'

'What are you getting at Lisa?' Penrose asked in a mystified voice.

'Last night the police patrol come into the Café Arnold. One of them, a big man called Lofty, talk to me. He want to go out with me. I tell him that you are my boyfriend. He tell me that you soon go back to England.' Tears welled up in her eyes. 'Is this truth? Why you no tell me?'

Penrose put down his coffee cup and took a cigarette from his pocket, which he lit and took a deep drag before replying. 'Lisa, you know that it had to happen sometime. Yes, I will be leaving in a month or six weeks time. My time is up here and there is nothing I can do about it.'

'What about me?' Lisa asked. 'What is going to happen to me?'

Penrose didn't want to commit himself. 'Don't worry.' he said, with as much conviction as he could muster. 'I'll look after you. I'll see that you are all right.'

A smile spread across Lisa's tear-stained face. 'You will come back for me? You love me?'

Penrose nodded, wondering how he had got himself into this situation. He decided to change the subject. 'Lisa, can I ask you about Manfred? Have you any idea how he came by the stuff you found in his room?'

Lisa shook her head.

'Are you sure that he only worked at the *Fischmarkt*?'

She nodded. 'That what he tell me.'

'How did you come to meet him and rent this room?'

'When I first come to Hamburg I share a room with another girl near here. When I walk I would meet Manfred in the street and we talk. Many times. One day he ask if I wanted to have a room in his house. That's how I come here.'

'Was there anything between you?' Penrose asked.

'What? You mean sexy?' Lisa let out a peal of laughter. 'With Manfred? He was an old man. He was no good for young girls.' She shook her head. 'He was just my friend.'

'Okay,' Penrose said, not knowing whether to believe her or not. 'Let's talk about the jewellery and gold. I'll talk to a man who you might be able to sell it to. I'll make sure that he will not cheat you.'

'You good to me Harry,' Lisa said, throwing her arms around his neck. 'We go to bed now?'

~ The Hamburg Dossier ~

'I'd love to Lisa, but I have to go to work.' Penrose replied before giving her a kiss. 'I'll see you tomorrow,' he said, turning to the door.

Blücherstrasse was a narrow street of what had once been townhouses and small shops. Penrose and Jones stood in a burnt-out shell of a bakery opposite Gross' building which was the only place in the street that had escaped major bomb damage. Most of the windows were boarded up but the masonry seemed intact. Bill Sharp and his partner had parked their jeep in an alley some yards away, well within shouting and police whistle distance.

They had been in place for over an hour. During that time the silence of the street had been disturbed on three occasions by the arrival, in taxis, of Tamborin ladies with clients in various stages of intoxication. One punter, who had emerged from the taxi with his penis hanging out of his fly, had been so eager that he lifted the girl's skirt, as she inserted her key into the lock, and tried to back her into the corner of the porch. His giggling companion managed to coax him into the house.

'This seems to be how it all started,' Penrose said, cupping a lighted cigarette in his hand.

'I wonder what happened to him?' Jones murmured.

Penrose looked across at him with a puzzled expression. 'Who?'

'That young squaddie with the big tom who was wearing his hat. Don't you remember? They stopped in front of us when we were doing the obbo at the beginning'

'Fuck knows,' Penrose replied. 'The only certainty is that he got his leg over. I hope he didn't regret it.'

'Have you got any regrets Harry?'

Penrose looked at him, a half smile playing on his lips. 'What do you mean?'

'I mean about all what's happened over here. The job, Inge and that new bird of your. We'll soon be back doing the business on the streets of London. Will you have any regrets.'

Penrose remained silent, realising that Inge had never been far away in his thoughts.

'Well Harry? Will you?' Jones asked quietly.

Penrose shook his head. 'What's that song Edith Piaf sings? "No Regrets" Lots of memories mate but no regrets. I'll just put it all down to experience.'

Headlights flooded the street and a black Mercedes stopped in front of the building opposite.

'That's him,' Jones said.

Gross got out of the car and stretched before closing the door. He was alone. Penrose stepped onto the pavement and shouted, 'Gross.'

Gross turned and his right hand darted into the pocket of his overcoat. Penrose knew that he was reaching for a weapon and calculated that he would be able to cross the narrow street before Gross could bring it out.

Then, from Penrose's point of view, everything seemed to go into slow motion. He felt his foot go into a pothole and he sprawled headlong. From his position on the ground he saw Gross levelling a Walter PPK and heard him shout, *'Du hast mir die Sache echt versaut.'* He heard two gunshots almost simultaneously and felt the compression of bullets passing over his body. He saw a third eye appear in Gross' face before the back of the head exploded onto the roof of the car and Grosse slowly collapsing to the ground. Behind him he heard a moan. Looking back, he saw Jones holding his left thigh, blood pouring through his fingers. Between Jones' legs was his Smith and Wesson .38.

Suddenly, the previously silent street became a hive of activity. As Penrose scrambled to his feet, the jeep containing Bill Sharp and his partner roared onto the scene, quickly followed by two German police cars, one from either end of the road. Klaus Rossmann was in one of the cars that told Penrose that they had been loitering in the surrounding area. Five scantly dressed women came out of Gross' house and stood in a cluster on the porch, horror showing on all of their faces. From behind them, three hastily dressed men, still carrying some of their clothing, pushed their way out and tried to scuttle away in the shadows only to be stopped and detained by a German policeman from one of the cars.

It was apparent that Jonny Gross was dead and that there was nothing that could be done for him. Other than Rossmann retrieving the pistol that had fallen from his hand, Gross was left where he lay whilst all the attention was turned to the living.

Although there was no apparent signs of arterial blood spurting from Jones' wound, Penrose ripped off his necktie and applied it as a tourniquet around the top of Jones' thigh. Sharp's partner brought the first aid kit from the jeep and used a wound dressing as a pressure pad over the bleeding gunshot wound. Sharp was talking to Headquarters on the jeep's radio transmitter, requesting that an ambulance be summoned from the British Military Hospital.

The ambulance was there within ten minutes and a stabilised Jones was soon whisked away to hospital. More German policemen had arrived. They set up floodlights around the scene after dispersing the curious crowd of onlookers, who had materialised from the surrounding bomb ruins, and sealed off either end of the street.

Five minutes after the ambulance had departed, Warrant Officer Lancaster arrived with the Commanding Officer, Squadron Leader Johnson, and a photographer.

'Not another balls up I hope Harry,' Lancaster greeted Penrose.

'No Boss. Just a necessity I'm afraid. May I suggest that you get the photographer to get a few shots of the Gross' before Rossmann's Medical Examiner arrives?'

Lancaster glanced towards Rossmann who was directing his team some distance down the street. 'Do you think it'll be ethical?' Nodding towards Rossmann, he added, 'Shouldn't we ask him? After all, Gross is going to be his responsibility.'

'As my old instructor at Peel House used to say, "Bugger the ethics, get the evidence." Anytime at all Rossmann's Medical Examiner is going to start moving that fat bastard around. Let's get a shot of how he is now. The way he was after Davy took him out.'

'So it was Davy who shot him?' Lancaster remarked.

Penrose nodded. 'Yep. He saved my life. The bastard was going to shoot me.'

'Where's Davy's weapon?'

'Bagged and tagged Boss. Bill Sharp has it.'
'And yours Harry?'
'Where it's been all night. In my holster. I never got a chance to get it out.'
'I'll have to have yours as well. The guys from Bückeburg will need to examine it.'
'You calling them in Boss?' Penrose asked as he took his pistol out of the holster around his waist and handed it to Lancaster.
'Have to Harry. There will have to be an internal inquiry. I sent a signal before coming here. Now I had better go and have a word with Inspector Rossmann.'

25

The next four weeks seemed to fly by for Penrose. On the morning following the shooting he had gone to Davidswache where he made a statement to Rossmann. That afternoon he had made the same statement to Flight Lieutenant Jack Adams from the Provost Marshall's office at Bückeburg.

Three days later he was again in Rossmann's office where Rossmann informed him that his forensic department had confirmed that the Walther found by Gross' body was the weapon that had killed Karl-Heinz Necker and Irma Stubbe.

'And what about the Tamborin Klaus? Did you find anything there?' Penrose asked.

Rossmann twirled a pencil he was holding. 'It's all closed up Harry. Gross's daughter has shut it down. All the employees have vanished and the paperwork sanitised. We searched the place but there were only the accounts for the business. No records of any former employees, no records of any other business that might have gone on there. Nothing.'

'Did you speak to the daughter?'

'I had her here for a day but she claimed that she was only involved in keeping the books. Said that her father kept his business dealings to himself.'

'Did she have no idea who *Taucher* might have been?' Penrose asked.

Rossmann spread his arms and shook his head. 'Nothing Harry. She said that she did not know the names of any of the people who worked there. Said they were... what do you call it... casual workers who were paid every night. I think she is one very smart lady. Anyway, what is the condition of your friend Sergeant Jones?'

'He's on the mend Klaus. The wound was not as bad as it was first feared. No damage to any of the arteries or bones. He will have to stay in hospital for a few weeks, walk with a limp for a little longer, but he should end up as good as new.'

'Is he not due to return to England at the same time as you?'

~ The Hamburg Dossier ~

'He should be,' Penrose replied, 'but I'm afraid that his departure will now be delayed.'

The RAF Board of Inquiry found that the shooting had been carried out in self-defence and that no blame should be attached to either Jones or Penrose.

Penrose introduced Lisa to Nick the Trader who agreed to fence the jewellery. Before the introduction he had advised Lisa to only accept payment in US dollars. He had also warned Nick not to have any thoughts of cheating Lisa as he had a file on his activities that might interest Honest Klaus. This revelation did not alter the expression on Nick's face; he just moved his cigarette from one side of his mouth to the other.

'Sergeant,' Nick said, 'I would not think of cheating her. She is a friend of yours and I am your friend. Getting rid of Jonny Gross has made you many friends in Hamburg.' He gave Penrose one of his rare smiles. 'You never know, maybe I can now become number one in the town.' He removed the cigarette stub from his mouth and lit a fresh one from it. 'You got Jonny Gross Sergeant but you did not find your killer,' he said with a sly look.

'Any ideas Nick?' Penrose asked.

'We all have ideas Sergeant,' Nick replied. 'Maybe you will have one someday and then you will find your killer. What do the French say? *"Cherchez la femme"*.'

Penrose brought his file up to date on the deaths of AC McNeil and Tiny Chapman but made no conclusions. The file also made mention of the murders of Willi Winkler, Pussy Averbeck and Manfred Haller because Penrose was convinced that they were connected, but he offered no opinions as they were the responsibility of Klaus Rossmann. The file would remain open, to be taken up by another investigator should any further evidence come to light.

~ *The Hamburg Dossier* ~

On his last afternoon in Hamburg, Penrose was at the British Military Hospital, sitting in the sunshine with Davy Jones. Wheelchair-bound, Jones was dressed in the hospital patient's uniform of a light blue jacket and trousers, white shirt and red tie.

When he had first seen the dress Penrose had joked, 'The outfit suits you Davy. Very patriotic. Do they make you wear that so you can't do a runner?'

'Chance would be a bloody fine thing,' Jones replied with a laugh, pointing to his leg.

Now they were talking about Penrose's impending departure.

'In a couple of weeks you'll be back doing the business in the Smoke Harry,' Jones said. 'I wish I was going with you,' he added wistfully.

'Cheer up mate,' Penrose replied. 'You'll soon be up and about again. You'll be joining me in no time. Then we'll be wishing that we were back here.'

'We've had a few good time here Harry,' Jones said. 'A few good laughs.'

They reminisced for another twenty minutes before Penrose said his good-byes and left. As he drove out of the hospital gates he had to brake sharply to avoid a pretty female pedestrian who had stepped off of the pavement and entered the gates without looking. She gave him a lovely smile and a little wave before going on her way. I wonder, Penrose thought, which lucky bastard she's visiting. For a moment he thought that she looked familiar.

Penrose did not hold a riotous farewell party. He had said his good-byes to those who mattered, except Inge and Lisa. Inge, because he was convinced that she would not wish to see him, and Lisa, to avoid complications.

He spent his last night in Hamburg having a quiet drink with WO Lancaster and Terry Reader at the Victory Club. Inevitable, their conversation turned to the murder file.

'Forget it Harry,' Lancaster said. 'You did your best. Without the evidence you couldn't do any more.'

~ *The Hamburg Dossier* ~

Penrose shook his head. 'I still feel that I missed something Boss. I'm sure the answer is in that bloody file somewhere.'

Reader emptied his glass and stood up to replenish the round. 'You win some, you lose some Harry,' he said. 'Get back to England and restart your life.'

From the concourse of Hauptbahnhof Inge Lang peered down at the milling crowd of servicemen on Platform 9 awaiting the military train that would take them to the Hook of Holland where they would embark for Harwich. It took her sometime to pick out Penrose, as she had never seen him in service uniform before. Eventually she saw him halfway along the platform, standing at the edge. The train steamed into the platform from its starting point at Altona station. Inge hoped that he would turn and glance up before entering the train, but he didn't. Nor did he open a window and look out. As she watched the train pulling away through misty eyes, she whispered, 'Good-bye my Harry. Have a good life.'

Stepping back from the railing she collided with a woman standing behind her, who acknowledged her apology of *'Verzeihung'* with a wane smile. Side by side they walked along the concourse to the eastern exit where they parted. They didn't bid each other farewell because they didn't know one another. Inge crossed the pavement to a Control Commission car that would take her back to her office. Lisa turned right and went down the steps to the U-bahn, back to her uncertain future.

26

1987

A hush descended on the chattering people seated around the twelve round tables in the banqueting hall of the Hilton Hotel in response to the spoon being banged on the top table. Colonel John Mackensie, the Managing Director of Nimrod Security International rose to his feet and peered around the room. All eyes watched as this tall, military figure extracted some sheets of paper from the inside pocket of his evening jacket before slipping on a pair of half-moon spectacles.

He began to speak in a well-modulated voice that had graced many an Officers' Mess dining-in night and countless boardroom meeting.

'Distinguished guests. I call you that because that is what you are. Amongst us tonight are a Commander and senior members of the Metropolitan Police, former Provost Marshals of both the RAF Provost Branch and Royal Military Police, together with high-ranking members of both Services. Also the Assistant Chief Constable and senior officers of the Ministry of Defence Police and several people who will only admit to being Government employees. Take that how you wish.' A rumble of laughter went around the room.

'The fact that you are all here only goes to show the esteem you hold for the man to whom we are saying good bye. Harry Penrose.' He indicated the place setting on his right where Penrose sat, a half grin on his face.

'I know that Harry has been through his before. Nineteen years ago, when a Detective Chief Superintendent, he took his leave of the Metropolitan Police Service. I have been reminded by Commander Redfern, who was a Detective Sergeant on that occasion, that Harry's leaving was a great loss to the force, being one of the few detectives who could claim a hundred percent record in bringing murderers to justice. Well, the Met's loss was our gain.

' At that time Harry could have taken the pick of the many prestige jobs on offer to him. Instead, he agreed to become the Operations

Director of our fledgling Company. In the ensuing nineteen years, his efforts have built Nimrod into one of the foremost security organisations, not only in this country but throughout the world. Our client base includes governments, both home and abroad, yourselves and, I am proud to say, even our cousins across the pond

'Our fax machines at the office have been clogged with messages of goodwill and wishes for a happy retirement from all over the world. Should he wish to take up just a fraction of the invitations to visit, Harry will not have the time to become bored during the next phase of his life.

'The modest man that he is, Harry has insisted that I do not bore his guests with a monologue of his achievements, nor did he want to be presented with a clock. As he said to me, he only did what he was paid to do and a bloody good pay packet at that.

'So, I will wish Harry all the best in his retirement and ask you all to raise your glasses. The toast is Harry Penrose.'

The applause died down to be replace by shouts of 'Speech'.

Penrose slowly rose to his feet. He was still a fine figure of a man looking ten years younger than his sixty-seven years. The only lines on his face were laughter lines, his hair was slightly grey at the temples and there was just a thickening around the waist. His grin widened as he looked around the room.

'Friends,' he began. 'I don't intend to keep you long as I could not start to match the eloquence of John Mackensie. If I went into a rambling speech I might cause some embarrassment because, remember that I know all you buggers. I know all your little secrets and where your skeletons lie.' After the laughter died down he continued, 'So I will just thank you for coming here tonight and thank you for your good wishes. No doubt we will keep in contact and I will meet you all again to spin a yarn over a pint. Now I ask you to enjoy yourselves at Nimrod's expense. Thank you.' He sat down to tumultuous applause, which was followed by a rendering of "For he's a jolly good fellow".

~ *The Hamburg Dossier* ~

It was almost two o'clock in the morning when the taxi dropped Penrose off at his Ealing home. He paused at his garden gate to look at the darkened house, knowing the feeling of loneliness and emptiness that he would experience when he entered. Although it was nearly three years since Jean had died, he still missed her presence, her smell and her cheerful greeting whenever he returned home.

It hit him the following morning. He got out of bed as soon as the alarm went off at seven o'clock. As had been his habit for many years, he went straight to the bathroom for a shower and a shave. Back in his bedroom he threw open his wardrobe and looked at the row of 'office' suits realising that he would not need to select one. Instead, he pulled on a pair of slacks and a sport's shirt, went down to the kitchen where he made a pot of tea.

Sitting at the kitchen table, sipping his third cup, he looked around himself. The unopened newspaper, which he had picked up from the front door mat, was beside his elbow. Other than glancing at the headlines, he had not bothered to read it, as he would have plenty of time for that. The quietness of the house seemed to bear down upon him. Is this how it is always going to be, he wondered.

The ringing telephone jerked him out of his melancholy. As he crossed towards it a faint hope arose that it would be the office wanting his expertise. He answered in the abrupt manner he had cultivated over the years.

'Penrose.'

'Hello Daddy.' It was his daughter Samantha who was living in Hong Kong with her husband, a Superintendent with The Royal Hong Kong Police Service.

'Hello sweetheart. What are you doing up so late?'

'Waiting for the man of the house to come home.'

'What's he at then?'

'Oh. the usual Daddy. Out playing his big boys' games. Cops and triads. I just wanted to know how last night went?'

'A great time was had by all. They gave me a good send off. So how are the kids?'

'Always talking about their Granddad.'

~ The Hamburg Dossier ~

A picture of his two grandchildren formed in Penrose's mind. 'It seems ages since I've seen them.'

'Well Daddy, you've got all the time in the world now. Get yourself over to Heathrow and hop on a plane. Then they can have you rather than just talking about you.'

'I'll think about it poppet after I've sorted things out here.'

'What have you got to sort? Oh, here come my Lord and Master. Do you want a word?'

'Sure. You take care now sweetheart. Talk to you soon.'

'You too Dad.'

There was a murmur of voices as the telephone was handed over.

'Hi Harry. How's it going?' It was his son-in-law Jim.

'Rushed off my feet Jim-boy,' Penrose replied, with a laugh. 'I never knew that a life of leisure could be so busy.'

'You want to sit down and write a book Harry.'

'You've got to be kidding Jim. That's been done to death. Every man and his dog leaving the Job are putting pen to paper. What more could I add?'

Jim's voice took on a serious tone. 'Harry. You can tell them how it was when detectives were really detectives. Those who were born and not made. When the Governor, and his Sergeant carrying his bag, went out and solved cases by deduction and intuition. When the boss had to be out on the job and not managing the investigation from behind a desk. When they didn't have the back up of a host of forensic and scientific experts. When Murder Squad detectives were household names and talked about as old friends in the public bar of the local. That's what you could write about Harry.' With a laugh, he added, 'There's not many of you left.'

'Good God Jim,' Penrose said, with a chuckle, 'what's caused you to jump on your soapbox? Are they putting you in charge of a desk? No, don't answer that. I'll let you get to your bed. Goodnight son.'

After replacing the receiver Penrose wandered into his front room and stood gazing out of the window at the quiet road. He smiled, thinking about the passion of Jim's tirade over the telephone. His thoughts drifted to the previous evening. What had they said? He had a hundred percent murder record? That wasn't strictly true. He may well have had during his service with the Met, but there were the murders that had occurred in Hamburg. As far as he was aware, there had never been satisfactory conclusions to them. The details were now vague. Other than Inge Lang, who he had often thought about over the years, he couldn't think of the names of the other people involved. He remembered that it had been his belief that the crimes had all been committed by the same person, but was that person ever brought to justice? He wondered if the file had ever been closed or even if it was still in existence. Acting on a whim, he returned to the telephone and dialled a number from memory.

Penrose shouldered his way through the lunchtime crowd in the bar of the Sherlock Holmes on Whitehall. Most of the customers, some of whom Penrose knew by sight, worked in the surrounding Ministries. Two Chelsea Pensioners, resplendent in their scarlet tunics, who were sitting at their usual table at the end of the bar, watched his progress, expectantly. When he reached their table, Penrose paused and greeted them.

'Hello Bill, Charlie. "Fraid I can't stop 'cause I've got a meeting with the man over there.' He nodded towards the back of the room. 'I'll stick a couple of pints behind the bar for you.'

'God bless you Governor,' Bill replied. Charlie just raised his half-empty glass and nodded.

Penrose made his way to the table where Group Captain Simon Rowe, the incumbent Deputy Provost Marshal of the RAF, was sitting, nursing a half-eaten sandwich in one hand, a half-pint of bitter at his elbow, pouring over the Times crossword. He looked up as Penrose approached. 'Hello Harry. I see your charitable causes waylaid you.'

'Who? Bill and Charlie?' Penrose laughed. 'I've known those old buggers since when the Yard was just around the corner. I don't know how they've managed to live so long.'

'Could it be that they are afraid they would miss out on the next free pint if they popped their clogs?' Rowe asked, with a sly smile.

'They've got gallons to drink yet. Are you ready for the other half?'

Penrose ordered his drinks and a sandwich at the bar, carefully watched by Bill and Charlie to ensure that he paid for their next pint, then returned to a chair opposite Rowe.

They talked about Penrose's retirement party before Rowe said, 'So Harry. To what do I owe this pleasure?'

Penrose's hand dived into his jacket pocket for a packet of cigarettes before he remembered that he had given them up fifteen years before. 'I was wondering if you could help me with something Si. If you can't I bet you know a man who can.'

'Go on,' Rowe said.

'When I had the honour to serve with your mob I was involved in a murder case in Hamburg.'

'I know,' Rowe said, with a smile.

Penrose stared at him in astonishment. 'How?'

'I was having a chat at your do with that old friend of yours. Kerry? Perry? That former Lieutenant Colonel of Military Police.'

'Oh Terry. Terry Reader. Yes he was with me on that. What did he have to say?'

'Well, not a lot really. Time had dulled his memory of the actual happenings. He just mentioned it in passing.'

'I've got the same problem Si. I can remember it but not the details. I was wondering if the file is still in existence?'

Rowe, who was taking a swallow of his ale, spluttered. 'You've got to be bloody joking Harry. That file must be over forty years old. Longer than I've been in the Service.'

'Yes, I realise that,' Penrose said, 'but surely it must still be around somewhere if the crimes were never solved?'

'God knows Harry,' Rowe replied, shaking his head. 'A lot of water has passed under the bridge. Over the years there have been reorganisations. Changes and movements. We have never had a presence in Hamburg during my time. The Headquarters is now at Rheindahlen and I can't imagine dead files being moved to there.'

'But surely records are stored somewhere,' Penrose persisted. 'They just can't be destroyed or thrown away.'

~ The Hamburg Dossier ~

Rowe swallowed the remainder of his drink and rose from his seat. 'I've got to get back to the office Harry. Look, I'll see what I can do but don't hold your breath.'

Penrose watched him leaving the bar before picking up his glass and making his way to where Bill and Charlie were sitting. 'So lads, what's the latest gossip?'

It was three weeks later when Penrose, who was aimlessly watching an afternoon television show, answered the telephone.

'Is that Mister Harry Penrose?' the caller asked.

'Yes,' Penrose confirmed.

'My name is Warrant Officer Jim Murphy of the RAF Provost and Security Services. I have a file that I believe you are interested in.'

Penrose shot forward in his chair. 'You have? You've actually found it? When can I have a look at it?'

'Whenever you like Mister Penrose. There is no hurry for it to be returned.'

'How about tomorrow?' Penrose asked. 'Where do I find you?'

'Tomorrow will be fine,' Murphy replied. 'We are at RAF Rudloe Manor. Leave the M4 at junction 17. Go around Chippenham and take the Bath road. Go through Corsham and we are about two mile further on the right. What time can I expect you?'

Penrose thought for a moment. 'I think first thing in the morning Mister Murphy. I'll make my way down this afternoon. Is there a nearby hotel I can book into?'

'The Rudloe Hotel is directly opposite our entrance. If you like, I'll nip over and book a room for you and then I'll see you in the morning.'

'Good man,' Penrose replied, before putting down the phone and dashing to pack a bag.

27

It was a fine summer's morning when Penrose left the Rudloe Hotel and crossed the road towards the entrance to Rudloe Manor. The previous evening he had walked down a small lane to where the elegant, stone-built manor house stood, facing across the Box valley towards Bath. Except for the ensign flying at the mast in front of it, no one would have suspected that it was a RAF Headquarters. Later, while having a nightcap, the hotel barman had acquainted Penrose with the history of the place and how the Air Ministry had taken it over during the Second World War. In a hushed voice, he had said that, in addition to the Box railway tunnel, there were a series of other tunnels below the surrounding countryside where, it was rumoured, all manner of secret work was carried out. According to the local population, the reason why the RAF Police made it their headquarters in 1975 was to protect whatever was happening down in the tunnels.

At the entrance of tree-lined avenue leading to the grounds of the manor was a blue sign on which was painted a RAF Police badge and the words, 'Headquarters Provost and Security Services United Kingdom' and 'Provost and Security Services (Southern Region)' The avenue led into the ground at the rear of the manor house where rows of prefabricated buildings stood on which once would have been gardens.

Following a sign pointing to reception, Penrose entered a flagstoned hallway through a weather-beaten oak door. Climbing a flight of stairs, he arrived at the Control Room where the Duty Sergeant contacted Warrant Officer Jim Murphy.

Jim Murphy was younger than Penrose had imagined him, having compared him to his memory of Warrant Officer Lancaster. But then Penrose remembered that he was now a lot older himself and, to him, policemen were looking younger than in his day.

Murphy led him along a long, stone corridor. 'It didn't take you long to track this file down,' Penrose said. 'I was led to believe it was almost the impossible.'

~ The Hamburg Dossier ~

'We had a bit of luck Mister Penrose...'

'For God sake,' Penrose interrupted, 'you're making me sound like an old codger. Call me Harry.'

Murphy smiled before continuing. 'Okay Harry. As I said, we had a bit of luck. It was the age of the file that helped. We contacted the MOD Depository at Hayes where we expected it to be stored if it still existed. They were able to track it down pretty quickly as it was forty years old and was due to be transferred to a Public Records Depository. Another few weeks and it would have been.'

Murphy stopped at a door. 'I've put you in here,' he said, opening the door leading to a small room containing a desk and two chairs. On the otherwise empty desktop sat the file. 'I'll leave you to it then,' Murphy said. 'I'll have some tea sent along and let you know when it's lunchtime. Are you okay for writing material?'

'Yes. Yes, thank you Jim,' Penrose said, his eyes fixed on the file.

Penrose sat down and stared at the file. It was only about three inches thick: somehow he had imagined that it was larger than that. He rubbed his fingers over the buff covered folder. How many times had he touch this file before? He looked at the charging list on the cover, the record of persons to whom the file had been charged out to by the collator. Penrose smiled as he recalled how the collator, Pete somebody, was a stickler for recording the movements of the files under his control. He recognised his own initials amongst the list and vaguely recognised others. Some, dated years after he had left Germany, meant nothing to him at all.

He opened the cover and leafed through the attached minute sheets. Now faces could be put to the signatures under the comments of the people who had handled the file. Warrant Office Lancaster, the OC, Squadron Leader Johnson and the neat, precise handwriting that he remembered so well; that of Inge Lang.

For a moment he allowed his mind to wander, wondering what had become of Inge? Was she still alive? Did she ever marry? Did she have children? He smiled at his own memories of her before turning his attention back to the file.

~ *The Hamburg Dossier* ~

The last enclosure dated January 1950, signed by a Squadron Leader Perry, who meant nothing to Penrose, was the suspension of the investigation. He skipped back through the previous ones, all periodic negative progress reports entered by various investigators, until he came to the last entry made by himself in 1947. It was apparent that little work had been carried out on the case since that time.

He turned the file over and, starting from the rear cover, began reading from the first enclosure, the Initial Case Report, remembering when he had entered it. The incidents and names came flooding back to him. The murders of Willi Winkler, Pussy Averbeck and Manfred Haller. The savage shootings of Karl-Heinz Necker and Irma Stubbe. The killings of Percy McNeil and Tiny Chapman. The meetings with Inspector Rossmann. Penrose smiled as he recollected the interrogation of Doctor Pick and thanked his lucky stars that the Police and Criminal Act had not been in force at that time. Manfred Haller brought thoughts of Lisa Lotte Klose, which intermingled, with those of Inge Lang. But despite all of his thoughts, he knew that there was something eluding him and his reading and re-reading of the file could not bring that something to light.

A knock came on the door and Jim Murphy poked his head into the room. 'It's lunchtime Harry. Are you going along to the Officers' Mess or would you like to join me in the Sergeants'?'

'The Sergeants' Mess is fine with me Jim. It's years since I've been in one. It will bring back old memories.'

They strolled along a path to the far end of the manor grounds. 'So, how is it going Harry?' Murphy asked.

'To be honest Jim, I'm no further forward than I was forty years ago.'

Murphy chuckled. 'I took the liberty of reading the file after I got it. It looked a right cow-son of a job. It seemed to me that you were being stalked, that someone was outguessing your every move.'

'Join the club,' Penrose replied, as they entered a long, low building.

'Do you want a full lunch or just a pie and a pint? Murphy asked.

'A pie and a pint will be fine.' Penrose replied.

~ The Hamburg Dossier ~

'After getting their beer and placing their order for food, they found a quiet table away from the crowded bar.

'What are your plans for this afternoon Harry?' Murphy asked. 'Are you going to have another bash at the file?'

'I don't think there is much point Jim. Know the bloody thing backwards now.'

'Good,' Murphy replied. 'The Commanding Officer would like to meet you. He wants to give you the grand tour.'

'That's okay by me Jim. I'd love it,' Penrose said. 'But can I ask you a favour? Is there any chance of me having a copy of that file? You know how it is? I might suddenly get a flash of inspiration.'

Murphy looked doubtful. After thinking for a moment, he said, 'The thing is about to go into the public domain, so okay, as long as you keep it to yourself. If the shit hits the fan I will say that you must have copied it when I wasn't looking. How much of it do you want?'

'The whole lot, from cover to cover.'

'You don't ask for much do you? I'll bring it over to the hotel this evening.'

'Better still,' Penrose said, 'Come and have dinner with me tonight. Bring the wife or girlfriend, both if you wish. I insist.'

28

'You're going where Daddy to do what?' Penrose's daughter shrieked over the phone.

'To Germany sweetheart. Hamburg. To solve a crime.'

'But Daddy, you're retired. You're too old to play games.'

'Not so much of the old young lady. It's something I've got to do Sam. If I can crack this job, I'll die a happy man.'

'Don't talk so stupid,' Samantha said, calming down. 'What if I want to get hold of you? Where will you be?'

'I'll stay at...' Penrose paused. What hotels were there in Hamburg? His memory could only bring one to mind, which he hoped was still there. 'I'll be at the Atlantic Hotel. I don't know the number but it would not be hard to find. It is, or was, the top hotel in Hamburg.'

Samantha heaved a sigh of resignation. 'All right. No wonder I married the man I did when I've got a similar fool for a father. Take care of yourself.'

Penrose laughed. 'And I love you too sweetheart. Bye now.'

Liverpool Street station had vastly altered from when Penrose used to catch the troops" boat train in the 1940s. Then, every evening, a boat train would depart on the hour, between six and ten o'clock, bound for Harwich Parkstone Quay. The "old sweats", those soldiers who had done the journey at least once before, would wait for the later trains knowing that those would caught the earlier ones would be detailed for boat duties on their arrival at the dock. They would await the later trains by drinking in Dirty Dick's, opposite the station in Bishopsgate, or in the station buffet where they would stare out at the Military Police patrols who were ambling up and down the platform, hoping to put some unfortunate, returning soldier or airman on a charge for some minor, disciplinary offence.

Penrose was catching a boat train that was leaving just after three in the afternoon. He had decided to go by train and boat rather than flying as he looked at the journey as a part of a pilgrimage. But he had

~ The Hamburg Dossier ~

opted to take a ferry direct to Hamburg rather than go to the Hook of Holland and another train journey from there.

Parkstone Quay had also altered out of all recognition. Penrose recalled that on leaving the train one went into a large, steel warehouse containing rows of army clerks at tables who would check travel documents and allocated berths for the voyage. At one end of the shed was a field kitchen where the desperately hungry could sample the army fare, usually bully beef and mash potato complete with eyes, slopped up out of serving dixies. Another large door led out onto the dockside where the rust-stained *'Vienna'* or *'Empire Wansbeck'*, the troopships which shuttled nightly across the North Sea, would be tied up awaiting the passengers. The dock would be a hive of industry with gangs of Pioneer Corps soldiers loading cargo nets, then shouting at the crane driver above to hoist then up.

Now, Penrose left the train and entered a building modelled on an airport departure lounge. Pretty girls behind a reception desk dealt with the documentation. An elegant bar and buffet offered the opportunity of refreshment before taking the covered walkway to where the gleaming, white ferry was waiting.

After a leisurely breakfast Penrose strolled out to the sun deck and found that the ship was steaming up the Elbe river. Finding a chair in the sun, he watched the passing countryside. Occasionally, huge, ocean bound container ships would hurtle past, so close to the ferry that it would make one think that it was possible to shake hands with the crew members leaning over the ships' rails. Slowly the river narrowed giving the impression that the outgoing ships were passing closer. Landing stages began appearing on the northern bank on which groups of people were standing, awaiting one of the river ferries that plied up and down the river.

The ship's tannoy crackled into life. 'Ladies and gentlemen. We are now approaching Wedel, the world-famous *Willkommhöft*, the welcoming point.' On the quay of the riverside restaurant, *Schulau Fährhaus*, the Hamburg flag, flying on a mast, was lowered in salute and the strains of God Save the Queen floated towards the ferry. The anthem was replaced by a recorded message, welcoming the passengers to Hamburg, followed by a rendering of Wagner's "Flying Dutchman".

The northern bank began to rise and form a hillside dotted with white buildings, as Penrose watched the ferry stage of Blankenese slip by. Slowly, the ferry edged round a left-hand bend and the buildings of Hamburg began to appear. Gradually, the patina domed Michaeliskirche came into view. Staring at it, Penrose felt that he had never been away.

Penrose disembarked at the landing stage opposite the Fischmarkt and boarded one of the waiting taxis. 'Atlantic Hotel,' he said to the driver, hoping that the hotel still existed.

As the taxi proceeded along Grosse Elbestrasse he couldn't help thinking that there was something different about the place. It wasn't the absence of bomb-damaged buildings or the massive Blohm and Voss floating dry dock across the river, in which the cradled ships in for repair looked like toys. There was just something different.

When the taxi turned left at St Pauli-Landungsbrücken and climb Helgoland Allee, around the knoll on which Bismark's statue stood, it came to him. The statue was screened by a stand of trees on the hillside.

'My God, there are trees,' he uttered aloud.

The taxi driver gave him a curious glance in the rear view mirror. 'Ja. We have trees here.'

Penrose laughed. 'The last time I was here, forty years ago, there were no trees. They had all been burnt down.'

'Ah, the British firestorm,' the driver said. 'My father told me about that. In the 1950s the city planted one million trees and now we have them.'

The taxi turned right onto what appeared to be a ring road, which Penrose didn't recognise. He thought that they should pass through Zeughausmarkt but he could not see the Café Arnold. Except for the ruined spire of St Nikolai church, he could not recognise any

~ *The Hamburg Dossier* ~

landmarks until they passed Hauptbahnhof. The exterior of the main station had not changed.

The classic style of the Atlantic Hotel, facing the Aussenalster alive with small sailboats weaving to and fro, was as he remembered it. The entrance lobby showed that the hotel had been restored to its pre-war glory. Penrose was given a room on the second floor that overlooked the lake. Stepping out onto the small balcony to admire the vista, he decided to forego unpacking and explore the town instead.

29

Leaving the hotel, he strolled along the bank of the Binnenalster to Jungfernstieg and then to the Alsterpavilion where he could not resist going inside for a cup of coffee. Sitting at a table in the window, he remembered that rainy day when he sat in the same spot awaiting the appearance of Tiny Chapman. How different the scene was now. The sun was shining down on the large department stores and boutiques on the opposite side of the road. The pavements were thronged with people who had cast off their post-war, dreary attire for attractive dresses and designer clothing.

Passing Büschstrasse, he wondered what had become of Nick the Trader. In Dammtorstrasse he realised that the trams were no longer in use. He was disappointed to find that Hamburg House, the Victory Club, had been pulled down and replaced by a glass-fronted bank. Welckerstrasse was closed and appeared to be ready for redevelopment. He wondered if Herbertstrasse had gone the same way and what had happened to the legions of ladies of the night who had plied their trade there.

Passing around the Rathaus, which was still as ugly as he remembered it, he strolled along the side of the Alsterfleet to Michaeliskirche. What had once been an area of total devastation was now row upon row of well-maintained, low-rise dwellings. The row of old town houses, where Lisa Klose rented her room from little, deformed Manfred, were no longer standing. Penrose spent some time gazing up at Michel tower, remembering that day when Tiny Chapman met his tragic end, before moving on.

When he reached Zeughausmarkt he realised why he had not recognised it when passing through on his taxi ride. Half of it was no longer there. The Café Arnold and the Anita Bar had vanished, making way for the new road. The English Church still stood at what remained of the apex of the triangle. The building that had been the Café Koch was closed and the Seaman's Club was now an estate agent's office.

~ The Hamburg Dossier ~

The Reeperbahn was more tatty than he remembered. Then, of course, it had been a bright spot in a sea of ruins but now the newly, rebuilt surrounding area seemed to emphasise the neglect of the most famous street in Hamburg. There were still landmarks that Penrose remembered, the Zillertal dance hall, the Café Keese, the Café Lausen and the Astoria coffee house but the other bars, with exotic names, offering all kinds of carnal delights, and the Euro-Laufhaus, a brothel supermarket, were all new to him.

It was too early for business in Grosse Freiheit. Now arches of flashing neon lights across the street indicated the locations of the Tabu, Safari and Regina bars. The Tamborin had been renamed Jambolia but had not altered in appearance. All were tightly shut but would throw open their doors as soon as the punters appeared to be enticed inside by the persuasive doormen.

Penrose crossed the Reeperbahn to Hans Albert Platz, the heart of Old St Pauli known as Kleiner Kiez, the little red light district. Wandering through the small cobbled streets he came to the rear entrance of Herbertstrasse. The barrier across the entrance showed that it was still in business although the warning sign painted on the barrier now prohibited entry to women and children under sixteen years.

Although the street appeared to have changed little over the forty years since Penrose had last seen it, there had been some refurbishment. No longer were the places of business single occupancy, Two or three establishments had been knocked into one with three or four girls sitting behind large, picture windows.

Penrose stood in the cul-de-sac as he had forty years before and looked across at where Pussy's room would have been. The four girls behind the window were all young, pretty, beautifully dressed and made-up, and would not have been out of place in any fashion magazine. The women that Penrose recalled as once plying their trade in the street would not have been able to compete with their successors.

He strolled the length of the short street, acknowledging the tapping on the windows with a smile and a wink, emerging into Davidstrasse.

In front of Davidwache was a small pavement kiosk where he sat down at a table and ordered a beer. He watched the comings and goings at the police station. Now, the colours of the police uniforms were tan and green: the patrol cars being the same colour. A distant clock struck eight when he noticed the appearance of young, mini-skirted girls who took up station along the pavement of Davidstrasse, each about five yards apart. He was not aware that pavement soliciting was allowed in Germany. In his day business was conducted either in the brothel streets or cafés and bars. Suddenly, the line of girls moved five paces to their left, then, after a brief pause, back to their original positions. He wondered if street soliciting was illegal after all and that the movement coincided with the arrival of a policeman at the station, but this theory was dashed when a policeman went to a post-box where he stood chatting to one of the ladies. Then, after some study, the penny dropped. The prime position was that at the corner of the Reeperbahn and Davidstrasse. The occupant of that position had the pick of clients in both streets. Should she move from her position on the corner to accost a punter on the pavement, the next lady in line would move into the prime position, followed by all the rest moving to the next station. If the first lady was unsuccessful and move back to her original position on the corner, all the rest then returned to their last positions. Penrose chuckled as he thought that only Germans could organise themselves in such a manner. He could never remember, when as a young copper working the streets of Soho, the wall to wall pussy acting in such a civilised way.

Still smiling, he finished his glass of beer and headed for the U-bahn station. Back to his hotel to prepare himself for work the next day.

30

The entrance hall of Davidwache was still as Penrose remembered it. Now a little smarter with a new coat of paint and a more comfortable waiting area. The grizzled haired, elderly policeman who watched him approach the counter could have been there for ever except for the new style uniform with four bronze stars on his epaulettes instead of silver stripes on his sleeves.

'*Guten Morgen Herr Haupwachmeister,*' Penrose said. '*Sprechen Sie Englisch?*'

The policeman smiled. 'Of course,' he replied, 'but you are out of date with my rank. I am now called *Polizeihauptmeister,* Sergeant. But how can I help you?'

'My apologies,' Penrose said. 'It is a long time since I had dealings with the German Police. I am trying to trace an Inspector Rossmann who used to be at this station.'

'Yes, we still have him,' the Sergeant said. '*Polizeirat* Rossmann. Captain Rossmann. Who is asking for him?'

Penrose looked astonished. 'My name is Penrose. But surely he can't still be here? He must be very old?'

'Not so old I think,' the Sergeant said, with a laugh. 'Please to take a seat,' he continued, pointing to the waiting area, 'I will call him.'

Mystified, Penrose sat down in one of the chairs, watching the Sergeant muttering into the telephone. Is this some kind of joke, he asked himself. Are they trying to take the rise out of an old man?

A movement at the top of the stairs attracted his attention. A tall, slim man was looking down at him. Penrose's heart gave a leap. It was Klaus Rossmann, just as he remembered him.

The man came down the stairs, two at a time, and, with a smile on his face, approached Penrose with his hand outstretched. 'Mister Penrose?' he asked, in precise English. 'It is a pleasure to meet you.'

Up close, Penrose realised that it could not be Klaus Rossmann. 'I think there has been some mistake. I was trying to trace an old friend who.....'

'I know who you are Mister Penrose and who you are trying to find. My father. I am Karl Rossmann, Klaus' son. My boyhood was full of tales about you and at last I am seeing you in the flesh. Come to my office where we will be more comfortable.'

The criminal department, on the second floor, had altered out of all recognition. It was now opened planned with Karl's office being a glass cubicle in one of the corners. Detectives of both sexes looked up from their work and gave welcoming smiles as Penrose and Karl made their way between the desks.

After they had settled down with cups of coffee produced by one of the policewomen Karl shook his head. 'This is a wonderful surprise Mister Penrose. My father will be overjoyed. Do you know that you were the first Englishman that he ever liked?'

Penrose laughed. 'You are as formal as you father. For God sake call me Harry. Anyway, how is the old fellow?'

Karl's face took on a serious expression. 'Not as good as he was Harry. After all, he is eighty-seven years you know. Some days he is better than other, but he is becoming very forgetful. At time he can remember everything and then, well he has difficulty remembering what happened the day before or even an hour before. There is nothing wrong medically, just old age.'

'Unfortunately, it happens to us all,' Penrose said. 'So how did his police career end up?'

'Oh, he made *Polizeidirektor*, Colonel, before he retired. When the Occupation ended and the force was reorganised they realised his worth. He was also happy that you progressed in your career, which he watched very closely. Whenever he read something about you in a police or security publication he would boast that you were his friend. So Harry, when will you be free to meet him?'

'Whenever it is convenient. I was hoping to talk to him about a series of murders we were working on forty years ago. I don't know if you know anything about them?'

Karl shook his head. 'It was my father's golden rule never to discuss anything about his work at home. If I asked him about his work when

I was a boy he would say that if I wanted to know anything about police work I should become a policeman. So, here I am.'

'Would there still be any records relating to the case?'

'I suppose there must be. We Germans never destroy anything. But why not talk first to my father and see what he can remember, if anything. You might catch him on a good day. Look, why don't you come to dinner, say tomorrow night? Where can I contact you?'

'I would love to. I am staying at the Atlantic Hotel. There is another favour I would like to ask of you. Can you trace two women for me? They may still be alive.'

Karl's eyes glinted as a smile spread over his face. 'Ah ha Harry. Secrets from the past?' He shouted, 'Helga' and the young policewoman who had served them coffee scampered into the office. 'Give Helga the names and she will see what she can do.'

Penrose looked at Helga who was waiting expectantly. 'The first one is Inge Lang. Of course she might be married now if she is alive. She worked for the Control Commission. The last place I know of was in the military legal department. The other is Lisa Lotte Klose. That's all I can tell you about her.'

'Leopard Mode,' Helga said.

Both men looked at her in astonishment.

'What?' Karl asked.

Helga laughed. 'You men know nothing,' she said in an attractive accent. 'Every girl between ten and eighty knows of Lisa Lotte Klose and *Leopard Mode*. All of them would love to afford her creations. She is the top fashion designer in Germany.'

'So where can I find her?' Penrose asked.

'Here in Hamburg. Her main office is above one of her boutiques in Mönckebergstrasse. She will be there if she is not in Paris, London, Rome or New York.'

'So, what's the name of this shop?' Penrose asked.

'Shop?' Helga hissed. 'You call it a shop? Anyone can walk into a shop, but to go into a *Leopard Mode* boutique you need to be carrying a suitcase full of money. It is called *Leopard Mode*. Her motif is a running leopard.'

Karl clicked his fingers. 'Now I know of her. My daughter and her friends are always talking about her clothes.'

'Clothes?' Helga tossed her head. 'They are creations.' Her face softened as she looked back at Penrose. 'Do you really know Lisa Lotte Klose?' she asked, coyly.

'A long time ago,' Penrose replied.

'Well, when you meet her again just remember who your friends are and who is helping you,' Helga said, with a smile.

'So, Harry, Until tomorrow,' Karl said, shaking Penrose's hand. 'I'll leave a message at the reception desk of your hotel with arrangements to collect you. In the meanwhile I will check the archives for my father's old cases and see if I can trace the file of what you were working on together. Helga will show you out.'

As Penrose followed Helga through the office she shouted a string of German which included the words 'Lisa Lotte Klose'. All the other females raised their heads and let out a collective 'Ooh'.

31

Penrose discovered 'Leopard Mode' halfway along Mönckebergstrasse. It was double-fronted without a name above the shop; just a running leopard. In each window was a single dummy draped in a dress, neither of which bore a price tag. Although he was not *au fait* with *haute couture*, Penrose could see that both creations had the exclusive look of the clothing worn by film stars and models at film premiers and the like.

He went closer and peered through one of the windows. The interior was small and tastefully decorated. There was no evidence of any clothing on display, just a scattering of comfortable chairs. A man and a woman, who both radiated wealth, were sitting in two of the chairs looking up at a model who, by twisting and turning, was showing a dress she was wearing. A third women, immaculately dressed, was talking to the couple whilst pointing out various feature of the creation on the model. The model noticed Penrose and said something to the other three. All turned and looked at him and burst into laughter as, embarrassed, he backed away from the window.

Next to one of the windows was a door, which bore a brass plate engraved with the running leopard and the words 'Leopard Mode'. He entered the door and came into a marble-panelled reception area. To one side was a slate and chrome low table behind which was a long settee covered in a leopard-patterned fabric. At the far end of the room was a slate and chrome desk behind which was a clone of the saleslady next door.

The clone gave him a flashing smile. *'Guten Morgen Meine Herr?'* she greeted him. *'Kann ich lhnen helfen?'*

Penrose approached the desk. 'I'm sorry, I don't speak German,' he said.

The smile returned. 'That's okay, I speak English. How may I help you?'

'I was hoping that I might see Fräulien Klose.'

The smile vanished. 'Do you have an appointment Sir?'

Penrose shook his head. 'No, but I ----'

'I am sorry. Fräulien Klose will not see anyone without an appointment. If you would like to leave your name and details of your business I will see that she receives it.'

Penrose knew that he was not going to get past this exquisite creature who was certain to have her foot on the panic alarm button. 'May I beg a piece of paper so that can leave her a note?'

Reluctantly, the receptionist delved into one of the desk's drawers and handed Penrose a sheet of paper. He retreated to the settee and bent over the table to compose his note to Lisa. He became aware of the noise of a lift descending and the swish of opening doors behind the receptionist, who rose to her feet.

Penrose heard the receptionist say, *'Fräulien Klose'* and a voice he remembered so well reply, 'Maria'. He glanced up and saw Lisa coming towards him. She had not changed in appearance; she was just a little older. The large sunglasses and floppy hat could not disguise those classic Slavic features. The slim figure still had the pose and the walk that would turn men's heads. As she passed Penrose she turned her head towards him and, with a slight nod, said, *'Meine Herr'* before moving on towards the outside door.

Penrose murmured an acknowledgement, 'Lisa.'

Lisa stopped. She turned, took off her sunglasses and stared at Penrose. Slowly, recognition appeared in her eyes and a look of concern on her face. As Penrose rose to his feet the receptionist darted towards him from behind her desk. Lisa, still staring at Penrose, waved her away. Slowly, she walked towards him and, intently, studied his face.

'My God Harry. It is you,' she said finally. 'What are you doing here?'

Penrose gave her a lazy smile. 'What I'm doing right now sweetheart. Seeing you.'

Lisa grabbed his hand and pulled him towards the lift door. 'Come upstairs so we can talk.'

'But Fräulien Klose,' the receptionist said in English for Penrose benefit, 'what about your meeting with ----'

~ *The Hamburg Dossier* ~

'Cancel it,' Lisa said, with a wave of her hand. 'If I let this man out of my sight only God would know when I would see him again.'

They exited the lift on the first floor into an anteroom panelled in the same marble as the reception room below. Behind a desk was another clone, this one a secretary, holding a telephone to her ear, who looked at Lisa with alarm. '*Was ist los Fräulien Klose?*' she asked in a concerned voice.

'Nothing Ingrid,' Lisa replied in English. 'Herr Penrose and I have a lot to talk about. I do not wish to be disturbed. Hold all telephone calls.'

Still grasping Penrose's hand, she pulled him into an adjoining office that was obviously hers. The room, this one panelled in pine, was large, dominated by an immense desk under the windows at the far end. To one side was a conference table surrounded by twelve chairs. In the opposite wall, above an arrangement of two leather-covered settees and a low coffee table, was a large picture window, draped with open, Venetian blind, giving a view of a large studio next door. Three women were working at easels on which they were sketching outlines of dresses, a large cutting table, heaped with fabrics of various designs and colours, ran along the centre of the room. At the far end were two effeminate men fussing around a live model, draping and pinning material around her young, slim body. All of them looked towards the window as Lisa closed the blinds.

She had thrown her outer coat onto one of the settees and Penrose saw that she was wearing a tight, low-cut sweater, which showed that her breasts were still as shapely as he remembered them. Around her neck was the jewelled leopard. A picture formed in Penrose's mind of a naked Lisa wearing the necklace, sitting on a bed in a garret, surrounded of pieces of jewellery and bundles of money.

'It looks like it did bring you luck sweetheart,' Penrose said, pointing to the leopard.

'That and a little bit of hard work,' Lisa replied with a smile. 'But let us sit down,' indicating the settees, 'we must look silly just standing in the middle of my office.'

After they had settled onto the same settee a serious Lisa looked at Penrose. 'So, why did you leave without even a good-bye Harry?'

Penrose shook his head. 'Stupidity, the folly of youth, embarrassment, fear. Take your choice.'

Lisa's expression changed to one of disbelief. 'What? You were not young and certainly not stupid. There was never any embarrassment or fear between us.' She turned her head away. 'Was it because of what I was?' she asked, in a quiet voice.

Penrose grasped her hand. 'No Lisa. That is all in the past. Times were different then. We had to do what we had to do. I never disrespected you for that.'

She turned back to him and placed her free hand over his. 'Then can we keep it that way. No one here knows of my past life and there are very few who might still remember it. Promise me that you will keep what you know to yourself.'

'I promise Lisa. My lips are sealed.'

She leant across and lightly kissed him on the lips. 'That is a seal of friendship,' she said. 'Now, tell me about your life. Are you married? Do you have children? Tell me everything.'

'Yes, I was married but my wife died. We have a daughter and two grandchildren. ------'

For the next twenty minutes Lisa listened in silence as Penrose related the events of the past forty years. Then he said, 'Enough about me. Now its your turn.' He waved his hand around the room. 'Tell me how all this came about.'

'Well, after you disappeared,' she said pointedly, ' I did as you said. With Nick's help -------.'

'So the old bastard came up trumps.' Penrose interrupted. 'How is the old villain?'

Lisa placed a forefinger on his lips. 'Questions later. First I will tell my story.

'When, with Nick's help, I had some capital in the banks that had opened for business, I told Nick of my dreams of becoming a dress designer. He found a workshop for me, material, three manual sewing machines and seamstresses who could use them. They would make

~ *The Hamburg Dossier* ~

up the dresses I designed and each week I would take what we had produced and sell them to the shops that had started to open.

'Soon the demands from the shops began to outstrip our production. Nick, who as you know always had an eye for a business opportunity, offered to become my partner. He found bigger premises, treadle sewing machines and machinists. And he also taught me how to run a business.

'With the profits we rebuilt his old warehouse by the docks about twenty years ago and turned it into a factory. Even though we were making a lot of money, I still had my dream of designing and making exclusive creations so, about ten years ago, I took a chance and tried my hand at *haute couture*. I guess that the rest is history.'

Penrose looked around the office. 'And this is the end result?' he said. ' An exclusive shop on Mönckeberstrasse with similar outlets in other leading cities.'

Lisa slowly shook her head. 'No,' she said in a quiet voice that Penrose remembered she used when embarrassed. 'This is where the *haute couture* is designed and made up in a workshop upstairs. I also have offices in Paris, Milan and New York, a number of factories supplying the lower end of the market, department store chains, all over the world and a sportswear division. The sportswear is being produced to our design in Thailand, Hong Kong and the Philippines.'

Penrose looked at her with mouth agape. 'Jesus Christ Lisa,' he spluttered. 'You must be as rich as sin. I bet old Nick's not flogging cheap watches and nylons now.'

Lisa eyes began to water. 'He is not, as you put it, flogging anything now. He died twelve years ago. He never lived to see all of this.'

'Oh I'm sorry,' Penrose said quietly. 'Were you and him er -----?'

'Remember our promise Harry,' Lisa said with a sad smile. 'What is passed will remain in the past.'

'Forgive me. But I am sorry that he is no longer here, I wanted to ask him things. I wanted to ask him about events when I was last here. I am sure there were things he knew but never told me.'

'What things Harry?'

~ *The Hamburg Dossier* ~

'Do you remember what I was working on before I left? The murders?'

'I can remember poor Pussy and Manfred being killed, the man you killed and that there were others, but the names and details escape me now. It was such a long time ago.'

'I never killed anyone.'

'Everyone said you did. That man who owned the club in St Pauli.'

'I was wondering if Nick ever spoke about it?'

'He may have done. In the early days he often spoke about you. Like me, he would wonder why you had walked away from me. But if he spoke about the killings, I can't now remember.'

'What happened to his effects? Did he leave any papers or anything?'

'Nick had piles of papers and notebooks. He kept records of everything and everyone. His protection he called them. His little black books.'

'Are any of them still around?'

'There might be some in the attic at my house. I haven't been up there in years.'

'Any chance of me taking a look?'

'Not at the moment. I have to leave for Milan tonight to make arrangements for our summer show. I will be back in three days then we can arrange something.' She gave him a sly look. 'Better still, why not come to Milan with me?' she added with a smile.

Penrose laughed. 'There is nothing better I would love to do, but I have some business to settle here. Give me your card and we will have dinner when you return.'

Lisa walked to her desk and returned with an embossed card that she tucked into the top pocket of his jacket. 'It is lunch time,' she said. 'I will buy you lunch.'

'That will be my privilege,' Penrose replied with a smile.

'No Harry. This is something I want to do. It is something special.'

Arm in arm they crossed from Leopard Mode into Gerhard-Hauptmann Platz that was thronged with a lunchtime crowd, all of whom seemed to be eating on the run. Penrose felt the admiring glances being thrown at Lisa and the envious looks at him, the man lucky enough to be on the arm of this beautiful celebrity.

They strolled into Spitalerstrasse, a short street of fast-food outlets, and approached a crowd of people standing at the far end. Penrose's senses picked up a long forgotten smell. The crowd of people was around a *brückwurst* stall. Lisa dived into the throng and soon returned with two polystyrene trays each holding a sausage, a hunk of bread and a dab of mustard.

'Remember?' Lisa asked mischievously as she handed him one of the trays.

'Could I ever forget? It's a part of the past that I will always remember,' he replied, looking into her eyes.

'Me too.'

They laughed as they both took a bite of their sausages.

'Harry,' Lisa said quietly, 'may I ask you something?'

'Ask away.'

'You never told me the name of your wife. Was it your good girl from Hamburg?'

'Who, Inge? No, I never saw her again. My wife's name was Jean. Anyway, what about you? Do you have anyone.'

Lisa shook her head. 'You know me Harry. Business is business but love is bullshit.'

Penrose nodded. 'But I also remember when it wasn't so,' he replied quietly.

They parted after finishing their meal with Penrose promising to contact her and arrange the dinner date. He walked back to his hotel and Lisa returned to her business.

~ 209 ~

32

Penrose idled over his breakfast wondering how he would pass the day. He had no new leads that he could follow up; he hoped that they would be forthcoming at his meeting with Klaus Rossmann later that evening. His mind went back to his meeting with Lisa the previous day and he remembered that she had said that the general belief was that it was he who had shot Jonny Gross. How could that rumour have started?

He went up to his room and poured over the file again. He reread his report of the incident in which he stated that his weapon had not been fired, Davy Jones' statement admitting that he fired the fatal shot and the forensic report which stated that the bullet causing Gross' death had been fired from Jones' pistol. The finding of the Board of Inquiry was perfectly clear; that Jones had killed Gross in self-defence. So why had it been generally believed on the streets that it was he who had killed Gross? He decided that he would go back to the scene of the incident where he might get some inspiration.

Blücherstrasse was unrecognisable. It had been completely rebuilt and did not have any resemblance to the street of forty years before. Penrose wandered along the street, trying to get his bearings, and stopped before a small bakery, remembering that he and Jones had been hiding in a ruined bakery. On the opposite side of the road was a small attractive hotel. He became convinced that this was the spot where he had sprawled on the pavement.

Staring at the hotel, trying to picture in his mind the events of that night long ago, he glanced over his shoulder at the bakery as if expecting to see Davy Jones standing there. A middle-aged man, dressed in white trousers and tee shirt, evidence of flour dust on his hair and face, was staring at him from the doorway. Penrose gave him a smile and, with a nod, said, 'Good morning.'

'English?' the man asked.

'Yes,' Penrose replied.

'I speak English good. You look for something?'

'Yes,' Penrose replied, 'But it is not here now. It was something that was here during the war.'

'I live here in war. My Grandfather was baker here. This his shop,' the man said indicating the bakery behind him. 'Not this shop, this new. Old shop go bang, all fall down. This my shop.'

'And what was there?' Penrose asked, pointing to the hotel.

The baker laughed. 'Before there was house for sex,' he said, emphasising his answer by moving his forearm and clenched fist backwards and forwards. 'Women lived there with big gangster.'

Penrose knew he was at the right spot. 'What happened to the gangster?'

'He dead. Big fight here. I see it all. Gunfight at OK Corral. Bang, bang, bang. Gangster kill many German police and British soldiers before he...' The baker tapped his chest with both hands. 'Many bullets here. I see it. I standing right here. I see him killed over there,' pointing to the opposite pavement.

'That must have been a nasty experience for a young boy.'

'I never forget it,' the baker said mournfully shaking his head.

Penrose thanked him before taking his leave. He smiled as he walked away. One thing he was certain of was that there had been no spectators before Gross had met his maker. He now knew how the rumour of his involvement had come about. Past events are exaggerated in the retelling.

Penrose was sitting in the lobby when Karl Rossmann walked into the hotel at six o'clock. A message had been waiting for him when he returned earlier that day and now he was looking forward to meeting Klaus again.

'I see you are ready Harry,' Karl greeted him, extending his hand for the customary handshake. 'My father did not believe me when last night I told him of your arrival. He asked me again this morning if it was true and that I was to be sure that I bring you home with me.'

'Well, we had better not keep the old fellow waiting,' Penrose said with a laugh. 'But, to tell the truth, I am also looking forward to seeing him again.'

They drove north along the side of the Alster lake into Sierichstrasse where Penrose recognised the former RAF Police headquarters, now, once again, a private residence restored to its former glory. Then north to Alsterdorf where Karl pulled into the driveway of a modern, detached house which backed onto the river. As they parked, a tall, thin figure rose from a chair on the porch and moved towards the steps. Although older, there was no mistaking Klaus Rossmann.

Her opened his arms towards Penrose. 'Harry, Harry, my friend. Welcome.'

Penrose was slightly taken aback by the warmth radiated by this formerly staid and very formal man that he could not resist giving him a hug after he had clasp his hand and said, 'It's good to see you again Klaus.'

Karl's wife came out of the house followed by a pretty teenager who reminded Penrose of his own daughter at that age. After introductions, Karl's wife, Ursula, said, 'You men sit here in the sunshine and reminisce whilst I finish preparing dinner. Heidi, go and fetch some beers for your father, grandfather and our guest.'

After they had settled into garden chairs around a table Klaus said, 'Let me look at you Harry. My God, you are as I remember you.'

Penrose laughed. 'You too Klaus, but regretfully many years have slipped by without either of us noticing.'

For the next thirty minutes they told each other of what had happened in the intervening years. Then Penrose broached the subject he had been itching to raise since his arrival.

'Klaus, I wonder if you recall the St Pauli murders we worked on together/'

The smile faded from Klaus' face. 'Harry, Karl spoke to me about them last night, but my memory is not so good now. Maybe if you remind me of the events I might be able to recall them.'

'I found your old file papa,' Karl said. 'I read it today so I might be able to help.'

Klaus slowly shook his head, the smile returning, 'My old file? Is that still about? So Harry, what would you like to know?'

~ *The Hamburg Dossier* ~

'You will remember Klaus that it started with the body of Gerhard Winkler being pulled out of the Elbe. He had been strangled.'

Klaus thought before slowly nodding his head.

'Then there was the prostitute who was murdered in Herbertstrasse. You might remember that you put me in the frame for that one.'

Klaus' smile widened. 'In the frame. Your English expressions. But yes I remember that one and I proved that you were innocent. Yes?'

'And then there was ....' Penrose went slowly through each murder ending with Tiny Chapman's fall from the Michel tower. Some event Klaus remember clearly, others, helped by prompting from Karl, he vaguely recalled.

His face took on a look of disgust when Penrose mentioned Jonny Gross. 'That man I will never forget. He was evil. His death was the happiest day of my life.'

Penrose smiled. 'Do you know, that there is a rumour that I was the person who killed him?'

Klaus nodded his head, his eyes clear and bright. 'Yes. His daughter. What was her name? Lilli? She came to my office and accused you of killing her father. She wanted me to arrest you. I told her that I knew who had shot him and that it wasn't you.'

'What happened to her Klaus?'

'She? She opened up her father's club again and ran it correctly. I did hear that she got married. It wasn't a German man. Then, of course, I left Davidswache when I was transferred to the police headquarters and I lost touch with her.'

'I spoke to the Vice Squad about her. She still owns the club,' Karl said, 'but has lots of other business interest now, All in the sex trade and all legitimate. There has not been any complaints made about her. She is married to an Englishman but his name escapes me as she still calls herself "von Grosse". I will check that out for you Harry.'

'Talking of Englishmen Klaus,' Penrose said, 'you always said that I should look for the murderer on my side of the fence. Can you tell me any more about that?'

~ 213 ~

The gleam faded from Klaus' eyes. 'It was so long ago Harry. I can't remember why I should have said that.'

'On the inside of the front cover of your file papa,' Karl said, 'you had written, in large letter, *"Taucher"* and *"Englisch"* with several question marks behind each word.'

'Did I?' Klaus said sadly. 'I'm sorry Harry. I don't know why I did that.'

Karl looked at Penrose and shook his head, a look of pity on his face. Before Penrose could respond Heidi came to the door. 'Dinner is ready,' she said with a smile.

The next hour was enjoyable, Delicious food and convivial conversation. Even Klaus seemed to comprehend talk of day to day matters and was able to take part. Throughout the meal Penrose noticed that Heidi kept giving him sly glances as if she wanted to ask him something. Suddenly she plucked up the courage. '*Herr* Penrose, may I ask you something?'

'Of course my dear, but please call me Harry.'

'Do you really know Lisa Lotte Klose?' she asked with a shy smile.

'Yes,' Harry replied, glancing at Klaus.

'Klose? I remember a Klose somewhere,' Klaus said placing both hand to his head, 'but I can't for the life of me remember where.'

'How did you meet her?' Heidi asked.

Penrose, fighting to stop himself blushing, noticed a slight smile on Karl's lips. 'It was many years ago Heidi. When I was a policeman here in Hamburg. Like your father and grandfather, in our job we meet many people. Some you forget and some you remember. I think I remembered Lisa because she was helping me in an investigation and also, of course, she was a very pretty girl.'

Karl's smile became wider. 'That reminds me Harry. That other contact you were asking about.' He reached into his pocket and pulled out a piece of paper. 'The only Inge Lang we could find married a Bruno Maier He was one of our leading criminal lawyers in Hamburg but, alas, he is now dead. I don't know if it is the lady you seek, but she is now living in Blankenese. This is her address,' passing the paper over the table to Penrose.

'Lang? Maier? More names I know.' Klaus muttered. 'I'll remember them very soon.'

'Is she as nice as she appears to be when we see her on T.V?' Heidi asked.

'She is a lovely person,' Penrose replied. 'What we English call a proper lady. I'll introduce you to her some day.'

A look of pleasure spread across Heidi's face. 'Harry, Harry,' Karl interjected with a laugh. 'Promise her that and the invitation will extend to half of her school class. Don't forget also all the young ladies working in my office. Since you left yesterday they have spoken of nothing else. You will need a bus to take them all to meet this Lisa Klose.'

'Lisa Klose? She I remember,' Klaus exclaimed loudly. A look of comprehension was back on his face. He opened his mouth to say something then stopped as he looked across at his granddaughter and daughter in law. 'Harry, Karl. Come to the study. We will talk there.'

After the three men had settled down, each with a glass of schnapps from the bottle that Karl had taken from a cabinet, Penrose looked expectantly at Klaus.

'Lisa Klose,' Klaus said. 'She was a friend of yours and her landlord was found hanging from a beam in her flat. I remember that we agreed that *Der Taucher* killed him but we never discovered who he was. We also believed that the same man killed the woman in Herbertstrasse.'

'That's correct Klaus,' Penrose agreed, 'but what are you driving at?'

'I remember now that it was my theory that *Taucher* was not a German, in fact I believed, although I couldn't prove it, that he was English.'

'Go on,' Penrose said quietly, glancing over at Karl who was listening intently.

'You will remember Harry that we had a long discussion on fingerprints, how neither of us had records we could compare them to.'

Penrose searched his mind before slowly nodding, amazed at the recall that Klaus was now demonstrating.

'We also spoke of body fluids and of my belief that one day it would be possible to match it to an individual.'

Penrose suddenly saw where Klaus was going. 'You mean...'

'Yes Harry, I think that day has come. There is this new research into DNA. It is still in its infancy but, from what I have read, I believe that it might be possible. My men took swabs of the semen found on the woman in Herbertstrasse. You will remember that we were able to prove that it was a different blood group from yours. Also, fingerprints from Herbertstrasse matched some of those found in the flat of your friend.'

'I didn't know about the fingerprints,' Penrose said.

'We might not have mentioned it to you Harry as both cases were a German investigation.'

'Would the print lifts and the body fluid specimens still exist?' Penrose asked. 'After all, we are talking about forty years.'

'Karl?' Klaus asked, looking at his son.

Karl nodded. 'The lifts are still in your file papa and there was nothing in it to indicate that the specimens had been destroyed.' He looked at Penrose. 'I think I told you Harry, we Germans never throw anything away if what it is connected to is still unsolved. They will be somewhere in the storeroom.'

'Even if they still exist,' Penrose said doubtfully, 'we still need a body to match them to and that is one thing we haven't got.'

Klaus smiled. 'I think you have the answer to that Harry. From all the detail you have been able to give tonight it is obvious that you have access to your old file. Search it Harry and find the answer. Then you and Karl together must bring this person to justice. Now, if you will excuse me, it is long past an old man's bedtime.' He slowly rose from his chair, crossed to Penrose and gripped his hand. 'It was delightful to see you again Harry. I hope you will come again before you leave and many more time after that.'

Penrose and Karl watched in silence as Klaus left the room. As the door to the study closed Karl slowly shook his head. 'My God Harry, its a miracle. I can't remember the last time I saw my father as articulate as that.'

~ The Hamburg Dossier ~

'Maybe he just needed to be stimulated by the thing he was best at Karl. As somebody once told me, "Honest Klaus was a bloody fine policeman." Maybe you should tear up his old rulebook and bounce some of your more difficult cases off of him. After all, there's a mine of experience in that head of his. Now, I mustn't keep you up any longer. If you can call me a cab I'll go and say goodnight to your lovely wife and daughter.'

'I'll run you back to your hotel Harry. I insist.'

During the journey they ran through a number of ideas that Karl said he would check out. As Penrose went to get out of the car at the hotel he hesitated. 'Er! Karl. May I ask you a favour? Um! Whatever you might have guessed about my relationship with Lisa Klose, please don't disillusion that lovely daughter of yours.' He smiled. 'I'll be in contact Karl.'

33

The taxi dropped Penrose outside of a long, white bungalow built into the hillside, which screamed a lot of Deutschmarks. As he walked up the drive and climbed the steps to the front door he searched the windows for signs of movement behind them. He pressed the brass doorbell and then turned to admire the vista of the river far below, ships moving in both directions.

He heard the door open behind him and then a voice he long remembered. *'Guten Morgan Mein Herr. Kann ich ihnen helfen?'*

He turned towards her. 'Hello *meine Schatz. Wie geht es ihnen?'*

Inge stared at him. He would have recognised her anywhere. Now there were flecks of silver in the golden hair, which only made it more attractive. Her face was unlined. A short flowery dress adorned her trim figure, revealing a pair of still very shapely legs.

Recognition slowly crossed her face. She clapped the palms of both hands to her cheeks. *'Mein Gott.* Harry? Is it you?'

Penrose only nodded, not really knowing what to say.

It was Inge who broke the silence. 'Come in. Come inside. What are you doing here? This is quite a surprise.' She led him down a hallway into a large kitchen, filled with top of the range kitchenware, and indicated a high chair at a marble topped breakfast bar. 'Why did you have to come here today Harry?' she asked.

Penrose stood up from the chair. 'I'm sorry Inge,' he said, embarrassment showing on his face, 'I should not have come. I'll leave if you wish.'

'No, no, no. Don't be so silly. I'm happy you came and it is lovely to see you. What I mean is that I have to go out. I work as a volunteer at Citizens' Legal Office and today is my turn to be on duty. We still have time for a cup of coffee, then we can arrange for you to come back later.'

The smile returned to Penrose's lips. 'I apologise. I should have contacted you before appearing on your doorstep.'

Inge busied herself setting up two mugs that she filled from a percolator. Penrose looked around the kitchen. Set into an internal

~ *The Hamburg Dossier* ~

wall was a large tank filled with tropical fish. 'This is certainly an improvement from Lattenkamp.'

Inge placed the mugs of coffee on the bar. 'That was a long time ago Harry, but Lattenkamp holds many memories.'

'So what has happened to you since Lattenkamp?' Penrose asked.

'We do not have time for that now,' Inge replied. 'That can wait until we can sit down without interruption. Now we must hurry as I have to leave very soon.'

Penrose picked up his cup of coffee. 'What do you actually do at this Citizens' Legal Office?'

'It is a charity for people who cannot afford to seek legal advice elsewhere. On one day a week I see these people and advise them.'

Penrose looked at her in amazement. 'Are you able to advise them?'

Inge laughed. 'Of course. I am a qualified lawyer. My correct title is Doctor Inge Maier. When the University opened again after the war I began to study law on a part-time basis. It took me seven years to qualify,' then I joined my late husband's firm. I practised until my husband's death ten years ago, then I sold the firm and became, what do you English call it, a lady of leisure?'

'My God Inge,' Penrose said in admiration, 'I'm proud of you. But then, I always was.'

'Were you Harry? Enough of this silly talk, I must leave,' Inge said looking up at the wall clock. 'Can you come back for dinner this evening?'

'If you want me to,' Penrose replied, displaying a look of pleasure.

'Good, then we will have all the time in the world to talk of old times. Come, I will give you a lift to the S-Bahn station.'

It was just after six o'clock when Penrose climbed out of the taxi in front of Inge's home. He was clutching a large bouquet from the hotel's florist, a bottle of Riesling picked up en-route from a wine merchant's and his briefcase containing the Hamburg file that he had picked up on a whim as he was leaving his room.

Before leaving, he had called the number Lisa had given him and found that she had just returned from her trip. She had agreed to join him for dinner at the hotel the following evening, so he had reserved a table.

Inge seemed to open the door immediately he touched the bell so he was sure that she had been watching out for him. She was clad in a short, black dress and appeared to be wearing a little more make-up than she had that morning. There was a look of pleasure on her face as she leant towards him and touched her lips to his cheek. He wondered if she would have thrown her arms around his neck, as she used to greet him in times past, if he had not been so laden.

'Come in Harry.' She looked at what he was carrying. 'What is all this?'

Penrose handed her the bouquet and the wine. 'Flowers for a lovely lady and wine to cement a reunion.'

'And the case Harry? Is it what you policemen used to call it when you were going out on a job, your overnight bag?' she said with a mock look of severity.

Penrose just smiled and shook his head as he followed her into a large lounge furnished with two settees, two club chairs and sets of occasional tables. 'I will take the flowers and put the wine to cool. We shall have that with dinner. But first we will have something special,' she said as she went out through a door. Penrose assumed that the door lead into the kitchen as in the wall next to it was the reverse side of the fish tank.

She returned with two champagne flutes and a bottle in a cooler. 'Sit down Harry, make yourself at home. Being together again calls for champagne.'

Penrose wondered whether to sit on a settee but then settled for one of the chairs. He placed his briefcase down beside him. Inge handed him a glass of sparkling champagne and, standing in front of him, touch her glass to his. 'To us Harry,' she said with a smile before turning towards the opposite chair. As she sat down Penrose couldn't avoid glancing at her legs as her short skirt rode up to her mid-thigh; legs that he had known so well.

Inge gave no indication that she had seen his gaze. 'So Harry, tell me what has been happening to you over the last forty years.'

~ The Hamburg Dossier ~

She listened with interest as he related his life, career and marriage, never interrupting him, only refilling their glasses as they became empty. When he finished she smiled at him. 'Any regrets Harry?' she asked softly.

Penrose remained silent for a while. Finally he said, 'Only one. I regret that we parted as we did and that I never tried to get in touch with you.'

'That was my fault Harry. I was the one who ran away,' Inge said, her eyes going misty. 'You will never know how much I wished that you had come after me. I knew that you had been asking questions of where I was working. Every time the door to Legal Services opened I looked up hoping it was you. Do you know that I did see you again?'

'Oh! When was that?' Penrose asked.

'On the day you left Hamburg. I went to the station and watched you getting on the train. I was willing you to turn around and see me, but you didn't. Still, we can't turn back the clock. I think dinner will now be ready. Let me take you to the dining room.'

Over a leisurely dinner Inge told him about her life over the past forty years. How her mother had died in 1950; her studies at the University; her marriage to Bruno Maier and his untimely death. After he had helped her to clear the table and load the dishwasher, they returned to the lounge where they settled into the chairs with a jug of coffee and a bottle brandy between them.

'You never mentioned if you had any children Inge,' Penrose said.

Inge crossed to a pier table and returned with a framed photograph of the head and shoulders of a young man in naval uniform, which she handed to Penrose. 'This is my son Harri, Harry.'

'Harry, Harry?' chided Penrose. 'The *Schnapps* must be going to your head.'

'No. His name is Harri,' Inge replied with a laugh.

Penrose's head jerked up in alarm. 'He's not er...'

Inge giggled, a giggle that Penrose remembered from years before. 'No, he is not your child Harry although there were times that I wished he was. No, it was just that I liked the name Harri.'

'Where is he now?'

~ *The Hamburg Dossier* ~

He is now a ship's captain, just like his Grandfather. He is based in Hong Kong where he is living with his wife and my three grandchildren.'

'What a coincidence,' Penrose murmured, 'my daughter and her husband are also living in Hong Kong. Considering what happened to your father were you comfortable with him going to sea?'

'It was his choice. You see that?' She pointed to the tropical fish tank. 'He bought that for me. He said that that would be the only Davy Jones' locker he would ever see.'

Penrose studied the tank. On the sandy bottom was a miniature wrecked ship, a small, opened treasure chest and a model of a deep-sea diver, a stream of oxygen bubbles coming from its helmet.

'Davy Jones. Now that's a name to conjure with,' Penrose said. 'I often wonder what happened to him? He never came back to the Met Police.'

'He stayed in Germany,' Inge replied. 'I thought you knew. After he came out of hospital he joined the Control Commission Frontier Service. He came to Legal Services on one occasion and we spoke about you. He looked very smart in his naval type uniform. I don't know what happened to him. After the Control Commission was disbanded the Frontier Service remained. You can still see them on occasions at the border customs posts. I did hear that he married a German girl, but I don't know who it was.'

'I remember that he was seeing some girl but I have no idea who,' Penrose said. 'One thing is for sure, I bet he fell onto his feet.'

'So Harry, don't keep me in suspense. What have you got in your case?'

Penrose glanced down at his briefcase. 'Believe it or not, but I have got you in there,' he said with a smile.

Inge frowned. 'Me?'

Penrose nodded.

'I don't understand,' Inge said, mystified.

Penrose picked up the briefcase and laid it on his lap. 'Well, a part of you. Your handwriting to be precise.'

~ The Hamburg Dossier ~

Inge watched as he unbuckled the case and withdrew the file. 'Besides coming to find you, this is another reason for my coming to Hamburg. Do you remember the murders I was working on? You should do because it was after you spent a day in Herbertstrasse that you decided police work and policemen were not your cup of tea.' He handed the file across to her. 'The murders were never solved and this old man, with nothing much else to do, wondered if he could rectify the situation.'

He watched Inge leafing through the file. Some of the entries brought a glint of recognition to her eyes. 'My God Harry I remember things in here as if they only happened yesterday. Do you think the answer is here?'

Penrose shrugged his shoulders. 'I don't know. I've read it and reread it. The answer has got to be there but, for the life of me, I can't find it.'

'Why not let me read it with a fresh mind Harry? I might be able to find something that you have missed.'

Penrose looked doubtful.

'Don't look at me like that Harry,' Inge said, a little irritation sounding in her voice. 'Over twenty years I read hundreds of files like this seeking something that would give me the edge in a court battle. Let me go through it with my legal mind.'

Penrose looked contrite. 'I'm sorry *Schatz*, I keep forgetting that your knowledge of law has now outpaced mine by a mile. Okay, see what you can find. Now I think that it is time for me to make a move. It's very late.'

Inge closed the file and laid it on the carpet at her feet. 'Yes, it is very late. Too late for you to go back to your hotel. You must spend the night here. I have made a room up for you anyway. You can check out of your hotel tomorrow and spend the rest of your stay here. No, don't argue. Your *Schatz* insists on it.'

34

It was nearly lunchtime when Penrose returned to the house in Blankenese. Over breakfast, Inge had again insisted that he spent the rest of his stay at her home, waving aside his protests. Before vacating his room at the hotel he had showered, changed and packed his suitcase. When checking out he had ensured that his table in the dining room was secure for that evening, upping the reservation to three covers.

He let himself into the house using the door key that Inge had insisted he should have. He dropped his case in the hall and called, 'I'm back.'

'I'm in here,' Inge answered from the lounge.

She was sat on one of the settees, the file beside her, idly watching the fish swimming around the tank. She patted the settee. 'Come and sit down beside me.'

Penrose sat down, glanced at the file before looking at her. 'So? Any luck?'

Inge nodded slowly. 'I think I have found something.' Penrose looked at her expectantly. 'Harry, I read your report of the night that Jonny Gross was killed. Do you remember what he said before he died?'

Penrose nodded. 'I'll never forget it. It is amazing how focussed the mind can be when you are looking down the barrel of a pistol.'

'So tell me again what he said.'

'He said "*Du hast mir die Sache echt versaut.*"'

'And do you know what it means Harry?'

'I was told that it was Hamburg slang for, if you will excuse my French, for "You have really fucked me up."'

'How well did you know this man Gross Harry?'

Penrose shook his head. 'Hardly at all. I first saw him two nights before. We had a bit of a spat which ended with me telling to stick his beer where the sun doesn't shine. The next time I saw him it was bullets flying.'

~ 224 ~

Inge remained silent, gazing into the distance. Then, softly, she said, 'He was not speaking to you.' Penrose stared at her as she continued, 'Your German was never your strong point like all the British soldiers. They were limited to buying a drink or asking their companion of the night if they could sleep with them. The correct grammar was never a part of their conversation.'

Penrose was listening intently. 'Go on.'

'Gross used the word "*Du*" which is the familiar usage of the word "you" or "thou". I would use it, or "*ihr*", when speaking to you because we are very close but if I was talking to a stranger, or someone I did not know very well, I would use the word "*Sie*". Even speaking slang, he would not have addressed you as "*Du*".'

'Then who was he speaking to? There was no one else there except...' Penrose's head swivelled in the direction of the fish tank and looked at it intently. 'Davy Jones?' he hissed. 'Fucking hell! – oh I'm sorry Inge – I can't believe it.' he turned to look at Inge, who was slowly nodding her head. 'Surely not Davy Jones?'

'He was taking a lot of interest in your file at the start of the investigation,' Inge said, picking up the file. She pointed to the cover page. 'Look at the charging list, the initials to whom the collator charged the file out to. HP, that is you, IL, that is me and then there are these entries for MJ.'

'But wouldn't that be the Squadron Leader, what was his name, Mark Johnson?'

Inge shook her head. 'No Harry, it didn't work that way. Remember, all of the files passed through my hands at sometime. When I had to make a translation or enclose entries from the German police. Files to the Squadron Leader were charged to OC, Officer Commanding, and those to Warrant Officer Lancaster as WO. Look, there and there.' She pointed to the relevant entries on the sheet. 'There was only one person with the initials MJ. Davy Jones. His correct name was Mike Jones. That is what the collator would use.'

'Christ, I forgot that,' Penrose said. 'We were all used to calling him Davy.'

~ The Hamburg Dossier ~

'Also,' Inge continued, turning the cover to expose the minute sheets, 'there is no minuted action as to why MJ would draw the file. There are no entries corresponding to the dates that MJ was given the file so he must have only been reading it. What I don't understand however,' she went on, 'is why he stopped.'

'I can give you the answer to that.' Penrose said tightly. 'It must have been after you left. I stopped leaving the file with the collator. I either kept it with me or locked it up in the Warrant Officer's safe.'

He rose to his feet and crossed the room to the fish tank where he stared at the small figure standing on the bottom. 'Excuse my language Inge, but I fucked up big time. My fucking mate Davy Jones. The Diver. *Der Taucher.* I'll find you if you're still alive you bastard and I'll fucking have you.'

Inge came up behind him and slipped her arms around his waist pressing her head to his back. 'Don't upset yourself Harry. All of us at times miss the obvious. This is so unlike you to act like this. Where is the man who, I remember, was always so calm in a crisis? What was it you used to say, "Don't get mad, get even"? Come, let us have some *Mittagessen.*'

Penrose clasped both of her hands and broke her hold. He turned to her and pressed his lips to her forehead. 'You always know when to say the right thing *Schatz.* I'm starving.'

Over lunch their conversation was inevitably about Davy Jones. 'What I can't understand', Penrose said, 'was that when some of the murders occurred Davy wasn't in Hamburg. He was away on jobs of his own.'

'Can you be sure of that?' Inge replied. 'From what I can remember of you people you came and went as you pleased. What if he went away later or came back earlier than he said? Once he left the headquarters no one would have known where he was until he returned. Just remember the times that you came to me late at night after finishing an inquiry. You wouldn't go back to headquarters until the follow morning with me. Did anyone ever ask what time you had finished working?'

~ 226 ~

~ The Hamburg Dossier ~

Penrose smiled. 'It was nothing to do with them what I did on my own time.'

'Exactly. Do you think you were the only one who wasn't where everyone thought you would be? she said, with a smug look. 'Anyway, where do we start looking for this man?'

'We?' Penrose asked. 'No, don't answer that, I can see by your determined look that you're going to be a part of the chase. Okay, we start this evening. We are having dinner with someone who might be able to point us in the right direction.'

'Interesting!' Inge said curiously. 'Who?'

Penrose tapped his nose. 'That'll keep. Its no one you know, at least not personally. It's also somebody from my past who, if I remember rightly, we once had words over.'

'Who is it?' Inge said, banging the breakfast bar top in mock anger.

'My secret. There are some things you don't know about me,' Penrose replied with a laugh. He climbed down from the bar chair, 'I had better dump my case in my room.'

She followed him into the hall, where he picked up his case, and then along the passage to the bedroom wing. She watched him open the door to the room he had slept in and stop short. The bed had been stripped of its bedclothes. He turned and looked at her, an unasked question on his lips. She opened the door to the master bedroom. 'I though you would be more comfortable in here,' she said softly.

35

In the lobby of the Atlantic Hotel, Penrose and Inge were each sipping a glass of white wine and studying the menus that a waiter had presented to them. Penrose was still trying to come to terms with the unexpected invitation to share Inge's bedroom that she seemed perfectly at ease with. She had demonstrated her lack of embarrassment when they were changing to go out by exiting the bathroom with only a towel wrapped around her head. Despite himself, Penrose couldn't help watching her put on her underwear before seating herself at the dressing table to dry her hair and apply her make-up.

A disturbance behind Penrose caused Inge to raise her head from behind the menu and look towards the hotel entrance. 'My God! 'It's some years since I have seen her,' she said with a smile.

Penrose turned and saw Lisa being escorted into the hotel by the doorman. The duty manager was hurrying from behind the reception desk to greet her. 'Do you know her?' he asked curiously.

'Only professionally. That is Lisa Lotte Klose, our leading dress designer. I don't expect that will mean anything to you.'

'What professional connections did you have?' Penrose asked, a half smile playing on his lips.

'Nothing personally. She was a client of the commercial lawyer at our firm. He dealt with her business matters. I believe that after I sold the firm he joined her Company. I only met her when she came to the office.'

The manager indicated an empty chair and table at the far side of the lobby. Lisa shook her head, looked around the room before moving in the direction of Penrose and Inge.

She seems to be coming this way. She must have recognised you,' Penrose said in awe.

Lisa stopped at their table. Ignoring Penrose, she looked at Inge. 'Frau Maier,' she said formally, extending her hand.

'*Fräulein* Klose,' Inge replied, shaking the extended hand. ,May I introduce *Herr* Penrose?'

~ *The Hamburg Dossier* ~

Lisa turned to Penrose who had risen from his seat. She lightly kissed his cheek. ,Hello Harry,' she greeted him, a smile playing on her lips.

Inge looked on in astonishment. ,Do you know one another?'

'For many years,' Lisa replied, still looking at Penrose.

'Let me make the less formal introductions,' Penrose said, 'Lisa Inge. Inge, Lisa.'

Lisa turned towards Inge. 'So you are Inge?' She studied Inge's face before nodding. 'Yes. Now I can understand.'

The manager, who had been hovering in the background, had been joined by the head waiter and the sommelier from the dining room, each holding their respective menus. Ordering another bottle of wine and an extra glass for Lisa, Penrose told them that they would be ready to order a meal in half an hour.

After they were seated, and the wine had been served, they sat looking at each other. Finally, Inga broke the silence. 'Is someone going to explain this to me?'

Penrose took a sip of his drink before placing the glass on the table. 'I first met Lisa many years ago, when I was working here. She used to pass me snippets of information that she thought would interest me.'

'Information? What kind of information?' Inga asked with a look of astonishment.

It was Lisa who answered. 'Information about what was going on in St Pauli.' Looking Inge straight in the eye, she continued. 'It was me who told Harry about Pussy.'

'Pussy?' Inge asked, looking at Penrose.

'The woman who was murdered in Herbertstrasse. You remember that you spent the day there with the investigators.' Penrose said quietly.

'But she was a prostitute.' She looked at Lisa. 'How did you know that...'

'Because Inge, I was earning my living the same way" Lisa said, still looking directly at Inge.

Inge stared back at her, her mouth agape.

'There was no need to have mentioned that Lisa,' Penrose said, slowly shaking his head.

'Why not Harry? I am no longer ashamed of it and I am sure that Inge will be discreet about anything she hears here.' Still looking at Inge, she continued, 'If the truth be known, most German women of our age would have to admit to have done it in one degree or another. It was the only way we able to survive at that time.'

A slight blush appeared on Inge's cheeks but she remained silent. Lisa smiled. 'Now that we have got that out of the way,' she said, 'let us talk of more pleasant things.'

'In a moment,' Penrose said quietly. 'I want to stay with those times for a while. I want to pick your brains and see if you can help me.'

Lisa's smile vanished. 'About what?'

'Do you remember a colleague of mine, Davy Jones? I thing I recall that you met him once when we were in the Café Arnold.'

Lisa nodded. 'Yes, I remember him.'

A look of surprise appeared on Penrose's face. 'Bloody hell Lisa, that was quick.' he said with a smile. 'I wish I could have instant recall about someone I had met once forty years before.'

'Not just once Harry. I saw him many times,' Lisa said. 'Two or three years after you left he came back to Hamburg and married his girlfriend. Nick pointed him out to me.'

'His girlfriend?' Penrose said mystified. 'I didn't know he had one. Who was she?'

'Lilli Gross,' Lisa replied. 'The daughter of that gangster you ...' She paused. 'The gangster that was killed. Nick told me that he had been going with her for a long time.'

A mental picture formed in Penrose's mind of a pretty woman entering the gates of the military hospital. At the time he had thought that her face was familiar, now, in retrospect, he realised that she had been sitting with Tiny Chapman in the Tamborin on the night of his altercation with Gross. The night before Tiny Chapman had fallen from Michel tower. Jones had been away from Hamburg that night and had claimed that he had not arrived back until after Tiny's death. Could he have returned earlier than he had said?

~ *The Hamburg Dossier* ~

Penrose realised that Lisa was still speaking.

'... married left the Control Commission and started a car repair business. Ever one knew that this was a cover and that he was involved with his wife in running the Tamborin. Slowly slowly they started to buy other properties in St Pauli. It is rumoured that they own half the bars on the Reeperbahn and even have an interest in the Euro Centre. When the car repair business became a taxi firm it became the big joke that every sailor coming into Hamburg would be paying Lilli and Davy to be picked up and returned to their ships, drink their beer and enjoy their times with the business girls.'

'Bloody hell Lisa,' Penrose said, with a laugh, 'they must be nearly as rich as you.'

Lisa shrugged her shoulders. 'Maybe richer. But then my job is harder. I try to put clothes on women, not take them off.'

Penrose became serious. 'Lisa, I would like to get what you told me into writing so I have something to put before Karl Rossmann in the morning.'

'No need,' Lisa replied, reaching down to her large sling bag resting by her chair and extracting a black covered notebook which she placed before Penrose. 'You don't think that what I just told you was in my head. I found this amongst Nick papers. It is notes he kept on Gross and his daughter even after he became a legitimate,' she emphasised the word by waggling her forefingers in the air, 'businessman. With Nick, old habits died hard. He would always keep a record of what his rivals were doing. He called it his insurance.'

Penrose flicked through the book, which contained German script in a neat handwriting, before slipping it into his jacket pocket. 'It looks like Inge will have a little bedtime reading tonight.' He smiled at the women. 'So ladies. I thing it is time to eat.'

On the drive back to Blankenese Inge was unusually quiet. Penrose suspected that there was something bothering her. During the meal she had joined in the general conversation and had appeared to have established a rapport with Lisa. Penrose had raised the subject of his rash promises to supply Lisa's brand named clothing to Karl

Rossmann's daughter and Helga the policewoman and asked, jokingly, what discount he could negotiate. Laughing, Lisa replied that she would arrange for a selection of 'seconds' to be sent from one of her factories and so keep his reputation intact.

After a final night-cap in the lobby, they left the hotel, escorted by the attentive manager and doorman, where Lisa's large Mercedes was drawn up outside. After arranging to make contact the following day, Lisa kissed both of them, to the delight of the watching hotel staff, which drew a nod of approval from the scowling giant of a chauffeur who was holding the open door of the car.

Lisa's notoriety seemed to have rubbed off on Penrose and Inge as the hotel manager insisted that a porter should go and retrieve Inge's car from the car park. With a flourish, he had held the driver's door open, to allow Inge to get in, then closing it securely after bidding them farewell.

It was Penrose who finally broke the silence. 'So, what's troubling you *Schatz?*'

'Nothing.'

Penrose grasped her right arm and gently shook her. 'Come on. I know there has to be something. There always was when you used to go quiet on me.'

Inge glanced across at him. 'Was she telling the truth when she said what she used to be?'

Penrose nodded. 'Yes. But she was the same lovely lady then as she is now.'

Inge remained silent for some minutes before saying, 'And you were involved with her? How?'

Penrose looked straight ahead. 'Inge, I seem to remember that we had this same conversation about forty years ago. My answer to your question now is the same as when you asked it then. In the intervening years I have had to deal with thousands of people. The dregs of society. Some good, some real bad bastards. Some were born bad and some went bad because of circumstances. As a criminal lawyer you must have met the same type of people. In my dealing with them, the good ones I would try to help, the bad ones knew that

~ The Hamburg Dossier ~

we were on opposite sides and that it was my job to put them away. I still occasionally bump into some old villains who are now well past it and have been known to have a drink with them and joke about old times. But I can tell you that of all the people I have dealt with, whatever their past, I have never met someone as genuine as the lady we had dinner with tonight. Let me tell you about her life.'

For the remainder of the journey Penrose talked and Inge listened. He told her of Lisa's escape from the east, her former life in Hamburg and the founding of her business empire. What he omitted to tell was his personal relationship with her. That had been a precious memory that he had never shared with anyone.

When they drew up at Inge's home she switched off the engine and remained in her seat. Penrose stayed silent. Finally Inge slowly shook her head and let out a sigh. 'Harry,' she said in a soft voice, 'we Germans have short memories. We do not wish to remember those times. We try to blot it out of our minds. Try to rewrite history. Lisa was right when she said that most women of my age prostituted themselves then to a greater or lesser degree. Even me.'

Penrose placed his arm around her shoulder and drew her towards him. 'Don't talk stupid woman. You never did.'

She lay her head on his shoulder. 'What about us?' she said. 'How would my mother and I have survived if you had not brought us food? Did I not repay you in kind?'

Penrose kissed the top of her head. 'Don't be so silly Inge. What we had was very different. I didn't bring the food just so I could get into your knickers. I loved you.'

Inge laughed. 'Did you Harry?' She kissed him on the cheek before withdrawing the ignition key. 'Come. We have got a lot to do before bed. We have to read Nick's book.'

36

It was just past ten o'clock when Penrose entered Davidswache. Before breakfast he had telephoned Karl Rossmann to arrange an appointment. As he crossed the lobby towards the reception desk the duty *Polizeihauptmeister* acknowledged him with a wave and lifted a telephone. A few minutes later Helga, the young policewoman, beckoned him from the top of the stairway and escorted him to Karl's office.

After the formal handshakes Karl looked at Helga. 'I know *Pilizeirat,*' she said, 'coffee, milk, no sugar,' as she sashayed out of the office, wiggling her pert behind.

'So Harry,' Karl said, 'we have made some progress. The man who married Lilli Gross was...'

'Mike Jones also known as Davy,' Penrose interrupted.

'Are you a mind reader Harry?' Karl asked, with a laugh.

'Feeble minded would be a better definition,' Penrose replied. 'He was an investigator with me here after the war. Practically my right hand man. Right under my nose and I couldn't see it. What do you know about him?'

'He is well known to the Vice Squad. He and his wife are big in the sex trade. That is a legitimate business in this country and there is no evidence that he is involved in any activities that would bring him to the attention of us in the criminal department. Unless, of course, you know different Harry.'

'He might be straight now Karl, but once he was dirty.' Penrose took Nick's notebook out of his pocket and tossed it onto the desk. 'It's all in here. Some of it will be negated by the Statute of Limitation, which I am sure your criminal law will have, but I am sure we can have him for the murders.'

For the next hour they poured over the contents of the notebook, periodically refreshed by cups of coffee supplied by the curious Helga. Finally Karl closed the book and massaged the bridge of his nose. Penrose silently studied him.

~ *The Hamburg Dossier* ~

'So Harry, how can this help us? This is all circumstantial. The author is dead and cannot substantiate it. We cannot bring Jones in on the basis of what is written in here.'

'I agree,' Penrose replied. 'But we have the fingerprints and the possible DNA. What about if he made an admission? That would be sufficient to pull him in and interrogate him.'

'And who would he make this admission to?'

'Me,' Penrose replied sharply.

Karl smiled. 'I am sure you have got it all worked out Harry. Tell me.'

'I'll arrange a meet with him. Nothing strange about that. After all, we were friends. I'll wear a wire. I'm sure you can fit me up with some sophisticated electronics. We'll just be two old men talking about old times. I'll shake the tree and see what falls out.'

'Take care Harry,' Karl said, gravely. 'Make sure you arrange the meeting where my men can cover you. This man could be dangerous and I don't want you seeing him where you could not get help.'

'I don't intend to. Do you have a contact number for him?'

'We have the number of his office.'

'Good. Let's get young Helga in and make a telephone call.'

'More coffee?' Helga asked in response to Karl's shout.

'No,' Penrose replied. 'I want you to make a telephone call. I want you to pretend that you are a hotel receptionist. Be vague as to which hotel. If a secretary answers, ask for H*err* Jones, then give the phone to me. If he should answer, just say a guest wishes to speak to him.'

Helga dialled the number and spoke for several seconds. When she passed the phone to Penrose she mouthed, 'Secretary.'

As Penrose put the phone to his ear he heard a male voice say, '*Ja bitte.*'

'Davy?' Penrose asked.

There was a few seconds silence. 'Who is this please?'

Penrose detected a slight guttural in the voice. 'It's me. Harry. Harry Penrose.'

Again there was a pause as if the person at the other end was delving into his memory. Then, 'Bloody hell Harry, what are you doing? Where are you?'

'I'm here Davy. In Hamburg.'

'How did you know how to get hold of me?'

'I was at a reunion a couple of weeks ago. I happened to mention that I was going over to Hamburg and someone, I can't remember who, remarked that you were living here and I should look you up. The rest I left to an efficient young lady on the desk here. How about a meet?'

'Of course. Tell me where you are and I'll get you picked up.'

'Can't make it today Davy. I'm booked on a coach tour. In fact the coach is outside waiting for me. How about tomorrow? Lunch time. Same time, same place as usual. Must dash. See you tomorrow.'

Penrose replace the receiver before Jones could reply.

Karl and Helga were watching him. 'You were very vague Harry. Will he know where to meet you?'

'I hope so,' Penrose replied. 'If not, we will have to go to plan B. Okay, we have some planning to do.'

Penrose paused as he turned into Krayenkamp, the short, cobbled street on which the entrance to St. Michaeliskirche was situated. He had not been in the street since the day he had identified the body of Tiny Chapman lying at the foot of the tower. The church was now on the tourist route and one of the *Hummelbahn*, the toy-like tour trains, had just drawn up at the entrance and was disgorging its load of eager tourists. He joined the shuffling queue to find that not only was there now a kiosk at which an entry fee had to be paid, but also, to his relief, a lift had been installed to whisk him up the 271 feet of "Michel" and so avoiding having to climb the 449 steps.

The viewing platform was crowded. Although there was still half an hour before noon, he had purposely arrived early, so he circled the area studying the elderly men in the crowd. He noticed that the railings surrounding the platform had been extended upwards to above head height and he wondered if this was a direct result of Tiny's tragic departure all those years ago.

Satisfied that he had seen no one who remotely resembled Davy Jones, he climbed two or three steps up the disused, central spiral stairway, which led up the overhead dome. There, above the heads of the crowd, he had a sight of the lift door. He thought of the many twelve o'clock meetings he had had in this lofty position and wondered if Jones would take the bait.

Just after the church clock struck twelve, the lift door slid open. A new group of viewers pushed their way through the throng of people waiting to make the decent. Almost the last to leave the lift was a person who had Jones' features. He was about 50 pounds heavier than Penrose remembered, completely bald and wore thick, steel-rimmed spectacles; a cartoonist's perception of a typical German businessman. Behind him was a leather-jacketed heavy who screamed 'minder', who moved towards the edge of the platform after a brief word from Jones.

'Davy,' Penrose shouted and waved when Jones looked up in his direction. He descended the steps and elbowed his way to Jones who received him with a hint of suspicion in his eyes. As Jones had not extended his hand for a handshake, Penrose grasped his shoulders. 'By God Davy! It's great to see you again.'

They moved to the railings on the east side of the platform where a trace of a smile at last came to Jones' lips. 'So, what are you up to Harry? Spending some of the pension?' he asked/

'Well, you know how it is Davy, The old clock's ticking on so I thought I'd have a last look around before it's too late.'

'You'll have seen quite a change Harry. Look at that down there.' Jones pointed to the rooftops of Baumwall. 'Do you remember the state that was in the day we found that bloke and his tart shot to death in one of the cellars. Now look at it. You would never think that a single bomb was dropped, except St Nikolai church over there.' He pointed to a church spire in the distance. 'They left it as it was destroyed to stand as a memorial. Anyway, did you do your full time in the Job Harry? I guess you made Inspector.'

Penrose laughed. 'A little bit better than that Davy. I got to Chief Super. Why didn't you come back?'

Jones shrugged his shoulders. ' You know how it is? After I got out of hospital I had to have a long session of physiotherapy. I had lots of time on my hands and got to thinking about my future. Did I want to go back? Back to low pay and dead men's shoes promotion prospects. I figured that there might be better prospects here so I applied for the Control Commission Border Service.'

'Did you get in?' Penrose asked.

'Yes, Spent a couple of years or so with them. Things had started to improve here, I was thinking of getting married, so I resigned and started a car repair business. Haven't done too bad, I have a taxi business now.'

'Who did you marry? Anyone I know?'

'I don't think so Harry.'

They had slowly circled the viewing platform to the north side. Jones looked down. 'That tart of yours used to live down there Harry. Do you remember?'

Penrose felt a surge of excitement. 'What tart?'

'I can't remember her name. She lived in the top flat of one of the big, old houses. They were knocked down to make way for that road.' Jones pointed down at Ludwic Erhardstrasse. 'Some little old cripple who lived with her got done in there. Don't you remember?'

Penrose stared hard at Jones. 'That's the second mistake you've made today Davy,' he said quietly.

The smile faded from Jones' face. 'What the fuck you on about?'

'I never told you where my tart, as you call her, lived. The only way you could have known that she lived there, in a top flat, was if you had been there and I most certainly never took you there.'

'I must have read it in your file mate. You must have showed it to me.'

Penrose shook his head. 'Wrong again. I know that you were always sneaking a look at the file when I wasn't around, but when the house down there was first mentioned, after poor old Manfred was murdered, I had long hidden the file in a place where only I could get

~ The Hamburg Dossier ~

to it. Was that what you were doing in the flat? Looking for the file? If I remember right, someone also broke into my desk drawer and the collator's filing cabinet about the same time. Did you expect that the flat down there would have been unoccupied? Unfortunately, poor old Manfred was there. He saw you so you had to get rid of him.'

Jones face and neck had gone puce. 'What was my first mistake?'

'Coming here today. We never used to meet here. I only used this place to meet with my informers.'

Jones let out a short laugh. 'And you thought it was a big secret Harry? How many phone messages did I and the rest of the lads take for you? "Tell Sergeant Penrose I'll see him at the usual place at the usual time." It was enough to make anyone curious and it wasn't too difficult to follow you one day.'

'And did your curiosity get the better of you when you received the phone call from Tiny Chapman and you decided to keep the appointment instead of me?'

Jones glanced over his shoulder to where his minder was lounging against the railing before grasping Penrose's arm and pulling him to the west side of the platform.

'Look down there Harry. What do you see?'

'St Pauli?'

'What you see Harry-boy is my town. There I am king. There is my protection. What I say down there goes. And you? Your are just a fucking old has-been and whatever you know will do you no good because you can do fuck all about it.'

'Christ Davy, you're talking like some cheap gangster in a second-rate movie.'

'I am a gangster Harry. The top dog.'

'In the shoes of Jonny Gross?' Penrose sneered.

'That was always to be Harry. After all, I did marry his daughter.'

'And you were always working with him. It was you who was setting the jobs up. And it was you who killed him. What does your wife think about that?'

Jones leant back against the guard-rail. 'Killing him was a spur of the moment opportunity Harry. He was becoming a liability and I not

~ 239 ~

only wanted his daughter but his business to go with her. The gods were looking down on you that night when you took a purler on the pavement because his bullet was meant for you. You were getting too close for comfort. He thought that you would be there alone I told him that you would be reluctant to use your weapon and that he would have no trouble in taking you out. But when he saw me, and that I was aiming my pistol at him, he must have realised that it was a set-up and tried to take me out instead. As far as my wife's concerned, you killed her father.'

Penrose stared at him with a look of contempt. 'And what about the others? Willi Winkler, Pussy and young McNeil? Were they too close for comfort?'

'Willi was. He had begun to sus me out. The tom? Well, she was just a tom who might have known something. If you had not gone to see her that night she might have been a happy, retired hooker now. McNeil? He knew who I was and could have pointed the finger at me. And as for your friend Tiny? He saw my name on a cigarette ration card in the Tamborin. All of them could have caused me problems and the loose ends had to be tidied up.' He glanced behind Penrose and slowly broke into a grin. 'It looks a good a time as any to finally settle the matter Harry,' he said softly, the grin fading away.

Penrose turned his head and saw that, with the exception of the minder who was standing by the lift door, the viewing platform, as if by magic, was empty. He moved to his right and linked his arm into the railings before glancing up to the top of them above his head.

'Even you will have a job putting me over this Davy,' he said, involuntarily tightening his grip.

Jones slid his hand into the pockets of his coat. 'More than one way to skin a cat Harry. My man over there is an expert at disposing of shit.'

The sound of the lift door opening and the footsteps of disgorging passengers was music to Penrose's ears. He saw Helga the policewoman, with a well-built man, saunter to the railing a few feet from him. Glancing to his left, he saw that Karl Rossmann was standing by the spiral staircase surrounded by a most unlikely bunch of tourists. There was no sign of the minder.

He looked back at Jones. 'Seems like you've missed your chance Davy. Now it's my turn. I'm going to make sure you go down.'

Jones laughed. 'There'll be another time, another place. Where's you proof Harry? You haven't got any evidence. I'll deny this conversation ever took place. Anything you say will be put down, not as evidence but as the ravings of a senile, old man.'

'Another mistake Davy. Our conversation has been recorded. Also there was evidence. Fingerprints were left at the scenes and, I don't know if you know anything about it, but this newfangled thing, DNA. Who ever killed Pussy left his semen behind which can now be matched to an individual.'

Jones laughed out loud again. 'Harry, you're talking of forty years. Do you think there will be anything left to compare after forty years? Except for you and me, I doubt if there is anyone who remembers anything about it. And anyway, after forty years, who the fuck would cares?'

'I care,' Penrose said tightly. 'That man by the staircase also cares because his father cares.'

Jones stared at Karl. 'Who the fuck is his father?'

'Ex-Inspector Klaus Rossmann. Remember him? The son is also a criminal detective. Between the three of us, we are going to put you away'

Jones went ashen and looked around for his minder. When he couldn't see him, he tried to barge past Penrose as Helga and her companion grasped him by the arms.

37

Arm in arm, Penrose and Inge strolled through the departure lounge of Fuhisbüttel airport towards the departure gate.

'Your stay has gone so quickly Harry,' Inge said, looking up at him.

'But a lot has happened in a short time *Schatz*. I've renewed old friendships, made new ones, cleared up my unsolved murder record and, most importantly, I've found you again.'

'Then Harry, can I ask you a favour?'

'Of course. What?'

'Will you turn and wave before you go into the plane? Then I will know that it will not be another forty years before I see you again.'

From the observation deck, Inge watched the line of passengers walking across the apron towards the British Airways Trident. When Penrose reached the foot of the aircraft steps he turned and waved. Ascending the steps backwards, he continued waving until he disappeared into the plane.

EPILOGUE

Harry Penrose and Inge Maier (née Lang) were married in 1988 and had nine wonderful years together, making up for lost time. In 1997, at the age of 77 years, Harry suffered a fatal hear attack while walking up the hill from the River Elbe to their home in Blankenese. Inge still lives in Blankenese between visits to her and Harry's grandchildren scatter around the world.

Lisa Lotte Klose still controls her fashion empire.

Mike 'Davy' Jones was convicted of the murders of Gerhard 'Willi' Winkler, Karen 'Pussy' Averbeck, Manfred Haller, Jonny Gross and the manslaughter of Sister Gisela Rasche, in the Central Criminal Court, Hamburg, in 1988. He was sentenced to 20 years imprisonment. In the unlikely event that he might have lived to complete his sentence, proceedings were started to extradite him to England to stand trial for the murders of Percy McNeil and Cyril Chapman. Three months after starting his sentence he was found hanging in his cell.

Following her husband's death, Lilli Jones (née von Grosse) sold their business interests and moved to Bangkok where she was last heard of running a bar cum brothel.

Inspector Klaus Rossmann died peacefully in his sleep in 1998 at the age of 98 years.

Izzy Finkelstein was sentenced to 180 days in the Military Corrective Establishment, Colchester, where, strangely, he learned to love the army. On his release he transferred to the Royal Corp of Transport where he rose to the rank of Warrant Officer. He was discharged on pension but the author has not been able to trace his whereabouts.

The Tamborin has had a number of name changes over the years and as the Jambolia is still one of the clubs offering live sex shows in Grosse Freiheit.

The Café Arnold was demolished to make way for a new road system.

~ The Hamburg Dossier ~

Herbertstrasse is still a 24-hour hive of activity.

The Astoria café still serves an excellence cup of coffee.

Sergeant Stephen Baker, a Special Investigator of the RAF Provost and Security Services, who was not even born in 1947, entered the final conclusions in the file in 1988. The Hamburg Dossier was finally closed after 41 years. It is now exhibited in the RAF Police museum.